Take a … g her home a… or the funlovi… espite her fla… steady young man, she soon … he men to the boys!

It's not long before she has several strings to her beaux—and all of them playing a different tune. Young Ernest wants one thing, the Colonel, his father, wants another, while sex-crazed screen idol Nathaniel has other ideas entirely. But whatever demands are made on her, she learns how to handle them all—and does, without losing anything by it . . .

'No one expects Molly Parkin, with her outrageous observations, her graphic accounts of every intimate encounter you could possibly think of and some, I bet, you couldn't, to come up with the definitive work on contemporary moral values. She writes bawdy, vulgar, honest, titillating books and she doesn't pretend they are anything else.' *Cosmopolitan*

Also by Molly Parkin in *Star*

LOVE ALL

SWITCHBACK

GOOD GOLLY, MS MOLLY

UP TIGHT

Molly Parkin

STAR

A STAR BOOK

published by

the Paperback Division of

W. H. ALLEN & Co. Ltd.

A Star Book
Published in 1976
by the Paperback Division of
W. H. Allen & Co. Ltd.
44 Hill Street, London W1X 8LB

Reprinted 1977, 1978, 1979, 1980

First published in Great Britain by
Blond & Briggs Ltd. 1975

Printed in Great Britain by
Richard Clay (The Chaucer Press), Ltd., Bungay, Suffolk

ISBN 0 352 39717 9

To Mama
who first thought of me

We sat in the crowded, chandeliered restaurant with his celebrated hand inside my Marks & Spencer knickers.

"Ooh! Ouch!" I said. "You're hurting! What's happened, I think, is that my pubic hair has somehow got caught in your watchstrap. Half a mo' and I'll untangle it."

It was just as well that we'd both ordered salmon for starters. I wouldn't have wished to taint the taste of, say, an artichoke or some other such dish of delicate flavour requiring fingers as forks. But by the time we'd reached the brandy stage he was back in there again. And what's more, now, was making heavy demands that I should similarly explore the ageing content of his own much more expensive underwear. But "No," I'd insisted. "Not here." Best that one of us at least should appear to have both hands above the table. I wouldn't have known how to walk out if the management had asked us to leave. "In any case," I'd added, "what about the time? I can't be late for school again tomorrow. I'm having a hell of a do these days with the Head!"

In the morning he drove me to school. "Oh, don't drop me right outside," I pleaded. "The girls will get the wrong idea." But he had, of course, right up to the main entrance, in amongst the greatest mass of them, laughing loudly as he pulled the powerful engine to a halt. They gathered like ants, amazed in the first place to see anything other than an industrial lorry, a costermonger's barrow, or the rag-and-bone man in the drabness of that street. Let alone the scarlet splendour of his Aston Martin Sports. I cringed in the low-slung seat, expecting the worst when they recognised his face—and saw me with him. He leaned across, preparing to embrace before them all, but I escaped in time. "Take care, little one," he growled affectionately. "You're a bastard," I said as I slammed the door and braced myself for the storm. I could still hear the hum of his departing car as I reached the staff-room door.

The news travelled like greased lightning. Miss and a film-star! Yes! Was he my boyfriend? He couldn't be, that old! Did he know my dad then? Grandad? Who, and why and where—and what was I doing in his car?

"If this stupidity doesn't cease this instant," I said, "you will all, the whole damn shoot of you, be sitting with your hands held on your heads for the entire lesson! No art class, none today, nothing—do you understand! Just sitting, looking straight ahead, not a word from anyone! Now what's it to be? Painting or a form of purgatory—I leave it to you to decide—"

"Oh, painting, miss! Yes, painting! Mmmmmm . . ." They droned and mumbled like a swarm of bees. And though their actual questions ceased, their curious eyes and lifted brows maintained the tense excitement of suppressed enquiry until the morning ended.

I couldn't wait till dinner break to pour it out to Winnie. We were in luck; it happened to be her playground duty day, which meant a good long gossip without too much fear of being overheard. We met in the upper staff-room, where several other of my colleagues—conscious that I'd been hauled in by our headmistress yesterday after they'd left—were waiting with Winnie to hear the worst. My unpunctuality had now become almost legendary amongst these fond acquaintances, despite the fact that I hadn't been teaching there for all that long. Almost a term, the same as Winnie. The first teaching post for both of us. She spoke up first, still patently concerned on my behalf—despite the blinding wideness of my entering smile. "Well?" She wavered anxiously. "How did it go with old Pritchard?" So much had happened, of course, since then that I'd almost forgotten that bit. "Oh yes," I laughed and allowed myself a leap of triumph up and on to a chair.

"Well, congratulations are in order! I've managed to lose my class! The final disgrace! Stripped of the form mistress's responsibilities! No more morning register to call, or dinner money to collect—or daily squatters in my art room! All back to what it always should have been—a straightforward specialist post!"

"It gives you a leeway of half an hour on either side in the mornings anyway," Winnie said as we walked around the playground. Two girls had evidently, from an over-excited, ever-growing group around the lavatories, locked themselves in together and were indulging in a rude and running commentary. "Oh leave them, Winnie. Why bother? It'll be Doris Wellington and that daft Pauline playing boyfriends with their pencil boxes, I expect. He rang again anyway last night, Nathaniel—I slept in his hotel, the Cadogan Court, can you imagine! What are you doing after school tonight? We can have a cup of tea and I can give you all the details!"

She shivered slightly. From the cold? Or was it pure excitement? "Oh yes, I've nothing on at all, except—" She hesitated. "I promised I'd help mummy in the shop. She's having trouble with the bacon slicer—"

"You're barmy, Winnie, living at home, especially in a shop! There's no hope in hell of you getting any sort of love life off the ground whilst you still stick on there. It's impossible! Blimey, look at how I used to be before I made the break. . . ."

* * *

"You should apply for a teaching job down here in Sussex, my girl. Be nice and near to give your mother a hand—she's not getting any younger. And business as it is, with everyone stocking sweets and bloody cigarettes—he's got them over in the greengrocer's now, you know—we're staying open that much longer to cope with the competition. We could do with a spot of help, come evenings. And teaching art, you won't have homework to mark. And there's your bedroom upstairs to do your paintings in—you want to think seriously what's best all round, now, girl!"

"Yes, dad," I said, "I am." I lifted the lid of the deep double fridge to lower the lolly ices. He came closer and peered over my shoulder at the shimmering moulded tray, frowning down at each of the twenty-four circular sections—and rearranged the wooden sticks of one entire line.

"Go easy, if these sticks aren't put in at the appropriate angle, the entire lolly falls to pieces when you're trying to get it out. Your mother has calculated that it only has to happen to as little as five for the whole profit margin to be wiped out on us doing these home-made lollies—"

"Yes, dad," I said. "I know."

"Anyway," he continued, "it beats me what it is you see in

London. You'll find the cost of living vastly different. No chance to save your earnings, none at all. So no one will see the benefit, least of all your mother and me, for all the years of education that we've given you. I'm not sure now I see the point. I honestly think that, given the decision all over again, I ought to have stuck to my guns and put my foot down and had you out in a job. It was your mother's doing, not mine, sending you on to art school. But it's my belief that artists are born and not made, and all that's happened is that you're ending up as a teacher anyway, so if you had to go on you may just as well have gone to an ordinary teachers' training college. Which would have made it at least only two instead of the five years—where are you going now? Out? Mind to be back before long. We'll be getting busy then and your mother's having a lie down—"

"Right, dad. I will."

"Where are you off to anyway?"

I hesitated before answering, but he pressed home irritably: "Eh, where?"

"I'm going to say goodbye to Derek."

His lip curled, he turned his back, but not before making sure I heard. "Goodbye! Good riddance! Jewboy! Bloody yid."

Derek was waiting for me at the entrance of the Palace Pier. My heart tilted over when I saw him. He was looking at another girl, appreciatively, appraisingly, from head to toe. And she was looking back, laughing over her shoulder as she passed. I could have slapped her on both cheeks. That wasn't unusual, not with Derek, I'd known it from the start, what a terrible flirt he was. I'd watched him flirting with everybody else whilst biding my time to catch him. And I had caught him too, at Christmastime. I hadn't known till then that he was my father's *bête noire*—Jewish, the thought hadn't occurred. He looked more French, more Continental in his clothes and with his well-cut beard. He seemed so much outside these things, more of the world, more cosmopolitan. Like all those London students in our final pedagogic year. He must have found the rest of us appallingly provincial. That spurred me on, of course, to catch him more, to prove that I was somehow just a cut above. And I was as well, as he so very soon had found out. The brightest student of my year, the most imaginative of the painters. The most original. Yes, I was just as much a catch. "Only in this setting," was what he said to me. I'd have had a bloody sight more of a job to shine in the metropolis. In a keener ambience, like a London art school, where the competition was more crucifying. "And the atmosphere more creative," I'd added. "I might in fact have done much better—" "No, you're not the sort to thrive in competition. There's too much that's misguidedly arty in you. A false fostering of sensitivity. That's the danger of these sort of places, out of the artistic swim. You're so conditioned, you, that you might find it rather better to remain a big fish in a small pond—"

They were challenging words, as well he knew, and I didn't believe them anyway. Even then, before I'd claimed him as my own, London was already my Mecca. And now, with everything in shreds between us, where else was there for me to go?

The turnstile to the Palace Pier was jammed; he helped me to jump over. "Thank you, Derek," I said, mock-formally, hoping he'd hold me longer. He couldn't meet my eye and, though he took my hand in his to walk along together, his fingers too felt cold and strained and even, now, unfriendly.

I'd wanted our last goodbyes to be back in his room. I'd wanted in fact to say goodbye in bed, but he'd said "No, the thing would be too searing, too painful, too emotional for either of us to bear."

"No more than it has ever been," I'd said, trying to make a joke. He'd looked at me like a stranger. I'd laughed, knowing I was batting on a very silly wicket, but still unable to stop. "Painful, I mean! It always has been that. Painful and impossible. But," I sounded desperate even to myself. "But," and now my voice was breaking, "it could be nice since it's going to be the last time, if we just got in and cuddled—couldn't it?"

"No. It couldn't."

We passed the candy-floss machine and stepped around the children queueing for ice-creams. "I made forty-eight ice lollies today," I said. "Twenty-four a day up on what we were doing this time last week. All orange, they go much better than the raspberry. Strange that, isn't it? You'd think it would be the other way around. I used to love dyeing my tongue dark red, the orange is much less lovely—it can look like catarrh."

"Spare me the details, please."

"Oh Christ!" I said. "I'll shut up then."

We'd reached the end. "We've reached the end." I took my hand from his and twisted round to face him. "Symbolical. Shall we go under?" That sounded symbolical too, I thought. He answered as I had expected. "No." But I led the way, down the open iron stairs, past the line of anglers, right on until I'd arrived at the grid-like darkened structures underneath the pier. He didn't follow, and when he did, his face was sulky, like a little boy's. "This is silly," he said when I pulled him close. "Pointless."

We were alone, it was a lovers' place, secret and unseen by all those crowds above us. We'd been there many times before, in the early days, before I'd been brave enough to be persuaded back to his bed. Ironic that, that in those days he was the one who was so much keener. He'd said that's how it would be, that once he'd started me off, there'd be no stopping. It wouldn't be long now before I'd be looking at every man like that. Wondering, so he'd said, what they'd be like as well. The idea had intrigued me, but I hadn't let on then. Though possibly what he'd said might well come true.

I put my hand in his trousers pocket, he shrank nervously away, but I persisted in my quest. "What are you expecting to prove by this?" My fingers closed around the stiffening shape. "I've proved it!" He shut his eyes, threw back his head, so handsome, bearded—weak, and groaned. "You look just like an El Greco. The crucifixion." My hand began to work relentlessly and as rhythmically as the restricting pocket would allow. He made no sound at all. I cleared my throat. "I'm playing the part of a philistine," I said companionably, and waited for the smile to hover round his mouth.

It didn't happen, if anything the line became a little bleak. I stopped what I was doing. Suddenly and without a word of explanation. His eyes opened sharply in surprise, but I gazed steadily back. "You're right." I spoke flatly. "It is pointless after all." He was speechless, unable to formulate his feelings now in words. Between us, sheathed in flannel, grey—reared his great erection. I pointed to it. "It looks like a broom handle under a blanket! Perhaps you'd better think of finishing it off yourself. I wouldn't like to walk along the pier, not with you and that. It could be construed as conspicuous!"

"He'd have made a shocking husband, Derek, anyway—everyone thinks that you're better off without him."

"Yes," I said dully, and concentrated on my tie-and-dye. It was going to be a brilliant emerald silky scarf, with a border of alternating white and lemon rings. A complicated process, involving lots of pebbles and pieces of string and various baths of brilliant colour. I wasn't very good at it, the discipline wasn't there.

"Am I doing this right?"

"Not really, the spacing's too irregular—anyway, you know you said he was catching the boat on Saturday, he couldn't have been because Fiona saw him standing at a bus stop in Portslade on Saturday—"

I swallowed. "What time Saturday? In the morning?"

"No, very late at night—"

"Um, alone?"

"No," she said brutally. "With one of those French girls—those students who are up at the 'tech."

"It's silly, this scarf. I've got nothing that goes with green—"

She came over and stood beside me. "Don't give up when you've gone this far—it'll be something for your final show. Shall I try and retrieve something for you? In exchange for some help with my self-portrait?" I nodded, feeling slightly bruised inside. Why had he lied about leaving on Saturday? And if he'd had to sneakily see that French student, why couldn't he just stay inside instead of letting half the college see? Especially Fiona.

We were in the textile printing room, Pat and I, as we spoke, preparing for our end of course exhibitions. Derek was missing his, not bothering, bound by now on a big boat to South Africa. Summoned by his father, a good way to avoid his National Service. He'd been at home in here, the textile school, they'd liked his sense of colour and the intricacies of his small designs. Mine were too wild and swirling, so they said, chaotic and emotional. As one would expect from a Fine Arts, Painting student. Derek was aiming for the world of advertising, he was a crack hand at layout with ambitions of becoming an art director. Even from that fact of our opposite artistic standpoints, the affair could be seen to be doomed. Without everything else.

"Haven't you spoken to Fiona yourself, then?"

"No." I shook my head. "I haven't."

Pat plunged my piece of now neatly tied silk scarf into a bowl of kingfisher blue, we both watched it soaking into its present brilliant yellow and gradually turn green. She prodded it to make quite sure it lay beneath the surface and then she ran cold water from the tap over her rubber gloved hands. "I bumped into her by the bandstand—"

"The bandstand, the bandstand Hove?"

"No, Eastbourne."

"I wonder what she was doing there—"

"Well, she wasn't sitting in a deckchair."

"A sports car, probably."

"With an appalling-looking chap—"

"No chin?"

"None! Lots of money by the look of him."

"That was Humphrey," I said. "He's a Hussar."

There had always been the three of us really. Pat and Fiona and me. But in the last two years we'd gone our different ways. Pat into textiles and fabric printing, an annexe of the art school, situated on the other side of the road so that physically it wasn't so easy to swap stories or pass the time of day on the stairs any more. Me into the rarefied regions of canvas and oils—and Fiona into the social whirl of her sub-deb world. We none of us had very much in common except that we were keen on boys, but each of us had come to art school for very different reasons. Sent by our parents: Fiona to while away the time in a socially acceptable pursuit and because her father had a weakness for water colours. On the walls of his prosperous lawyer's office. Pat to better herself by hopefully marrying one of the qualifying architects in the affiliated architectural school, instead of doing as her mother—now widowed—had done, that is, married a well-to-do master plumber. And me, well me to make good too, but in a different way. To excel. To be brilliant. To be a credit academically. "Did you come top?" "No, Dad. Second." "Who came top?" "Someone else." "Next time then, see it's you, my girl!"

Not that I knew either of them that well. They spent a lot of time out on the town, hours which I preferred to spend on work. And they lived the sort of lives which meant a lot of coming and going into their various homes. I didn't have a home as such, not living above the shop—it was only in the last three years that we'd managed to make our outdoor lavatory in. And as well, compared to them, I was a late developer, filled out with under-the-counter chocolate, too fat to fit into the latest fashion, still wearing in fact my old school skirt for the first term. But even so, head bent and shoulders hunched, before I'd fined down to my present curves, both of them had sensed oncoming competition.

I came, strangely enough, into my own at the very point of separation. That is to say after the first two years of Intermediate had ended and everyone had decided in what to Specialise.

Fiona after deciding on Illustration, had suddenly switched to Painting, but at the end of her first disastrous term—which ended with her in tears and her father being advised to save his money—she was taken away. I saw her in the Christmas holidays. "I've got four portraits on the go," she boasted confidently.

"Have you? How impressive!"

"Yes, all friends of daddy's."

"Men of good standing—"

"It's not at all difficult." She leaned forward confidingly. "I'm doing them all from photographs actually . . ."

I tried not to show my distaste, and made an effort at sustained interest. "That's nice—." So much so, in fact, that she insisted I join her for coffee, with her paying. I was flattered, it was the friendliest gesture she'd so far made.

She steered me into an exclusive olde worlde coffee shoppe, full of refined old ladies and rich retired gentility, and cheerfully sat down at the nearest table. A pinafored waitress swept across towards us. "This way, madam, please," she said. I'd already put my handbag down on the table, preparing to take a chair. But now I picked it up again. Fiona didn't move. "This suits us fine," she said and smiled, firmly. I shrank and picked a nail, I never liked a fuss. Fiona looked up and waved her arm at me and then said, simply but with a certain sharpness, as if commanding a rather dim domestic animal: "Sit!" I did.

That was the start, I suppose in fact. Her inexplicable loneliness and apparent need of an audience and my ridiculous pleasure at providing simply that, the someone to listen. She'd drop in on our Life Drawing Class or when we'd embarked on a long-term project involving Pictorial Composition encompassing Perspective, and she'd stand waiting wistfully till someone should enquire as to what she was up to now. It was always me. And then she'd gush in answer. "Had lunch in London yesterday at the Chelsea Arts Club, and can you imagine—I was actually invited to become a member! As a Professional bona fide Artist!" And she'd take out a cigarette and place it in an amber holder. "Lovely colour," I'd say, and point at it to change the subject. But it wasn't until she invited me to her twenty-first birthday party that we ever broached the subject of sex.

Pat had been invited to the party too, and so had her cousin, a medical student at Guy's Hospital up in London. Actually it was because of the cousin that Pat had been invited. "He's the smart side of the family. My mother's sister, she married a dentist who did awfully well in Rottingdean. They've always had money. He's got his own car, Mark—shall I get him to pick you up?"

"Oh no, don't do that. I can get there on the bus." I said it quickly.

She looked doubtful. "I'm not sure that they have buses round Fiona's. It's what's called a very residential area."

"I'll be all right. One of our neighbours can give me a lift." Ted Grunt, the greengrocer's son, could drop me off in his van. On the corner, of course, not right up the drive to the actual front door! "What are you wearing?" I asked a little fearfully.

She'd shrugged her thin and elegant shoulders. "Oh, I never know till the night before. And then if nothing seems nice, I get old mum to fork out for something special on the day."

That was one of the things I'd noticed about Pat right away, her incredibly narrow body which, but for the looseness, the athletic grace with which she held herself, would have been merely scraggy. She hadn't any breasts at all, but instead her legs reached up to her ears. She dressed in clashing, primary colours with calculated confidence and incredible style. The clothes themselves were rather cheap and badly finished—it was she who made them marvellous. Her mouth was always immaculately outlined and carefully painted in to exactly match her nails. These days she favoured a stinging pink, with violet variations in whatever it was she wore. Apart from her legs and the magically achieved elegance, her crowning glory was her hair, side-parted very low down on her head so that the rest hung curtain-like across her face, below the level of her neck. "What are you, anyway?"

"Black, I expect, as usual."

"Smashing!"

It was in my first year of painting that I'd taken to black, in fact, after seeing a snap of Juliette Greco, and very soon after a French film about existentialists. My father nearly went mad, but I took no notice. "You're not minding the shop with that muck on your eyes, my girl! You're not making a fool of your mother and me turned out like an undertaker—"

"Right then, I won't—"

"That's it, good girl." He turned his back. "Soap and water."

"Mind the shop."

"What!"

"That's it then," I said. "I said I won't mind the shop!" And I won, that time. If I'd shown the same gumption over Derek, I might have won there too.

But it worked a treat, my black, especially with my white face. And even with my brown, I found in summer. I'd done it overnight almost, everything I owned straight into the four-hour funeral service at Sketchleys. And less than five shillings spent on mascara, a soft black pencil and a box of magnolia pale powder from Woolworth's. It wasn't Pat's style, but it was just as strong. It wasn't Fiona's either. Hers showed a penchant for pastels and pearls, and fine tweed skirts and flat-heeled shoes, shone conker bright. And well-cut, glossy, county hair. And very clean teeth, and fresh complexioned cheeks. She smelt very good—always as if she'd just got out of the bath. But her legs weren't good. And as well as that she wore glasses.

"It'll be a good do! Posh. Plenty of nobs. Have you asked across the road? He'll drop you off, Ted, in the van—"

"Yes, dad, I've asked already."

"That's settled then. I'll come up too. Just to see you in, girl."

"Don't! There's no need! I'll be all right! Honestly!"

"Well," he sniffed huffily. "If what you're saying is you don't want me. You'd rather I didn't. You prefer to straggle in like some stray cat without a family, I quite understand, my high and mighty miss! You needn't think because—" But in the end he gave in. After I'd pleaded desperately for him to come.

Fiona's father opened the door. My own mistook him for the butler because of his evening suit, but I was the only one who blushed; both men appeared to take the situation in their stride. "Well, sir," my father spoke in a strangled, high, affected voice, quite unlike his own. "I shall depart leaving my precious daughter in your undoubtedly capable hands. Should transport be required for her return, you have only to ring our good neighbour, the greengrocer, Mr. Grunt, and hey presto, her carriage will await!" He turned with a flourish of an arm towards Ted in the van on the kerb. Ted, taking it as some sort of signal, hooted back on his croaky horn.

"*A la* Cinderella!" uttered the charming host.

"Quite, sir," answered my father.

I didn't stop sweating for an hour.

"Do you have a number, little one? I'd like to get in touch."

"We're Number 20—20 Station Street—"

"Telephone number, ducky." I flinched at the insolence of the drawl, the implication of extreme boredom in the tone. I couldn't for the life of me see why he was bothering, or indeed had bothered almost within minutes of my arrival at the party. "My!" he'd said, when Fiona's father had done the introductions. Even before I'd taken my coat off. "Here, let me help you," My lining was torn, with help the sleeve could easily turn inside out. "I'm better off doing it myself, I think." But he'd stood there waiting, watching me, with half-closed eyes sliding up and over my body. I knew that he'd ruin my evening, but there was something about him you couldn't shake off. Like Fiona had been with the waitress.

We danced a lot, he held me terribly tight. That part of it was best in fact—it was the talking that got me down. "Cigarette, sweetie?" "No, thank you very much, I don't." "You don't, dontcha! What do you do then, eh?" And he leaned forward and deliberately pinched me on my botty. What answer was there to give?

I sat there smarting at his mimicry of my accent, giving no answer at all. If I could have managed it I wouldn't have spoken anyway, not in my normal voice, all evening. It must run in families, I thought, this failure to stay yourself. After several hours I could hear myself making a deliberate effort to ape the intonations of everyone around me. They seemed mainly to fall into two categories. The short and sharp, and the long-drawn-out. The first required an ack-ack style delivery, the clipping off of word endings and between the staccato bursts, quite long, abruptly started pauses. While the long-drawn-out was simply that—achieved by running each word right into the next, essentially low-pitched rather than high. Like his voice, my constant companion's, now. But I hadn't done my homework, hadn't sat down long enough to study it, simply because before it hadn't seemed necessary. Fiona had waved across the room. "Everything all right?" "Lovely," I'd lied, lifting my glass of champagne.

"But at least you got a man." Pat sounded despondent. "Who wanted to see you home. I seemed to be stuck with Mark all night, but he was so depressed over his trouble I had to be with him if only to see he didn't get too sloshed—"

"He's nice, isn't he? When's he going to have to marry the girl? If she's five months gone it'll be showing already."

"Bitch. That's all they go in for nursing for, you know, most of them—to nab a nice young medical student. My mum was thinking of it for me. I wouldn't have minded either, but I didn't get a good enough School Certificate. You have to be a bit brainier than me to be a nurse. No, it wasn't a memorable evening. Wasn't the food appalling? Mum does a much better spread than that. You haven't been to our house, have you? I never get on that well in those sort of do's. She's a shocking snob, isn't she? Fiona. The whole family in fact. My dad used to know them when they started. Yes, he fitted their upstairs lavatory. An ordinary house they lived in then, my auntie lived up the road. She said they'd never speak to anybody. Terrible social climbers. And as mean as hell as well. They kept him waiting a whole year, quibbling about the lavatory bill. Fiona's like that too. Haven't you noticed?" She laughed. "They must have shat themselves to see you getting off with who you did. He'd be the ideal in their eyes as a son-in-law. Isn't it funny that they don't put Fiona into those new contact lenses—those glasses of hers put the kibosh on things a bit, I think. Don't you? My mum would have me out of them in a trice, I know. But that's the difference—she spends on important things —they'd probably see it as extravagance! Anyway, enough of that. What happened? Did he kiss you? Yes? And what else? Anything?"

Fiona had asked that, too, the very next morning. But the call had come at a busy time, just as the pubs were emptying and lots of men were coming in for peppermints for facing their wives at home. Our telephone was just inside the shop, put there, despite the inconvenience, to make sure that the shop was never left empty and the telephone never left unanswered. It rarely, if ever, rang for me. My father didn't encourage either my mother or myself to give the number freely. "How did you get my number?" I said to her in surprise.

"From Piers of course. He was raving about you. Hasn't he rung you yet? No? Oh he will, I'm sure of that. He's super, isn't he? Frightfully well-to-do—has his own aeroplane, can you imagine! In Scotland, to survey the scenery I believe. Much of which he owns, of course. Or will do when dear daddy dies. I'm dying to hear all—oh don't go!"

"I've got to. Really."

"When shall I see you then to get the gory details? Would you like to come up to tea today? Mummy'll be here, but we can go out for a walk—"

"That's better, yes, the walk I mean. Why not meet down at the Pier?"

"Why not? Which one? I have to confess I've hardly been on the Palace Pier—except once, when taken by a rather common nanny. I'm sure mummy must have given her the sack, I know there was a frightful fuss—"

My father had started shouting. I managed to get in "West Pier then, at five o'clock!" before he forcibly removed the receiver from my hand and replaced it with a heavy jar of Trebor Extra Strong.

There wasn't that much to tell about Piers. There might have been, but by then I was much too miserable. My answers now were almost monosyllabic and as well I was worried to death about where to tell him he should drop me. It couldn't possibly be outside our shop, that was for sure. I couldn't have stood the comment. I could hear it already. "How frightfully smart. A shop girl." On the other hand, if I were to pretend to live in Fiona's area it meant a hell of a hike home. So I settled for the seafront, which was relatively nearer. Then having done that, having given him directions, I started agonising over Station Street. Would he remember I'd called it that? Hadn't he only written down the telephone number? "I have to go in," I said. He'd switched the engine off, lowering his head to peer up with what seemed approval at the Regency terrace I'd chosen. He'd slipped his hand straight up my skirt, right past my stocking top, clear over the suspender, bang on to the knicker itself. The bit between the legs. I curled with embarrassment. I knew it was wet. Not wet, but without doubt damp. Damp, from having sat so long in his overheated car. Already damp, in fact, from simply dancing with him close. And damper too from having been excused before we'd left and unable to adequately dry my pubic hairs on the cheaper brand of toilet paper they used in Fiona's house.

"You're damp!" I didn't think he'd let it pass. Were there no limits to which he'd stoop to make me feel embarrassed? "Am I?"

My voice was barely there. He forced the gusset to one side pulling with it a painful displacement of hair. "Ouch!" I said and tried to push his hand away. "Ouch! Ouch! Ouch! Just what are you ouching about, my sweet?" And he pushed his fingers even further and more brutally. "Eh? This?" The tears were coming in my eyes, just from the sheer discomfort. "It's hurting."

He pulled his hand away as roughly as he'd put it in and brought his fingers to his face. "Mm. Mmmmm. Mmmmmm! What fragrance! The best of Billingsgate!—Here, how do you like yourself?" And before I was able to say anything at all, he'd forced his fingers in my open mouth, unfastened the car door, pushed me out, shouted "Sweet dreams!" and driven off into the night.

"I don't like him, Piers, you know, not at all, Fiona. And he doesn't like me either, not really. He's playing a game, that's all."

"Shall we have a Kunzle cake each? I can't resist them, can you? They cost a shilling though, that's the only thing . . ."

"Have one," I said. "I'll pay. Oh listen to this, it's one of my favourites. *My Foolish Heart*. Did you see the film? Susan Hayward. She had a wonderful figure in it. Very high here—" I touched my sweater. "She'd pulled her straps up extra tight. When I got home, I did exactly the same to mine. Don't they sell them low in the shops? And people go round with them like that as well. Someone should say—"

"I'm wearing a new one, first time on. Do you see any difference in the profile?" She turned to sit sideways in her seat. The Palm Court Orchestra swooped to a crescendo, drowning the hum of conversation from surrounding tables. I made as if to measure, with my arm outstretched and one eye closed, my thumb upturned as we'd been taught to do in drawing. "Bit bigger, I think. And far more pointed. Nice. Where'd it come from then?"

"Harrods. Mummy got it when she was up. It's padded. Feel."

"What without you trying on? How on earth did she know it would fit? I'd never do that."

"Greatly Reduced. She couldn't resist. Less than half price, so she said. A fifty per cent saving and more! Anyway, with me and what I've got, the fit is not important. Mind you, I've got much more than Pat. I wouldn't care to see her stripped, would you?"

"Oh, I don't know, she's got dreadfully good legs."
"Straight, you mean?"
"Well more than that . . ."
"I'd rather have your figure. That bosom you've got is bloody good. That's what Piers said. He said that's what he noticed first, your terribly high round titties!"
"He couldn't have. I had my coat on when he saw me first—"
She clucked impatiently. "Well, anyway, I suppose he meant that when you took it off. It looked good, the dress, I must say. It showed enough, even daddy said afterwards, what a fine-looking girl you were. He said your father seemed a grand chap, with rather a sense of humour, is that right?"
"No," I said. "It isn't. But anyway now, about Piers. . . ."

When I got home he'd phoned.
I'd never known my father so excited except once many years before, when he'd recognised George Formby in the street. "George Formby, I presume!" And he'd placed himself squarely in the poor man's path, doubled in a deep curtsey, doffing his trilby and offering his hand! Squirming.
"He's an Hon, this boy, and double-barrelled to boot!" He propelled himself along the counter pinging each toffee jar with a blunt pencil, as one might use a tuning fork to test the quality of crystal. "You've done it this time, girl! Me and your mother could be out of this little lot and living in the lap of luxury before we know it, if you play your cards right! Now this is what you do, you see to it he doesn't go too far. Eat his oats before autumn, as it were! No point running for a bus once you've boarded it—any man would say the same. Stick to your standards, my girl, no shilly-shallying, you understand! These young rakes, a chap like that, the world at his feet and so much wealth to grease his elbows, will expect to just play fast and loose with everyone. Well, not with a daughter of mine! No sir! And I would say as much should the occasion arise. Though I think it won't with you, you know. I gave him to understand on the telephone that your father and family were forces to be reckoned with. You may have been brought up in business, but no one can call you shop-soiled." He stopped

short at that and peered at me, suddenly anxious. But through my numbness and growing despair I managed to shake my head and still his worst fear. He beamed. "Wholesome. And educated. I wouldn't be surprised if the silly girls that he's been used to can only just about tell the difference between a samba and a serviette. That's all they teach in these finishing schools—the superficial niceties of life. At least you know which artist lost his ear. You must show him your paintings—you never know, he might even buy one!"

"I'm not going."

"Oh yes. You're going my girl. She's going, isn't she, mam? What, after I've arranged it all, my girl—I'll say you're bloody going. You take this chance—how many more of these do you think will come your way?"

I took change from the till and went out to telephone. "Fiona? I'm seeing him again. Piers. Yes. My father arranged it all behind my back for the day after tomorrow, Sunday. He's meeting me at Lancing Station some time in the morning—I shall be with him all day."

There was a silence at the other end. "You lucky thing," she said.

"I don't want to go—"

"Oh you do, you'll have a lovely time. I bet he tries to seduce you."

"Yes."

"I'd give my life to be right there myself!"

"Oh I'd love you to be. Much nicer than being on my own."

I knew it was wrong when I boarded the train, my black. It had turned out to be a brilliant day, billowing with air and sun and early spring. The sort of light that called for white.

He'd greeted me with some distaste. "Why, duckie, you look like a spider! We're going up on the Downs, not into some dark bordello in the Boulevard St. Germain! You surely possess something slightly more suitable."

"I'm sorry." I sucked the inside of my lower lip between my teeth, a childish habit to stop me crying. I saw his eyes fall to my shoes, frail and fragile, almost non-existent ballet pumps.

"Why in hell have you come in your bedroom slippers?"

I hung my head. The train went back on the hour. I could stay of course; I could sit all day in the station Ladies and pretend to my father that I'd had a fabulous time.

The curtness cut through the sun, a nearby bush of premature blossom shivered when he spoke. "Coming!" And he turned on his heel and strode towards his waiting car. "Here. I'm sure I have some Wellingtons in the boot. They're mine, but you can wear them."

I stared at them stupidly. "What, without socks?"

"Wot, wiv out socks?" His upper lip curved high over his teeth, almost nearly to his nose. Perhaps he should be wearing the Wellingtons to deliver a crisper kick? "Sweetie, unless you have a set of extremities out of all proportion to the rest of you, I think we both accept that my Wellingtons will be too large. A pair of socks is neither here nor there. Nothing will balance the difference!"

"Socks would mean I won't get blisters." I spoke stubbornly, staring no higher than his lapels. Tweed lapels in shades of lovat blue. Pat would know which make it was and probably which mill had woven it. They did that over in her annexe—wefts and warps. She'd explained it all to me one day how she'd cleverly copied a woven herringbone and turned it into a fabric design which could be stamped on oilcloth. But I'd been doubtful, until she'd elaborated further. "It's a gimmick you see. It means that you could have it for bathroom curtains. Or kitchen tables covered in the stuff." "Oh, eating off tweed, a tweed tablecloth, I get it! Very good!"

"Blisters! Blisters! Bloody blisters! What are blisters to me!" He was shouting at me now.

"They're nothing to you if they're not yours. But they're something to me if they're mine." I couldn't believe I'd said it. Been so unbelievably inarticulate. Me, who'd always come top in English. Especially English Grammar and elusive Sentence Construction. Whichever voice I said it in, I knew what to say. Normally I knew. No one could have accused me of lacking in vocabulary, not when I had a father with the gift of the gab like mine. My eyes stayed glued on the same spot, no higher or lower. Neither of us spoke. In the distance the Downs lay rounded as a pregnant girl. Was that why we were going there, for us to do it in the open? "Anyway," I said, defiance rising in the silence. "I'm not that keen on ten-mile hikes—"

"No, duckie. And nor was Jesus Christ. He seemed incapable of organising his feet as well. But at least you haven't his furniture to carry on your shoulders. And nor am I 'thet kin' for that matter either on marathon marches. My plans *à propos* the Downs are merely to exchange the time of day with archaeological pals of mine who are involved in some sort of dig."

I swallowed, everything including my pride. I could see the stupidity of ballet shoes at digs. "Well, I'll wear the Wellies if it isn't far—"

But he was waiting now with the car door open, my side, which showed some manners. "Suit yourself," he shrugged. "I simply now have lost interest!" Which didn't show manners at all. His moods seemed to come and go at will; I couldn't make head or tail. We drove, his hand upon the wheel, the other one round my neck, its fingers fondling round my ear. I found it very off-putting until he turned his head to smile at me.

"What ho my beauty! And what have you been up to? Since we met?"

I enunciated as carefully as I could, taking care to avoid the tricky vowels. The Woolworth's imitation of Julie Andrews. "I had a nice tea with Fiona."

"Did you now, and how was that?"

"Oh, that was very nice." I coughed. "Thank you." I added.

"It was nice, nice, nice, nice, nice." He turned it into a chorus. "They did it twice, twice, twice, twice, twice." I started sweating.

I refused to go further and meet his friends; I could see even at a distance that they might prove the final straw. I could see from the clear canary of the women's Jaeger cardigans and the quality of the cavalry twill on all the men. And in addition, due to the excellence of the atmospheric conditions, I could hear their voices well enough in advance to know they'd paralyse mine, possibly for good and all. It wasn't a risk I was willing to take, not with teaching as my chosen career. I'd sat down on the lower slopes. He couldn't believe his eyes, not when he turned around to view the distance of the twenty yards between us. It had been twenty yards for more than a mile, his Wellies were playing havoc with my heels. And not only with my heels, but underneath my flowing dirndl skirt as well, cutting viciously into the back of my knees. At the thought of walking this way back to the car again I would have gladly stretched my length and died. Could my father have sued for the cost of the coffin? Or for the use of one of theirs with a crest on, because their son had been in on the kill?

"Okay. Okay, kiddie. Bye for now. I shan't be long. Why not take the instruments of torture off and get a little air to your tootsies. . . ." And then his voice began to mingle in with theirs, each braying in a slightly different key. "Henrietta!" "Why Piers, old chap!" "Well, blow me down, I don't believe my eyes!" "How's things then, Hugh?" I shut my eyes and went to sleep.

"Why did he want you to take a bath?"

"Because of my blisters, he said."

Fiona sighed. "He's divinely decadent. Do go on. What a day you do seem to have had!"

"Yes, it was horrible. The most horrible day I've ever had. Tell me, Fiona, quite honestly, how do you find my accent?"

She opened her eyes as wide as they'd go and slowly removed her spectacles. "I can't see it," she said.

"What, my accent? You're not meant to, not see it. No, do be serious—"

"The point. I can't see the point of the question."

"Well, what I mean is that I don't sound like you, for instance. I don't even sound like Pat—"

"Heaven preserve that you should. It's frightfully artificial, isn't it? Really suburban. I mean, have you ever listened to the way she says 'Really'—it's absolutely ghastly. I'm sometimes embarrassed for her in company—but she does have that super cousin, of course."

"He's getting married—did you know? He's got to, she's pregnant. A nurse."

"Oh Christ, really? I shall have to cross him off our list of eligible men. Anyway, to get back to eligible men, what happened then?"

We were walking along the undercliff route to Rottingdean, she in a second-hand sheepskin, another of her mother's bargains, and me draped in moth-eaten fur, reaching right the way down to my feet. There'd been a violent change in weather since the excruciating Sunday.

"What I found so unforgivable was the way he made fun of my accent, that's what I mean."

"Did he?"

"It put me off. My father was furious when I told him."

"I should think he was. It's rather rude, apart from anything else."

"Yes, he was furious. He said that Piers was perfectly right and I shouldn't have taken umbrage. He offered me elocution lessons!"

She stopped in her tracks. "Elocution lessons? That's crackers! Piers offered you elocution lessons—but that's one of the things he liked about you. The fact that your voice was different, otherwise, he'd have spent my party with one of us—" she blinked— "oh, I didn't mean that, but you know—"

"My dad." I said it wearily. "He's the one who suggested it. But it isn't just the making fun—the rest was awful as well.'

"Wakey wakey! Time for off. How were your forty winks?"

I opened my eyes, Piers blotted the view: the sun, the sky, the whole of the Downs. I steeled mysef, waiting for the worst, but in fact he seemed now in fine fettle. He'd been with his own kind again and life was obviously more agreeable to him. "How are the toots?"

"Terrible."

"Take heart, fair damsel, all is not lost. It's perfectly possible, my sweet, for me to fetch the car and pick you up from here. Stay put—I shall run all the way."

"Why," I asked, "did we have to walk in the first place?"

"Good for you, duckie! That's why. A fellow always has to have the say—lay down the law, all that sort of thing. It's probably put you in your place, I'd say. Shown you who's the master." He glanced at me, a curious, almost tender, certainly sensual look about the eyes. "Sorry about the feet—I shall have to kiss them better." And after that he didn't speak again until we reached our destination when I saw quite clearly, as he was getting out of the car, that something had caused him to swell.

There was no one at home. The house was empty; I sensed it as soon as we got there, an imposing building set in its own estate, of course. And arrived at by a curving drive flanked with herbaceous borders and overhung with the heavy branches of ancient evergreens.

"You'll be partaking of the Sunday roast I shouldn't be surprised with Mater and Pater et al. You know how to cope with the cutlery, girl. Start from the outside and then work in, you shouldn't go wrong sticking to that. And remember, when in doubt drop your hankie and let everyone get on with it first, then do as they do." "Oh dad, don't keep on." "What's up? You're not getting nervy? You'll be all right, just take everything in its stride."

"It's wonderfully peaceful here," I said, standing beside the car. "Not a soul in sight." No sound at all! Weren't places like this meant to have lots of dogs and things bounding and barking and wagging their tails? Steady Rover! Steady! Steady! Yes, old chap, I've missed you too, y'know. And old retainers tweaking their forelocks, with wives behind them wiping hands on their pinnies? Why, Master Piers! If it isn't you, I'll be bound!

"My folks are away. The house is virtually shut up except for me—when I choose to use it." He turned his head and the key in the door—and winked. I gave a sickly answering smile. What for? Use it for what? "Allow me, madam, to carry you over the threshold."

I would have liked time to make a show of reluctance, to have said—look here, I'm not coming in. Not on the maid's day off. My dad will want to know what veg we had with dinner, and whether your father carved the joint or not. And he'll want to know what we had for pudding, and was there a choice of tea instead of coffee. And I'm not very good at making up, he's better and always remembers exactly what you've said, which means he can trip you later on when he knows you'll forget—But I wasn't given the chance. Piers moved so quickly, quite literally sweeping me off my feet so fast that a Wellington boot fell off my leg to the floor. He kicked it out of the way and, carrying me still, he crossed the sort of hallway that you see on stage in heavy costume dramas. I felt for quite a flattered moment much like Scarlett O'Hara, except that instead of him sweeping me up the staircase, he dropped me on the bottom step.

"Whew, duckie, have you put on weight since last we met? I need a gin and tonic, what about you? Or should you be on a diet?"

"Nothing for me, thank you." He'd touched a sore point. I was indeed perpetually on a diet.

"Don't be silly, duckie—I'm hardly likely to be drinking on my own! The thought strikes, however—how about some champers? How indeed! Hold still my sweet, don't move."

I did move though, just to rearrange my skirts which had fallen round my middle. And to take off my remaining Wellington boot. My feet were filthy, though I'd washed them before I'd left home and cut the toe nails too, in case. I tried to cover them by sitting so to speak side-saddle, still there on the bottom step.

"What the hell are you doing crouching there, you funny little creature? Here, cheers!" He held a glass of bubbles in each hand and offered one to me; it meant me standing up. "How awfully short you are, robbed of your layer of rubber—don't leave it lying around, someone could break their neck," he said and kicked the Wellington boot.

We drank the bottle between us, I think we did. At any rate next time I looked it was empty and by then we were up in his bedroom.

"You're to have a bath, you little heathen!" I resented the implications, both of them, and coloured up a dull brick red. "Best thing in the world for blisters. Wait on, and I'll put some salts in the water."

"Oh yes, I love a lovely smell. What sort do you have? I'm not mad on pine. It's what we have at home—"

"No, duckie. Epsom Salts. Excellent for surface abrasions of the skin—"

"Oh dear! Will it make me need to go? It's not a corridor train. . . ."

He obviously didn't know what I was talking about, but it didn't matter because, when he'd left the bathroom after pouring in the salts to return to his adjoining bedroom for a minute, I quickly managed to lock the door. It left me on my side and him on his. I took no notice of the pounding fists, but kept my clothes on and merely soaked my feet instead, by sitting on the edge of the bath. I didn't need one, I knew that, by sniffing beneath each arm and bending my head to sniff as well under my billowing skirt. Quite all right. Billingsgate indeed! But I couldn't resist his perfumes—they occupied an entire shelf, the largest bottles I'd ever seen. And half of them not even opened. And I couldn't resist his talc as well and woofed it just where I'd been sniffing. When eventually I emerged I found him lying on the bed, a freshly opened bottle by his side, a half-full glass still in his hand and on his body—nothing at all.

"What sort of dick did he have?" Pat moulded her hands in the air as if enclosing a very large marrow. "Oh I see," she said at the expression on my face, and held up her little finger.

"Well, to tell you the truth, I tried not to look. And even when he forced it in my face, I shut my eyes—" I shut my eyes now, remembering. "He hit me with it though—"

"Where? On the body?"

"No, right across the face. The impact made him shoot off in my ear. And I'd only washed my hair the night before, it was terribly hard to get out—"

"You should have left it there to dry, and then you could have brushed it out. Mark tells me all about these things. He says the feminine equivalent of spunk can ruin a suit, if not treated right away. But men's stuff works the other way around. That's why very young boys and dirty old men have slightly chalky areas round their flies because they haven't brushed with enough attention. It's all a matter of grooming."

"Well anyway I'd only got my comb on me and the teeth are set too far apart. You need a nit comb for a job like that."

"He was cross then, that you wouldn't give it?"

"He seemed to be. Terribly cross. He called me a tart for being a virgin!"

"We're all tarts then!"

"Apparently. It's a strange conclusion to come to, isn't it?"

"I think he must have got it wrong—he really meant prick teaser."

"I wasn't teasing though, but I didn't terribly want to, you know. With him. Afterwards he could barely be bothered to drive me to the station, but when we got there, he said Cheers and he'd see me next week!"

"Oh, I'm sure you'll hear from him again!"

"I don't want to. I hope to God my dad doesn't answer the phone!"

He did though, answer it. And more than that, he made another date, giving—I couldn't believe it—our address for Piers to call. "It's a good sign that, girl. This coming to pick you up. It means he wants to meet your family. Get acquainted with your mother and me."

"I needn't be in. He can get acquainted, he can get acquainted all evening with you on his own. I can go to the pictures by myself."

"Now stop all that, you understand. He must see something in you or he wouldn't have called again—"

"Oh, he sees something in me all right—"

"Don't try to be bitchy, my girl. The fact that he tried to force his attentions was entirely your own fault. You should never have entered that empty house in the first place. It was asking for trouble—"

"How was I supposed to get home, dad? Stuck out there in God knows where?"

"You might have merely stood your ground, politely and in the nicest possible way. That, you see, that course of behaviour, would have earned his respect. He wouldn't then have dreamed of doing anything untoward. As it is, however, you haven't obviously burned all your boats. Now think of us, there's a good girl."

I could tell when Piers had arrived by the shuffling of my father's feet; he was scraping them like a horse, jog trotting on the spot from sheer nerves and pleasure.

"Here she comes ,my little beauty." But dad's eyes were not on me, so that when I neatly side-stepped the approaching outstretched arm, he lost his balance and fell heavily against a newly delivered batch of Barker & Dobsons, which in turn displaced the entire display of Craven A Cork Tip.

Piers didn't blink. His lounge lzard eyes remained as usual remote and uninvolved.

I didn't care. I'd gone past caring. I'd come out in my second best and hadn't even bothered to wash my hair. With what had happened last time, there didn't seem much point.

"Martinis at my favourite pub—the Grand Hotel?"

"Great!" I felt his glance.

"You feeling yourself, duckie?" Feeling myself? No, not at this moment, no. I have my hands upon my lap, not venturing between it. Not slowly sliding down inside, and touching my slit till it tingles. Later perhaps, when I'm in my bed, I shall pull my pyjamas down or my nightie up. But not at this moment, no, I'm not. Is that what you want to know?

"Yes. Completely myself. Why?"

"No reason. Unfortunate about your father. Could have been a nasty fall! But he seems a cheerful enough chappie. Nothing could throw him too much, I should say. I pride myself as a judge of character and he's an optimist if ever I saw one! Right, my old china?"

"Right! Yes, he's an optimist all right!"

"Perhaps it was your fall, dad, that put him off. He might have considered clumsiness to be hereditary. After all, you can't have heirs to great fortunes, and all that, moving around like mental defectives, knocking things over when they're called upon to open country bazaars. On the other hand he probably thought you'd had a drink—" My father groaned. He'd been groaning for the past fortnight. The pain was purely internal, it had come from the cruelty of circumstance and the obvious cessation of further telephone conversations with Piers. He hadn't called, simply because I'd said that he was not to, I felt that we weren't suited, was how I put it.

"Suited! Suited! Suited! Suited! Of course we're not bloody suited, but that's the beauty of it, don't you see, duckie? Good God, my forebears would no more dream of being seen in public with a person such as yourself than, well, than almost anything. Now, doesn't that stir the soul to think that democracy is such today that you and I can sit here drinking in the Grand Hotel as if for all the world we were equals?"

"No. It doesn't stir me very much. I might have more fun with a parrot, if I needed everything repeating. Or a bunch or radishes for that matter—"

"Radishes? Radishes? Radishes? Radishes?"

"Yes," I explained patiently. "Very bad for indigestion!"

My father patted me brokenly on the back. "You did your best, my girl. I'm sorry if your old dad let you down. Not too good an evening that, one way and another. A whole carton of Craven A gone west from falling into the fridge. I didn't notice. I didn't find it till the morning. Frozen solid, of course. And stuck to the block of vanilla ice. Was able to salvage that, fortunately though."

"Never mind, dad, it'll teach you not to play Cupid. You do it too clumsily."

But it had pulled us much closer together, Fiona and I, the incident of Piers. We met now every weekend, on Saturday mornings if she was here, to go over what she'd got up to. My examinations, my finals, in the painting school, were approaching, and every minute counted away from my work—which meant that socially I had little to report. Her own progress in the world of art had dwindled down to nothing. Her father said she must think of doing something constructive, either that or seriously consider getting married.

"Who to though, Fiona?"

"Oh, anyone with the right income and an appropriate background would do for daddy."

"Well, why don't you then?"

"It doesn't just seem to be happening."

"No, not when you go out looking for it, but I expect it will one day. Why not think of taking a job?"

"What sort of job?"

"Oh, I don't know. What jobs are there?"

"Plenty of secretarial—but you have to do shorthand and typing really for that."

"Why don't you then, learn? Take a course. I would if I was you—then, when I've finished next year, doing my Fifth and passing the Finals—we'd be able to leave here altogether. Go to London, both qualified, me to teach and you working in an office and marrying the Chairman's son!" That's how it came about—the original plan—but then, of course, Derek happened.

"I'm engaged!" I'd said. "This boy has asked me to marry him!" I stood just inside my parents' bedroom addressing their sleeping bodies. "Yes," I said. "His name is Derek and we've fallen in love. Oh, and by the way, dad"—I backed out on to the landing —"I forgot to say—he's Jewish."

"Daddy's the same about Jews. That's something they have in common. It's ghastly, isn't it! Here, have a cigarette, it helps to calm the nerves. I'm frightful these days, I can't seem to give it up. I go to these awful do's, get drunk and then start smoking. Smoke non-stop. Just for something to do whilst I'm racking my brains for something to say. They're so unutterably tedious, mummy and daddy's crowd."

"Poor old Fiona—what about the young Hussar?"

"Humphrey?"

"Isn't he around?"

"Yes, he is. He stayed with us last weekend."

"Well?"

"Well, it's not like you and Derek. I'm not in love, and nor is he. Oh, I meant to ask—how can I tell him about his halitosis?"

I stopped to send a pebble skimming over the sea. "It's like a millpond today. Look how calm. Are you good at bouncing them?" I bent down. "The flatter the stone the better. Here's one, hold on.

You try." I watched as she crouched slightly, then clapped as her pebble travelled the shining surface of the water creating ever-widening circles where it touched. "Six! That's superb." I said. "I shan't beat that." I aimed my stone, it sank at once. "What did I say! You win! Now, Humphrey's halitosis! Has he had his tonsils out? You could start off by asking that. I don't know what you do if he says yes, unless you suggest the surgeon may have left a bit behind. That happens sometimes, doesn't it? They leave a sliver of skin—causes a murderous stench I believe!"

"That's what he has—it's terribly tricky. I can't stand it when we're kissing!"

"Have you tried turning up with a peg on?"

"What do you mean—a peg?"

"A clothes peg. On your nose. When you go out to meet him. He might get the message then."

She sighed. "I doubt it. He's dreadfully dim."

I thought carefully. I understood the problem. My mother had put me to have music lessons at one time, but I hadn't physically been able to continue because of the piano teacher's pong. Bread-and-butter breath was what she'd had, and the curious mustiness of over-milky tea. 'This child's nausea isn't natural,' our family doctor had said. 'I think the world of music is going to have to reconcile itself to the grievous loss of her talents! Either that or find instruction elsewhere. To force her to continue with Miss Philbert would be not only foolish and uncommonly cruel but might well lay the foundations for a distressing medical condition known in layman's language as psychosomatic stomach! The symptoms are clearly here already.'

"Oh dear!" I said. "Honestly, Fiona, you deserve a medal. I'm afraid I couldn't stand it myself. I'd be bound to be bilious. That's one of my things. I have a horror of halitosis. Couldn't you just come straight out with it and say 'I'm sorry, sweetheart, but the way things stand, your rather bad breath is coming between us.'? Couldn't you?"

She shook her head. "No, I shall probably soldier on. Apart from that you see, he isn't all that bad—I mean, he fits the bill from daddy's point of view."

"What a shame. I'm sure it's simply a minor matter, something up with his sinuses or an ingrowing epiglottis—can't he have an enema? Or better still, what do they call it? Yes, a colonic irrigation? That's meant to clear the pipes you know, right the way up to the neck! Get your father to suggest it, man to man."

"Oh, I don't for a minute think I could get daddy to start discussing enemas! I doubt if he'd deign to mention diarrhoea! He's incredibly fastidious, my father! They seem to be, don't they, men—more than women."

"Not in our house. No!"

"I'll be buggered before I'll have that circumcised sod as a son-in-law! I'll swing for him first, so help me! I'll start on his balls with scissors!"

"Is it because I'm Jewish do you think? Perhaps that's what he has against me?"

"No, honestly, Derek. Really!"

"Mam, mind the shop for an hour or two while I walk this girl amongst the tribe along the esplanade. I'll shove the bloody chosen race right up her throat to give her some idea of what her in-laws are likely to be! And see if an unadulterated diet of astrakhan collars, fur coats, fallen arches and Manny and Izzy and Ikey can't do the trick!"

But it was all a wasted effort. Derek's family got in first. "A gentile girl, you say! Your mother is wearing black today—we mourn your death, my son!" That's what his father had written back at Derek's news of our engagement. And what's more he'd cancelled his allowance, withdrawn all possible financial support until the boy had come to his senses.

"But you said they weren't orthodox, Derek."

"They're not," he'd answered flatly. The money hurt. The pinch of poverty.

"Would it help if you sent my photo? I can look quite Jewish myself."

But he'd shaken his head in sorrow. "They'd know," he'd said. "By the nose."

It was his buttocks that drew me to him first, the way they came straight from the waist and then tilted up and out before they turned into his thighs. Like a small and sexy black boy's, with a very straight backbone above and arms that hung slightly away from the main body of the thing. Like the sleeves of a coat in a cupboard. I noticed them, his buttocks, within a week of his arrival, walking behind them up the stairs to a class we shared on Calligraphy. It surprised me, that, being drawn by a bum, and I'd run on ahead to purposely get a good look at the rest of him. He saw me looking, so he said. And had himself, even as early as that, been making surreptitious enquiries as to my availability. But I'd forged a name for having my nose to the grindstone and for being hard to get, and so, he'd given up without trying. "Hardly the spirit of endeavour," he'd agreed much later. "But there again, if you've already got a field full of cattle, why bother chasing one cow!" I'd made him pay for that—but in the end, we both lost.

"It's perhaps because you're nervous, you're tensing it up inside!"

"I'm not, honestly, Derek. Not nervous a bit. Go on, I promise I shan't shout this time. Just push harder, it's bound to go in somewhere!" And all the while I kept thinking what a terrible waste it was, this stud, the sexiest thing in the whole school, searching the length and breadth of my privates for a suitable place to put it! My husband to be! The love of my life! Obviously blind down below! "Shall I have a look for you?" I'd offered. "If you pass me my handbag mirror and I hold it just so—"

He'd said to try and show a little sensitivity please, that the fault lay with me and not him. It became a marathon effort for each of us until in the end we gave up. But the trouble was that by then he'd well and truly whet my appetite. I really couldn't wait to have another go, exactly as he'd predicted—with anyone!

"I don't really mind, Fiona, about you spotting him at the bus stop, but it might have been better to have told me instead of Pat. You know how she is—it's all round Brighton by now—"

"Well, everyone knew what a two-timer Derek was, but I was so shocked when I saw him after you'd said he'd gone, I had to tell someone. Can we meet for tea?"

It was months since we'd done that, Fiona and I, simply because of me being so tied up with Derek. Pat was the one I'd been seeing much more of, from doing our finals together. But now I was alone again and available to everyone.

"He said we were sexually incompatible, you see. Some couples are, apparently. It's to do with the right fit, like having the wrong glove. Nobody's fault."

"Perhaps it's just as well. He was frightfully good-looking and sexy I know, but he would always have been carrying on behind your back. In any case, you'd have had to take on his religion."

"Have plastic surgery and a hook put in my nose? My father wouldn't have stood for that for a start."

"He must be pleased."

"Over the moon! Especially pleased this week with me—my window-dressing won first prize in the Fry's Chocolate Counter and Shop Front Display! Five pounds! That will go on my fare to London for the interview on that job."

"Will they let you know on the spot?"

"Apparently, yes. Wish me luck!"

The District Inspector at County Hall was tall and extremely *distingué*. Middle-aged. A lady's man with lots of concertina creases across his lap. A sedentary post apparently, with a wife not too hot on the iron.

I'd just travelled up with a whole load of them—commuters coming to London—and would probably be travelling back with them, no doubt, much later on at tea-time. I was amazed at how alert they'd seemed for such an early hour, but then my father was the only man I'd had to go by in the mornings, and he didn't come alive, could hardly be called even human, till well past ten, with five cups of tea and fifteen Woodbines in him. They'd all had trouser creases too, splayed like crows' feet, ladies' laughter lines, over the top of each leg. So that the eye, starting from the outside edges, could run from one side of the carriage all the way to the other, window to window, covering the contours and counting up the cocks, I worked it out that, including those who passed along the central corridor, pressed occasionally almost in my eager face by the motion of the train—there wasn't a single erection from Brighton station all the way to Victoria. Derek would have said that was unusual. Most men, so he claimed, grew excited by a general jogging. I'd had to content myself instead with sussing out which side their sausages sat. And whether their sets were nestling nicely like a hen on eggs or if, in running to catch the train, they'd inadvertently rearranged themselves in some more awkward order. Before Derek, of course, none of this might have entered my mind. But now my interest was bordering on obsession. The District Inspector dressed on the left—was that the norm or not? I couldn't remember now. I know when Derek had told me first, I'd gone home and furtively studied my father. But as far as I could tell, he seemed hung straight down the middle. Either that or it was empty, living in vacant possession!

Yes, he dressed on the left, the District Inspector, and had wonderfully fine filbert nails. A sign of breeding, so Fiona said. He offered me them in a swoop, bending forward over the width of the desk between us, his flies well in evidence against the edge. I took four and allowed his thumb to wander where it would. It rested rather limply on my knuckles until we both withdrew our hands and sank into our opposite seats.

On the desk lay many applications for the post that I was after. I'd been warned it wouldn't be easy. We'd all been discouraged from applying for a teaching job in London, the competition was too keen. Everyone aimed for these jobs. They'd all given up in our year except me, but I had more reason to hope. My reports, I felt, might justify my optimism. And apparently they did. The District Inspector was speaking. I barely liked to look up, from modesty.

"It's frankly years since I read an assessment like this . . . will undoubtedly prove an invaluable member of staff . . . A highly talented and original artist . . . a sensitive, imaginative and resourceful teacher. . . ." He had a narrower mouth than I would normally have liked in a man and was rather too long in the jaw, with a definite suggestion of an Adam's apple immediately above his tie. But his complexion pleased me, its spotlessness, the age so far removed from acned youth. Even Derek just in his twenties had still been prone to passing boils and unexpected pimples. The District Inspector's skin was dry, its surface lightly scored with criss-cross lines—exactly like an etching. He would have made, for that matter, an excellent subject to etch. In the manner of Rembrandt—all shadow and scratch.

Something in me was moistening up, I could feel it twitch in my knickers. Oh Christ, I thought, it can't be starting up again. But it was, without a doubt, trundling up into my finger-tips, sizzling along under my skin, nothing necessarily to do with anything at all, except an uncontrollable sense of excitement, a washing over. A feeling of being very much alive as opposed to being half-dead. It kept coming, more and more, these days. Up and out of nowhere, suddenly, like the sun—as if I'd started to *shine*. Had he noticed, the District Inspector? Was my warmth making itself felt, filtering across his files? Firing into his fine filbert nails? Something had caused him to stop! Had even occasioned him now to stand and step around his desk towards me, his arm again outstretched. But this time in congratulation, so it seemed! I prepared to stand myself, and would have swooned against his stomach but mercifully dropped my gloves instead. Those interview gloves my mother had urged me to wear to make a good impression. Picking them up I passed his concertina zone so close I could have kissed it. The second went. He shook my hand. After five years of being a student, I was suddenly now employed!

"They should say something on the wireless perhaps. Put it in a special news bulletin. Warning all Londoners that we're coming. About to descend!"

"On the men!"

"I know," I said. "Honestly, Pat, can you believe it, I was only there for the day! The District Inspector for a start, I could have had him. Then the bus conductor on the way to the Tate. That Norwegian dentist at the National Gallery. A Serbo-Croat who chased me down the Strand—I spent an hour in Peter Robinson's trying on dressing-gowns to get rid of him! And at the end of it all there was this Press photographer who picked me up coming back on the train. He stared at me all the way to Burgess Hill and didn't start talking till then. Bit of a waste really, but he dropped me home at least. He kept his car at the station. That was a help because by then my feet were killing me. But it shows though, doesn't it, what can be done up there! I wish Fiona were here—it would cheer her up a bit."

"Mm."

I was sorry I'd said it then, brought Fiona into the conversation. The difficulties of sharing a flat with the two of them was now becoming more apparent. But at least that wouldn't take place for a while; Fiona wouldn't be joining us until her shorthand and typing course was finished, in something like three months. "That will be better really, Fiona, for all the Christmas parties. We'll have got in with lots of people, by then, Pat and me—"

"That's what I can't bear though, the thought of you two living it up without me. Or even just the thought of you with Pat—I shall be so jealous! Don't look like that. I shall! I've never been that keen on her in any case. Why do we have to have her?"

"Don't be silly. I can't afford not to share. We have to have her," I sighed, "because you've been dilly-dallying around for so long thinking secretarial work was beneath you, that you've only just got around to taking the course. If you remember, I told you to get on with it as long ago as last year."

She started pouting. "Yes, well it still looked as if Humphrey might pop the question then. And in any case since then it didn't look as if we'd get to London, what with you and Derek—can I take a chocolate from this tin of Mackintosh's?"

She'd arrived at a happy lull in the shop, knowing it was my night for minding. Every Monday my parents went to the pictures, whatever was on, it didn't matter. And then straight over to the Seven Stars for a pint or two of Merrydown. It was her first visit, in fact, to the shop. She claimed to find it entrancing. "How County one feels behind the counter! The owner of all one surveys! Oh, do let me serve someone, please! This next person coming in. . . ."

My toes curled over in my shoes. "Best not, Fiona. They're a funny bunch, our regulars. A strange face can throw them sideways. They like to know where they stand." And I'd put her to sit on a stool by the biscuits cutting Kit-Kat bars into bits.

"What am I doing this for?" she'd said, stripping off the silver paper.

"The mice have been at the box, that's why. We just snip off the teethmarks like that and sell what we salvage much cheaper."

"Wouldn't it be simpler to keep a cat?"

"We can't have cats, we've tried. It meant my mother spending every day swabbing down bottles from where my father was sneezing on them. He develops dreadful hay fever with furry things in the room. Even caterpillars—he found one once, a pet of mine, that I'd nearly nursed through to a chrysalis, and he was so cross, he dropped it in his cup of tea and stirred it round with a spoon. Strangely enough it didn't drown, what killed it I think was the heat. Yes, take a Mackintosh—I'll tell you which one to try. That, there, the triangle in the veridian wrapper. Milk. Marvellous. Customers used to complain, you know, that our Mackintosh's never had milk chocolates. And they didn't either because I'd eaten them, that's why I was so fat. Do you remember that, how fat I was four years ago? I do!"

"I'd like to lose a bit. I'd like to lose a bit on my legs."

"Oh would you?" I lied. "There's no need!" There was nothing in fact to do except lie about Fiona's legs. The ankles were so tragically out of proportion, nearly as wide as her knees, some said —Pat mostly, whose own legs were so indescribably elegant.

She stretched them before her despairingly. Oh dear, oh dear. "Now tell the truth. What would you do if they were yours?"

I cleared my throat. "Well," I went carefully. "I would probably burn my skirts and stick to trousers." It was out now, at least!

"Daddy would never wear them!"

"What?"

"Not on me. He says they're not lady-like. Mummy bought slacks for the summer in Fortnum's Winter Sale and he sent her all the way back to change them for a suitable skirt—"

"They won't change things in sales though."

"No. She was so upset at the thought of wasting that much money and so concerned by what daddy would say if she came home with the slacks again that she just swapped them herself without saying. And came away with a skirt which actually cost twice as much as she'd paid for the slacks! She didn't tell daddy of course. He'd have gone berserk—"

"He would have if she'd been caught. They make it their business in these places to prosecute regardless. That's one of the things, isn't it, about the menopause—secret shoplifting. They make scapegoats of the ones they catch just to put off the others. Pat's got an auntie who's always at it. I'm not sure it isn't Mark's mother. Someone quite close in the family. He's married now, isn't he, Mark?"

"With a baby. They're awfully unhappy. I'd love to be married with a baby, wouldn't you?"

"That's what Pat said to me the other day. In fact, I said I wouldn't—"

"But then you've just been engaged. We haven't, you see, that's the difference."

"I don't think the being engaged is what did it, but the being in bed might have done. It would be nice before we moved in all together, if the two of you could even up a bit. What about when you go to Scotland? Any chance of a bit up there?"

"There never has been before."

"I think it's really an attitude of mind. If I said to you our life together depended on it, I'm certain you could lose it."

"Oh, I think I've lost it already, the actual skin bit, I'm sure. On a leather saddle in a riding stable. Most girls do on a horse, or a bicycle seat for that matter. I've looked as well. I can see the little hole!"

I was impressed, why hadn't I? Who would have thought it of Fiona? Perhaps she'd show me where I should look.

It was Pat who'd managed to find us a flat. A dismal affair in a basement, with one window looking out on a wall a foot away from your face. And it was Pat's mother who paid in advance the whole of the first three months' rent. When Fiona saw it first she point blank refused to live there. I didn't argue with her, there was no reason since she wouldn't be sharing till Christmas. "We can find somewhere else by then," I'd soothed. "This will do Pat and me in the meantime." I personally found it marvellous. "Do you want to see it first? Before we finally decide?" Pat had said. "Nope!" "Aren't you amazing! I would never dream of moving into somewhere that I hadn't seen first—" "It's in the centre, isn't it? And in London. That's enough for me. Anything as long as it's not at home!"

Pat had not managed to get a teaching job in central London. Somewhere in Essex was what she'd found, which meant that she'd have to start travelling each morning at something like half-past six with three changes on the train and a bus the other end. I thought she was crackers.

"You're crackers. How in hell's name can you afford the fares, for a start?"

"Mum's paying my fares. She says it's worth it not to have me at home!"

"Really?"

"No, not really. She's just paying them because she knows I've been longing for London. Anyway, she claims to be considering it an investment."

"How's that?"

"Because of Roly Balls. He's at Guy's with Mark, but it's his last year. If I don't catch him now, I never will!"

"I've never heard of Roly Balls before. Is that his real name?"

"Roland. He's fabulous. Fat. I like them fat. Something nice and soft to squeeze. Like you."

"Thanks!"

"Meant as a compliment, of course."

I watched her munching up a Mars bar, having just polished off one already. A large saucepan full of spaghetti sat bubbling on the ancient gas stove. We'd only been in the flat several hours and in all that time she'd been eating non-stop. "Do you usually eat as much as this? Or is it just the excitement?"

Her jaws stayed open in surprise. "Eating? Oh, I love eating! I could eat all day, couldn't you?"

"Don't you ever find you get fat?"

"Fat? I wish I could. I'd love to be fat, wouldn't you?"

"I have been. Don't you remember?"

"You're always saying that, but I don't. Here, are you having some of this spaghetti? No? Not any? I'll eat it all myself, I'm warning you! Oh, come on—you can't survive on boiled eggs!"

It was Sunday, the day before we started work. I was looking forward to it myself, but by nine that night Pat had made herself sick with nerves. I held her head while she vomited and turned my face away not wishing to catch a glimpse of her regurgitations. "You shouldn't pump food into your stomach at such a rate, you know. It's a natural reaction, not just nerves. In any case, I don't think I am going to be able to stand it, seeing you eat like that. It'll lead me into bad habits again, and I shall lose this new found figure."

Pat's alarm went off at six o'clock, efficiently waking me with it. She switched the light on—one barely shaded central bulb hanging from the ceiling, shining straight down into my eyes. It was late summer, the start of the autumn term, and had been a particularly mild season. Even so the room was freezing, icy cold with overtones of damp and a fearful condensation dribbling down the walls. "This basement in accord with recently passed bye-laws, has been relined throughout. And freshly decorated to render it fit for habitation," the landlord had assured us on arrival. "Yes," I'd replied. "You can tell it's just been done." The cement was still sweating.

Pat, in her pyjamas, stood shivering violently beside her single bed staring at the floor on which she'd placed, the previous evening, alternatives to wear. I sat up in my bed; we both sneezed together. "Bless you." "You too." "Christ, it's cold! Can't you plug the heater in?" "Have you got money for the meter?" "Not change, no." "Nor me."

I stared at her, fascinated by her naked fragility, unable to look away. She looked so touchingly thin, it made me want to blink. Or take her into my bed and cover her from the cold. She was very brown all over, browner than you'd expect from just meeting her face to face, except for two milky horizontal strips above and beneath her middle. I watched whilst she drew a defensive arm across the flatness of her chest. "Bloody awful aren't they! No boobs as such to speak of!'

I continued to stare. "They're sweet," I said. "Like a child's!" And they were, I couldn't even remember the time when mine must have looked like that. Ten years ago or more. And as well I was struck by the profusion of her pubic hair; there was almost as much between her legs as I, with my tangled tulip cut, had on my head. "Do you shave every day, Pat?" For I was noticing now how neat and nice she was beneath her arms.

"Every other. Why, do you?"

"No, only when I see it sprouting over-long. Actually though, in wintertime, I let it grow. For warmth."

She'd put a pair of knickers on, surprisingly large, white cotton. Aertex. With loose wide legs like a boy scout's shorts.

"They're big enough, Pat!"

"My brother's. A family joke."

"Does he wear yours?"

"However did you guess? He's like that though you know, a bit. I'm sure of it, I keep saying so to mum, but she turns a blind eye. He lives there with her, left school when my dad died, to help mum run the business. The apple of her eye, of course, he can't stand me. Well, we can't stand each other—he always was a terrible cissy. He's only got one friend, Maurice, an old man in his forties. They go to concerts together, or out around the country in the car! But it doesn't bother me too much, he takes mum and the business off my back."

"You're going to be late if you don't watch out. How long will it take for your face?" I'd been amazed the night before to see her taking it off; at the end of ten minutes she'd looked almost a different person—eyeless and pinched and pale. Fiona would be pleased. 'What a particularly plain person poor Pat appears to be underneath!' I could hear it already.

"My face? Oh I shall leave doing my face for the train! Each eye takes twenty minutes at least!"

"Does it? But you'll have to do one on one train and the other on the other! What will people think as they pass you on the platform? I'd never . . ."

She'd slicked herself now into a lacy black uplift brassière, like a kid trying to ape its mother, each side gaped loose and empty. "Oh, very seductive," I said. "Especially with the aertex!"

"I'm going to be late. I'm starting to flap. Quick, tell me what to wear."

I got her out by half-past six, then fell asleep myself, right through the second setting of her alarm so that today, of all days, on my very first, I turned up late for work.

It was an eventful journey, our basement lay on that bend of road where Old Brompton turns into Earls Court. And it was from that station, the Earls Court one, that I'd taken my tube, slap bang in the middle of the rush hour without even time to clean my teeth and render my breath inoffensive. Standing room only. Six stations to go till I reached Westminster where I'd catch a bus on to Elephant and Castle.

It seemed to start as soon as I stepped in and by South Kensington I knew it couldn't be my imagination, that what my journey had lacked from Brighton was being made up for this morning. "The way to tell if a man is past his prime is by whether he wakes in the morning with an erection or not!" That's what Derek had said. I hadn't known that, I'd thought that everyone woke like that from wanting to have a widdle. I mean to say that I'd thought that's what it was full of. But he'd said no, I wasn't to confuse the two. Sometimes, so he claimed, he'd had to put a book on his boko to aim it down at the pan in order to piss. And then he'd had to wank after in order to fit in his trousers. I'd taken it as gospel, though I could never imagine my father having to follow the same procedure. Was that why our outside lavatory had always looked so dribbly, from the inaccuracy of his portion's aim, due to the lack of a book? Was that in fact why men liked taking literature to the latrine? Would a rolled newspaper carry sufficient weight?

There weren't many wankers in my carriage, they'd been saving it for sardining up to me. One was so large indeed that by Westminster it was almost in my pocket. No one looked at me at all:

from their faces, the calmness of their eyes and the immobility of their mouths, no one would have guessed how vigorous were their lower portions. I held my face up like a flower, studying the coloured map of the London Underground. I smiled at it and once or twice I even shut my eyes, so enjoying myself was I. I'd started throbbing of course, that now familiar surging on the first furtive fingering feel. My mouth had dried, my teeth grew tight, my jaw fell slack and loose. I saw for one swift instant my strange face staring back at me, reflected in the glass-panelled door, as heads had swayed suddenly to one side and caused a sudden gap. We thundered through the interminable black tunnels, now underground, and underhand and under everything. I tried to hold a glance—with anyone, but no one would. They turned their eyes deliberately away as if I was the one who over-stepped the barriers of formality. It had happened before in the cinema; people, strangers tickling my tips and nobbling my knees and generally trying to get chummy—then rushing out before lights up, not even exchanging a name. But anyway, it made no odds, travelling to work this way. Was this how it was going to be every single day? I looked round happily at the shy and stony faces. No one to fancy, not really, not a single one, not like Derek. All more like the District Inspector, nice family men I'd have said. And different women with disappointed mouths and brassière straps all hanging on the slack. Fiona had sent a card this morning, a letter would have been better. "Lots to tell." That's all it said, with an upturned mouth like a melon slice. A very good sign that we'd preplanned to show she was possibly getting it. Pat was all who needed some now—it didn't matter how little. Just so we started the same. And in the meantime, as to me, I had my journey to work—would the going home be as good though? Derek had made no general statement on genitalia at late afternoon.

My Headmistress's name was Mrs. Pritchard. She was big and juicy and nice like an extra large portion of apple pie, with the bitter surprise of a clove. I could sense it, the bone at the centre of her sunny butter as soon as she shook me by the hand.

"You're young," she said, "and inexperienced. Not normally

what I would welcome in a school of this size, but"—my blood ran chill at her iron smile—"we've been led to expect extraordinary achievements from you." She smiled again, this time as soft as a cushion. "Whatever sort of spell did you cast on our District Inspector? I've known him many years, but I've never before seen the dear man in quite such a dither!" To my deep annoyance, I began to blush. She found it charming, of course, and at the same time chose to see it as an acceptance on my part of some sort of guilt and thus a complicity with herself. She wagged her finger. "It's all girls together here, I'm sorry to say! Unless you count Cunzle, our caretaker." She leaned forward and lowered her voice. "I wouldn't myself count Cunzle!"

"Kunzle like the cake?" Perhaps it was true about Fiona's meanness—I'd ended up paying for three Kunzles, and she hadn't offered anything. Mrs. Pritchard flung a spontaneous outstretched palm against her Spirella'd stomach—the surging slap ricocheted around the room and finally got gagged by her gurgle. "With a C, but similar enough to remind of one's weakness I am afraid! Now, my dear, to get down to business—I'll tell you what I've given you. . . ."

What she'd given me, and what I didn't like, was a form, a class of my own. One to take care of and chivvy. One to be on time for in order to do their morning register and count up all their dinner money. One to house in the hallowed sanctuary of my art room, so that they would be forever at my elbow whining about the whereabouts of their Wellington boots and playground plimsolls. And what she'd given me as well were oddment classes here and there like Basic Arithmetic, Remedial Reading and Junior Netball. "No. Not netball. I haven't played that since grammar school. I barely remember the rules."

But she'd smiled the smile of a stick insect this time, ready to spring through the leaves. "Miss Megaphone will refresh your memory. Our capable Senior Sports Mistress." Hardly that capable or she'd be coping with Junior Netball herself.

"Even so, I'd rather not, Mrs. Pritchard. This is a secondary modern school I know, attended by girls who haven't managed to pass their Eleven Plus. It would seem to me terribly unfair that for Games, of all subjects, they should be taught by somebody who finds no enjoyment in it herself. These things, as you know, are so easily transmitted. It would distress me very much to think of somebody unenthusiastic attempting to teach Art, my subject—"

"Yes, well, I hardly suppose, my dear, that for you to stand in a playground with a whistle round your neck and a ball in your hand simply frowning a little, is going to do that much harm to our girls. There'll be nothing more for the moment. Could you kindly tell your colleague, Miss Einstein, to come in on your way out?"

Pat was already in by the time I got home, painting the kitchen floor with purple lino paint, but leaving a narrow strip along which to walk whilst the rest was drying. The place looked transformed. I stood at the doorway not daring to enter. "What a palace, when did you do all this?"

"They let us off early, because of it being the first day. I've just been shopping—everything came from Woolworth's. What do you think? I thought I'd cover the length of this wall with some of my fabrics. I brought them up as teaching aids, but you should see them! Practically all cretins—including the bloody staff. I don't know how long I can stick it. I think my Headmistress is a Mongol!"

"You're lucky," I said. "Mine's not! Golda Meir—sharp as a tack, tastes like a strawberry! Dreadful building, all dust and dried lice! You know the sort of smell. Mixed bag in the staff-room. Hardly a surfeit of equipment in the stockroom. School dinners as appalling as you'd expect. But, I had a good day's teaching though—"

She looked up. "What already?"

"Yes, I spent the whole time telling them off. Every single class that came in, I just stood there in front of them laying down the law as to what or not they might expect to get away with. I needed to as well, Christ, you should see them—as tough as old boots. Like street-walkers, the ones you'd get in Soho, some of the sixth formers—frightening, honestly. And huge great things as well. They'd hit you as soon as look at you. But by the end I had them like mice. I'm going to do that with each lot that come to me, just to show who's boss, otherwise everything will be up the wall. I believe in that, ruling with a rod of iron—one of the other teachers was crying by the end of the day. Sitting in the staff-room crying her eyes out. She's in the next room to me—I could hear her lot through the wall, bedlam, poor bugger. She was new as well. There are two of us new—what about you?"

"Oh, my lot have been there since the Boer War, I should think. I'm by far the youngest."

"What was the journey like anyway?"

"Oh dreadfully dreary. Almost deserted actually, because everybody else was travelling in the other direction. I felt like a leper. Good for doing my face though. And I got there on time."

"I didn't. I was late."

She stood up to survey the wet and shining surface of the floor. "It's a good colour, this. Or do you think red might have been better? Well, if we get tired of it, I can always do it over."

"Can you?" I said. "It's funny, that. I'd never have thought of painting the floor. I'd probably just have left it with that awful pattern on the lino. It doesn't worry me that much what a place looks like. But you'll make a wonderful wife—the homely touch!"

"Well that's no change, your being late. You're always late. Wc all know that."

I laughed. What a nice life, coming home like this. Carrying on so cosily. No father to shout. No shop to have to serve in. No customers irritably tapping the counter with their coins. "Well, I have to go easy with this Head. She caught me coming in—and what's more she's given me my own form, which means I've got to do all that register thing and take them into Assembly. Unless I can train them up to do it themselves. Perhaps if I make a real balls-up of it, she'll take them away. That's probably my best plan. And the same with Remedial Reading and bloody Junior Netball—"

"Has she given you that? All those things?"

"I'll get rid of it all somehow. Yes. ID, that's my form. D for duffers! The bottom stream. Poor little sods. Have you got a class, by the way?"

She shook her head. "No. And not a bad building either. Quite new I think. A bit like a public lavatory. Cold-looking. Clean. By the way, are we going to have some sort of rota here for the cleaning?"

"Cleaning?" Cleaning hadn't occurred to me before. And nor had things like cooking or who should buy the soap. "I leave it to you," I said. "You work it all out and I'll do whatever you say. We'll get on best you being boss. These menial things don't interest me."

She raised her brows sarcastically. "*La vie bohème*—I get it!"

"I'm afraid I'm awfully untidy, you must tell me if I get terrible. Start nagging me, I shan't mind."

"Oh no, I'm not doing that. I do a lot of throwing away though, I may as well warn you now. I've had a bit of a clear-out already. Perhaps you'd better look in the dustbin; there were lots of bits and pieces I've cleared. Nothing very important, I don't think. . . ."

I walked along the corridor away from the kitchen, past the bathroom and into what could loosely be called our bedsitter. In one sense the term was quite accurate since there were only the beds there to sit on. The beds, the dressing-table, mirrored, and a corner cupboard for both our clothes. "I can see you've cleared up, Pat," I shouted back at her. "Thanks for making my bed." I looked around the room, missing my own familiar mess. Where the hell had she put everything? I cleared my throat and returned to the kitchen; she'd finished the floor and was cleaning the kettle, her paintbrush already neatly standing in a container of turpentine. "Oh, are you good with brushes? I shall have to give you all mine. I'm awful at cleaning them after. Every single one is quite stiff. It's like painting with a palette knife. I just use them for laying the pigment on the canvas, that's all. No niceties of stroke."

She paused. "I've thrown them away, I'm afraid. They're in the dustbin. I didn't think you used them in that state! Sorry! Shall I get them back?"

I looked at her, appalled. My brushes! She'd gone and thrown away my brushes! In the Painting Department a person's brushes were their soul! Sacrosanct! Their prized possession! Nobody touched another's brushes. But Pat had thrown mine away! The sheer vandalism rendered me speechless. I walked out wordlessly in the direction of the dustbins to retrieve the discarded tools of my trade. They lay reproachfully beneath two over-ripe tomatoes, a torn Ryvita wrapper, an old *Picture Post*, a banana skin and a whole gaggle of stuff amongst which I noticed my favourite lipstick and the now crumpled letter from the District Inspector informing me officially of my employment. I came back with both hands full.

"What are you doing?" Pat looked genuinely astonished.

"I'm rescuing my belongings!" I answered stiffly. "This, Pat" —I held it up—"is my favourite lipstick!"

"But it's all used up. There's nothing left!" She looked perplexed and puzzled. "I opened it. If there'd been any there, of course I wouldn't have thrown it away."

"That's beside the point. There may be other reasons why I might wish to keep it. Like needing to take it to the shop when I get round to replacing it. To match it up, I mean. You didn't jot down the make or the shade I shouldn't think, did you? And in any case"—I took the top off and began to unscrew—"there is some left, just here, look, right at the bottom. I manage all right with a matchstick—" She curled her own immaculately coloured upper lip disdainfully and began looking disagreeable, but my adrenalin was now too high to stop. "And"—I flourished the District Inspector's letter in her face—"this. I was keeping this."

"Keeping it? What for?"

"Keeping it to keep."

"I see." Her voice took on a note of flat finality. "Keeping it to keep! Is that what you are then—a hoarder?"

"No, not a hoarder. But you have to keep some things. As mementos. Nice reminders. Like small landmarks in your life. You have to do that surely. Like this letter. I'm not going to get this letter again, am I? Not telling me about my first job, I'm not. That's what makes it special. And come to that even the lipstick. I shan't necessarily throw it away even when I buy a replacement, an identical replacement. The first will remind me, you see, this one here will of different times and things. Kisses, you know. Evenings out. Everything like that—"

"A hoarder. You're a hoarder all right. A bloody magpie. Not whilst you're living with me though! Right? We'll make a pact now that when I'm clearing up, I can throw away whatever I think, if it's lying around the place. If you want to hoard, you hoard in your drawers, or your part of the cupboard, not on communal territory, okay?"

I turned on my heel, my arms awash with my bits and pieces, and made an attempt at dignity. "That suits me fine. Oh, and before I forget. It surely is unprofessional to throw out the *Picture Post*?"

"Why on earth should we want those, once we've seen them?"

"Pat!" I managed to make my voice as reproving as possible. "Our teaching aids, remember!"

It was our first unpleasantness and, dreading unpleasantness as I did, I made the first move towards a truce. "Any plans *à propos* your Roly then?"

"Plans?" She repeated coldly.

"Yes, plans. Have you a plan of action for the capture of Monsieur Balls? Are you considering asking him round or inviting him out or anything? Or will you be leaving it all to him?" I was on the right tack, I'd known I was before I started. She'd already begun to melt. My God, but this sharing stunt was less easy than I'd envisaged. We needed a suitable social life if she wasn't to get on my nerves. I'd have enough to tell old Fiona anyway.

"Well. What do you think? I was hoping that Mark might manage something, but of course now he's married, he's no longer as available as he used to be. What I'd like is to have a party. Perhaps at the end of the week, if we can jolly the look of the place a bit. That's why I'm doing all this, trying to tart it up."

I looked at her doubtfully. Did we know enough people yet? "But who could we ask, do you think? Wouldn't it be better to wait a bit until we know a few more?" I was unfamiliar with the art of party-giving, never having given one before. It was a mystique to me, though one which I was most eager to become acquainted with.

"Oh, giving a party is the best way of getting to know people. You tell everyone you ask to bring someone and a bottle, and automatically, your circle widens. That's what I've always found works best. What about you? You must know at least one person in London, surely. However slender the thread? What about the ones that Fiona knows? She was always coming up to London, wasn't she? Or was it all eyewash, do you think? When is she back in any case, from Scotland? If she's back in time she could come."

"Yes, she could. No, I don't know anyone, isn't it extraordinary! Oh, except Derek's cousin. I know him. Michael, he's a solicitor. Or will be when he finishes. He's frightful though, you wouldn't like him. Smarmy. He lives in Battersea. I've got his number here somewhere. Derek stayed with him when he came to London."

"Well, there you are, you see. Why not give him a ring? Go on."

"What? Right now?"

"Yes, why not?"

"And say what?"

"Say hello. That's the way, I promise you—"

He was in, the dreaded Michael, as it happened, but only just, it seemed. "You've caught me with my coat on! How awfully nice to hear you. So sorry about the dooming of your love affair. Had a card from Derek, strangely enough. Posted on board. Have you heard from him? No. Ah well. Perhaps a clean break is for the best. I say, look here, have you eaten? What about having a bite with me? Yes, do bring your friend, by all means! Is she as glamorous as your good self? I have to meet an old school friend for a drink first, but if he's free, I'll ask him to join us. He has a hell of an eye for a pretty girl, I must warn the pair of you—"

"That's it then, Pat! We've bloody done it! Let's dosh ourselves up! We're going out to dinner!"

Michael's club was in Swallow Street, just off from Piccadilly. We went there on the tube. A rather different ride to the one I'd had this morning. Pat, strangely, had claimed to find my revelations mildly revolting. "Really?" I'd said. "But why?" The fact of the furtive fingers. The impersonal pushing of the penises. "Wouldn't it be penii, in the plural?" I decided to ask Michael. He was well up on Latin being a legal person. I wondered if his old school friend was a legal person too. My father was very fond of lawyers. Legal beavers, so he claimed, were the most prestigious of the professions. "You come back with a barrister, my girl, and you'll have gladdened your old dad's heart. Don't go squandering yourself now, on any old Tom, Dick or Harry. You could get anything if you put your mind to it. You've had a lucky escape with the yid, now see to yourself and aim for the stars!"

I'd met Michael before, of course. Twice—the first time in those early idyllic days with Derek. And then later on when things between us were going badly off the boil. Both times had been in Brighton, but I knew about this club of his already. The Studio Club it was called, Derek belonged and had managed to wangle Michael a membership, not being strictly to do with the Arts. "You should join as well. They have women. Painters, writers even actresses—"

"This is the club that Derek said I should join. It doesn't cost that much, Pat. It's exactly for people like us. On our own." I was over-excited. We were going out. All my doing. Our first date! I squeezed her arm as we came up the steps of Piccadilly station and got caught in the roar of the town. "Oh, look around!" I gawped. "What do you think! Isn't it wonderful!" I went like that in cities, warmed to the hum and the heart. The width of the pavements and the height of the poles. The telegraph wires and the traffic lights, and the shimmering shine of shop windows. The magic of the metropolis.

But Pat appeared unmoved, even faintly irritable. The people of Piccadilly milled around us. "Oh don't they get on your nerves—all pushing! Honestly! Did you see that woman then? Right on my toe—and she didn't even say sorry!"

"Oh come on. I'll say it for her—sorry!" I wanted it to be perfect, our first night out. Why on earth did she need such cajoling? I did a little skip as we passed Swan & Edgar's and laughing linked my arm in hers. She looked at me. "Calm down." I clamped my teeth together and silently counted ten. "Oh, come on Pat! Cheer up! Calm down indeed—what's wrong?"

I wasn't interested to hear, in fact. At even the slight suggestion of her shrug, I could feel my spirits evaporate. She was opposite to Fiona, that's what I now began to tell myself. Our sharing had been a mistake.

"Will we like them? That's what's wrong. I don't want to waste time with two drips—"

I stopped walking. "What?"

"Well, we'd be better off washing our hair and tidying up and having an early night than—"

"Pat"—I spoke so severely, as if addressing my girls at school, that for a second she looked quite startled. "Pat," I repeated. "We're never going to be better off having an early night. Not at our age. Got it?"

She hung back reluctantly. "I'm having second thoughts. I don't feel up to going in. I don't fall on my feet with strangers—not like you, you know—"

"Fall on my feet? Who, me? I don't fall on my feet." I was quite genuinely amazed. It was happening more and more these days it seemed to me. People making absurd assumptions. Attributing me with quite extraordinary qualities. Placing me an alienating distance from themselves—accepting their own inferiority. When I would have preferred the camaraderie of being equals. "No, it's not my feet. If anything, it's probably more my mind. I like to keep it open. That's why I never shut doors or drawers, or anything, even my handbag if I can help it—" We'd reached Swallow Street. I started searching for the entrance to the Studio Club. "And when I eventually get going, I hope to apply that very same principle to my legs. Keeping them open I mean, if you'll excuse the coarseness."

The Studio Club had a peeling painted door, which had at one time been Thames Green. A favourite shade from the Festival of Britain. Pat viewed it approvingly. "We could do ours that, you know. Our front door in the flat. Thames Green. And the inside of the toilet." I turned the handle. She kept saying toilet. Fiona would have condemned it non-U, but was there a nice way of warning Pat? No.

"Anyway, you never know, you may well meet your future tonight."

"The school friend, you mean?" There was actually now a break in her voice! Not of nervousness, surely? Never!

"That's where you go wrong you see—pinning your hopes on an

actual person. Like Roly Balls, for instance. Worshipping from afar. I'd never do that. If you want somebody, you wangle it that you get them. But otherwise, just living in hopes at a distance, you're bound to be disappointed. What I mean is that your future could present itself at any turn of the corner. It doesn't need formal introductions before you start speaking to people, surely. I'd forget about the school friend for a start—he's bound to be bloody awful. Blind dates almost always are."

He wasn't though, not bloody awful. In fact he was quite the opposite! And Pat obviously thought so, I could tell from the way she blinked. It smacked of success, the whole evening, from the second we stepped through the door. A heady mixture rose to greet us of perfume and garlic and wine, mingling with music—modern jazz—and the tantalising subdued snatch of low talk. We walked self-consciously down the stairs, aware of the waiting eyes beneath. A man with a beard barred our way. He looked like Augustus John but turned out to be the Club Secretary. "Ladies?" I explained that we'd come as guests, just as Michael appeared from the Gents. He kissed us both before he signed us in and then introduced the school friend, Douglas.

He wasn't at all my sort of chap—too much of the Anglo-Saxon. Too fair and smooth and well-turned-out, like a walking shop-window dummy. The sort you'd come across in Austin Reed's Regent Street window—we'd only just passed them this evening. The look of the young executive, complete with executive glasses. Douglas. "As in the Isle of Man." Pat laughed delightedly. Exactly her level of humour. He turned and smiled at her appreciatively, deliberately lingering on her tidy lips and nattily manicured nails. I saw him approve her arrow-straight seams as she turned to take off her coat. I reminded myself to have a word with her over her aertex underwear. It would be heartbreaking to ruin what could be a promising relationship for the sake of her brother's bloomers.

Michael was smiling at me admiringly; I forced myself to smile back. I'd forgotten how awful he was. And what was worse—how short. Had something happened since we'd met? Had someone sliced off his ankles? He slipped his arm ostensibly around my waist, it ended encircling my buttocks. And it was in this bizarre fashion that we entered the bar of the Club. "What will you have?" He looked up at me. I quickly slipped on to a stool to render us more on a level. People were dancing—merely feet away from us—between the bar and the trio who played far beyond. My heart sank, it meant, of course, that we'd be doing the same. Me and Michael. "A very large gin for a start!" Drunk, I could dance with a dwarf!

The two of them, Michael and Douglas, had had quite a few already. We needed ours large to catch up, but by the time our table was ready, both Pat and I were aglow. "Which way to the Ladies' Room?" I whispered quietly to Michael. "The Little Girls?" he shouted back, and stood up to point with his finger. Several men at the bar crowded round to clap me on my way.

"Are you coming, Pat?" I wanted to know, suss out the state of the nation. "No, I'm all right," she started. I pulled a face. "Oh, yes. Wait, I'm coming!"

"What do you think then?" I said as soon as we got there.

"Phew!" she went. "What do you?"

"He's it, I think, Pat. You've done it!"

"Do you think so? Yes! So do I!"

The thing was, where though? I was more worried about that than her. Douglas still lived with his mother, who was widowed—the same as Pat's. I watched them over dinner, they certainly suited each other. When they got up to dance I turned to Michael. "They seem to have hit it off—your school friend and my flat mate. We should congratulate ourselves! Does he have many other girlfriends? I mean, where would he entertain them?"

He wasn't so bad, old Michael. He understood right away. "Oh I say. Yes. I'm sorry I can't be of assistance. The only girls I've ever met of Douglas' have always had pads of their own. One assumes the worst would take place back there. How large is your flat, by the way?"

"Not large enough, I'm afraid."

"On the other hand, would you like to sleep with me tonight? Strictly as friends, of course?"

"How sweet of you Michael—some other time. But not tonight I think."

I shut my eyes very tight, though there wasn't any need in the dark. And pushed a finger in my one good ear to blot out the sound of her groans. My deafness would seem now to be standing me in good stead. A mastoid operation in early childhood. My only physical disability the resulting deafness. But when at last I let my good ear go, I could tell that they'd fallen asleep from the absolute steady silence. I opened my eyes again, still whirling from what I'd been drinking. We were all whirling by the time we'd left the club. And possibly because of that, the lightness of the occasion and the lateness of the hour, it had seemed quite perfectly natural that Douglas should accompany us down. And of course there seemed no reason why he shouldn't come in, once in the basement.

I'd left them kissing in the kitchen, and gone to clean my teeth. Thankful only that Michael had finally seen reason and relinquished all hopes for my favours. And from cleaning my teeth and running my new blue flannel around my face, I'd fallen quite giddily into bed, and left the light on for Pat. When I woke up it was off. But they were both in her bed. It shouldn't have shocked, but it did. Her doing it there the first time! It seemed to me, like throwing away my brushes, to smack of such insensitivity! I wouldn't have done it, not even drunk. I'd have wanted to have a word with the one that you give it to first. Perhaps that's what had put poor Derek off. The attachment I'd shown then to talking. If I'd kept my mouth shut, he might have made more progress opening up my other end.

What did her groans mean? I wondered. I lay there now, flat on my back, my good ear, like a piece of fine electrical equipment, picking up the lightweight cadences of their combined sleeping breaths. And the relentless ticking of her alarm. Had she remembered to set it? I strained to see in the dark. It seemed right, those luminous lines, as far as I could tell. That was one alarm call I should sleep through. To let them get dressed on their own and spare us all the embarrassment, mutual, of a morning confrontation.

That wasn't actually how it happened. They both woke me up with some coffee and watched me drinking it starry-eyed, on the edge of her bed together. They held hands and kissed a lot, oblivious of my presence. Pat had been to bed with all her make-up on, her eyes looked bleak and black with smudged and stale mascara. And on her mouth remained a faintly carmine tinge—I didn't think I'd ever seen her look so bloody beautiful.

All their clothing lay littered over the floor, they'd obviously undressed in a hurry. Stripped in haste. Peeled off at a speed. Hardly able to wait. To fall upon each other like two lustful ravenous beasts! My sleep-drugged sluggishness jolted at the thought. I felt appalling now. I was awake but half-dead, with a diesel drill doing its damnedest in my head. I cowered over my cup of coffee, barely able to bring myself to meet their eyes. But it was obvious that I was the only one of us embarrassed in any way by the intimacy of the situation. I cleared my throat, I felt clogged internally. "I've got a hellish hangover, haven't you two? Shut your eyes while I slip out of bed—I was so far gone last night I couldn't even find my nightie."

Pat looked blank and utterly beguiling. Wide-eyed but not quite with us, like someone in a dream. Was she still drunk? Douglas leaned over and teasingly tried to flick my bedclothes to one side. I snatched them back beginning to be alarmed, but he just gave a good-natured frown.

"Oh, don't be a spoil-sport, old thing! Let's take a peep at the beautiful bod!" He was wearing one of Pat's dressing-gowns. A floral Acrilan affair. Man-made fibre, covered in crimson carnations. American. Sent from San Francisco by another of Pat's aunts, who'd been the first of the GI brides. Wash'n'Drip Dry. Faced by the multitude of many such enviable gifts that Pat received, I might well have wished that my mother too had had sisters. Or my father, come to that. It barely met across his front, hardly covered up his nipples. He had a particularly smooth and hard and hairless chest, I noticed, and a mannish nice long neck, muscled somewhat like a giraffe's. And now without his glasses and his Board of Director's suiting, he looked less spruce and taut, more appealing altogether. I didn't let my eyes fall lower down. I didn't dare. In any case it would have seemed like poaching on poor Pat's territory. I coughed. He was sitting discreetly cross-legged, no chance of a glimpse of anything. It was only if he stood, that I'd be privileged.

Pat spoke at long last. "It's all right! We're all pals together. Let him see, go on!" And as if to illustrate the all-encompassing extent of our togetherness, she deliberately tugged her own sheet to one side and stretched without self-consciousness towards the ceiling. She yawned as we both watched the sinewey lines of her becoming taut then slackening gracefully away. Her hair hung tangled and uncombed around the suntanned shoulders; the entire shape seemed mysteriously more seductive than I had previously judged before. She settled back, the sheet fell even further so that now I could see her navel and the subtle swell of one hip. Her tiny nipples were now erect, had come to a life of their own. Even the colour seemed different—a delicate terracotta where before they had merely been brown.

I swallowed. No one spoke but now they were looking at me—expectantly I thought, as if waiting for what I was about to do. Douglas made the first move, he slowly stood up, allowing the American bride's Drip Dry to fall away and reveal his own personal properties. The clock said ten past six. I would have had to admit that I enjoyed the sight of his offering, despite the reluctance I felt. I'd always liked looking at Derek's, unhealthily much, so he said. He'd taken a bath, that very first time, and had casually called me in. "Soap it!" he'd said. And had offered the two together—first the Palmolive and then his penis. He'd shown me how to run the bar around the rim, with a hand beneath the balls. I'd enjoyed it all, the feel of it stiffening up—like a lighthouse surrounded by surf—that's how it looked by the end, I said. And I'd swilled all the bubbles away with his super de luxe bath sponge and water straight from the tap. Much too hot! He'd squealed like a stuck pig, struck a new note in the musical register for a full five minutes or so. As a matter of fact I'd felt quite scared believing I'd done permanent damage.

Douglas' looked rather similar, as far as I could tell in the light. "It's a fair size," I said conversationally. "Did it hurt you?" I turned towards Pat. I'd got over my initial embarrassment. Why not involve oneself after all? Since Pat didn't appear to mind—but I felt worried even so on her behalf. "Keep an eye on the time, Pat," I warned.

But she lay back with even greater abandon, slanting her eyes provocatively from one of us to the other. "Perhaps"—she spoke very slowly—"I shan't go in today. Not turn up to work at all!"

"Pat! What? You're still drunk!"

She shrugged. I looked at her amazed. Could one single sexual experience have wrought such a positive change? Had deflowering divulged an unexpected streak of Patty-Devil? Not go in? What gross irresponsibility! I gasped at the very recklessness, barely aware of what Douglas was doing now. He'd disrobed, let Man-Made drop on to the floor and stood with his cock at a sly wild salute. It waved there bravely though unsteadily, due to a lack of support, towards the upstairs tenants. A circumcised sod, so I saw, to quote my articulate father. A carefully clipped poodle, a well-pruned privet, a sharpened propelling pencil. He propelled it down now with both hands.

I swallowed again. An inexplicable supply of saliva was pouring into my mouth. Drowning my front teeth and the tip of my tongue, and drumming out into the back of my tingling ears. All my orifices in fact were receiving emergency oil of sorts from somewhere! Every pore was opening up, extending itself in welcome. "I need to go," I said. "I think." Something was happening under the sheets, some strange and unbearable pressure, high up in what I took to be my bladder, but at the same time further through than there, was the certain sensation of oozing. This can't be correct without contact, prior to all the palaver, without the excitement of stroking—to be so seduced—on sight! I crossed my legs and squeezed together tightly with my upper thighs. But it seemed if anything to make the matter worse, the unspecific centre of the surging pleasure was becoming more sharp and intense. "Oh dear," I said it quietly and to myself. And without giving a second thought I slid a hand in down over my own now hard (and normally so soft) nipples, pausing a second to pass over them another time, so natural did it seem and nice. Down I went over velvety skin until I came to rest in the entrance of my open crinkly nest of hair. My clitoris felt swollen, wonderfully wobbly and stiff. I pressed it hard, and surreptitiously began to rub, holding the bedclothes well up with my other hand.

Douglas raised his elbows away from his body, wriggling his wrists in the air. "Look, no hands!" And tensing himself, started thwacking away on his stomach. A performing penis, like a seal. What a house pet to have in your pants! How much murkier, marshier, messier women's parts were! Like school atlases, the hillier bits brought out in lighter shades, and the rest all dank and dark and uncharted. Layered like ripe pickled onions and prone to the same sort of smell.

Pat had brightened up a bit and had even begun to clap. "Oh," I winked at her. "Congratulations yourself, by the way. You look better now you've lost it!" She smiled and so did Douglas. "Your turn now," he said, and in one quick movement, had tossed all my sheets to one side. "Caught you!" He tapped my manipulating fingers. "Here, let me. There's no need for that with me around, kiddie!" I shuddered dangerously inside to feel his hand touching the swell of my stomach. "It's full," I said. "I'm afraid I shall have to be excused."

"All piss!"

"That's true—"

"All piss and ignorance! Gives the best fuck in the world. A full bladder!"

That's not what Derek had said. Go now if you want to, before we start, for God's sake! Now are you certain you don't feel the need? "The pressure, you see," Douglas spoke with enthusiasm. "Tremendously exciting! Cliff-hanging stuff, so it seems! I promise you. Had a girl not so long ago—we all had her if I remember rightly—the whole of the rugger club. Her speciality was pissing on a chap. Really hot stuff on it she was. A rather chilling experience in the front seat of a parked car come winter, I can tell you! And positively anti-social in the rear of the coach for that matter! Yes, she was a sort of mascot for a time. Can't think what happened—proved too expensive probably. The dry-cleaning bills, y'know. Flannel pants need particular pressing and so do club blazers, come to that. Also I believe the coach company registered a formal complaint—the upholstery becoming discoloured and sustaining an unpleasant smell."

I listened closely. Could it be true, what he was saying? Surely not! "Liar!"

"No. Scout's Honour. S'true, old thing! On the absolute point of orgasm. She'd release all inner tensions! The whole lot let rip!"

"A form of enuresis? Incontinence under sexual stress!" I was fascinated by what he was saying. Who would have guessed it to look at him! Michael had said he was good with girls. What a mine of marvellous information—I glanced at Pat to see how she was taking it. She was leaning forward, seemingly not listening, but staring intently at me. My insides lurched.

"I'd best go," I moved. "I'm almost sure I shan't hold out—I like to empty the reservoir first thing in the morning before I can face the day. Sorry, Douglas—"

"I'd go on the side of the bath if your legs don't reach up to the sink. Just run the tap, that's all—saves time." Pat turned to Douglas. "That's the worst thing about this flat, the bog being out by the dustbins. You have to go right out to the outside corridor. I cock a leg over the sink. You're lucky, you boys, I learnt it from my brother." Yes, I'd seen her do it the very first day. "You don't mind, do you? Old habits die hard." Her wide-legged knickers had helped, of course. She'd drawn the gusset to one side, lifted her left knee over the porcelain and aimed at the ancient plughole. Muscles like a man! I wondered now, with everything more open, as it were, whether there'd be the control.

I stirred myself, not too ashamed to stand and show my body. In fact quite proud these days. "Christ, you're beautiful!" Derek had said. "You honestly bloody are!"

"Am I?" I'd still been anxious then. "Not too fat?" I'd said. That would always be my worry. It had been my worry from the time my father had noticed me starting some shape. "Have you been at the strawberry sherbets? You're putting some weight on, my girl! I've a good mind to move these Maltesers out of temptation's way as well. Don't think I don't know when you've been dipping in—"

"Fat, my foot! Hourglass! Pocket Venus." Derek had given me confidence.

"Isn't she gorgeous, Douglas?" Now Pat was being generous! Douglas was sweating on his upper lip. "I could tell what was there in her clothes."

I held my shoulders back and tried my best at sucking my stomach in as well as I could in the circumstances. "I'll be back in a sec, where're my shoes?" I'd slipped them on and gained another several inches, but I still didn't quite make the sink! It was 6.24 exactly, I'd looked at the clock to make sure before bombarding the ancient enamel over the edge of the bath, cold tap full on, top pelt. "Are you sure," I shouted above the din and deluge, "you're definitely not going to school, Pat?" She didn't answer until I returned.

"I'd rather stay here and watch you."

"Watch what though? Won't you mind?" I felt the need to know. I thought it only nice to ask. I would have minded with Derek. If he'd have invited another. Oh, all men would like it with two girls. That's one of the most normal fantasies! Is it, Derek? Really? More than alone, being in love? But he hadn't answered. Sometimes being in love could make it less successful.

Douglas pulled me very close; in my high heels, I reached almost to his ear. "Oh come on, I'll be gone tomorrow, kiddie."

I reared back. "Gone?"

But Pat answered cheerfully. "Off to Malta to start a new job! So it makes no odds either way. We may just as well both benefit. Go on, get a move on, you two. It's terribly exciting—"

She seemed at home now, Pat. As at home as I had ever seen her. This wasn't the first time she'd done it—she'd never have been so relaxed. Or eager either, come to that, to be merely an excited spectator. Didn't *two* girls mean having both? But Pat it seemed would remain an observer. "Have you done this sort of thing before, Patsy?" I managed to ask as Douglas prepared to kiss me. Her mouth curled up each end. "Millions of times with old Mark. He always let me in on things. The taboos were too great for him to have me—"

Douglas knew his way around all right. "Stand very still," he said. And led me towards the wall. "I want to feel just what it is I'm getting!" 6.37 I saw. I'd worked out to leave by 8.10. My conscience could never have allowed any careering off on my part. Part of my attitude to life was to try to cram everything in.

He started with my earlobes and travelled round my neck, tickling with his finger-tips and touching with his tongue. It made me shiver, the skill which he employed, although I felt so much less sexy now. Perhaps then what he'd said was true, the fullness of the bladder had triggered off that very special tension. Because right now, despite the nearness of his bulging dick—which after all is what you're meant to like—I'd begun to *separate* inside. I still felt swollen, as it were, and my nipples were still erect. I felt the need to quicken his desire. I loved the *thought* of Pat as an onlooker—in fact I purposely posed myself in what I knew to be provocative angles. I thrust and trembled and sighed and shut my eyes and smiled. I pushed myself against Douglas and I smouldered in Pat's direction, even licking my lips in quite uncharacteristic lewdness as if to arouse her licentiousness. But all the time I was aware of an alienation—and I was waiting for when he'd go in. 6.57 went the hands of the clock, three minutes more made it 7.00. He was still stroking—one hand concentrating on my upper zones, the other on my lower. Pat was beginning to wriggle. He'd placed an index finger between my lower lips and had begun a delicate movement, encompassing with each further subtle swoop a greater expanse of that inner skin. The rubbing of Aladdin's lamp, a magical affair, intended as in the tale to open up the pleasures of Heaven and Life's unparalleled pleasures. But I knew where he was aiming for and had got my needles ready. They were knitting and knotting despite myself. "Shall we try the bed, madam?" I allowed him to steer me in that direction, willing myself to unlock. He smiled at me. Sweet. And Pat smiled as well, like a sister, a loving well-wisher. I longed not to let them down.

It was 7.15 exactly by the time we'd got into position. Missionary style for starters, that's what Douglas had said. I'd never known another way. "Yes, that's how I did it before—him on top." Douglas had laughed. "Glad to hear someone has broken the ice already!" I kept my mouth shut, my misgivings were mounting—

broken—cracked it, maybe! Or possibly merely scratched it, like something diamond sharp on glass. Fiona had done that in our shop, drawn on the window with what she claimed to be a diamond. A glinting splinter of a thing hanging in an antique ornament from her ear. "Oh don't," I'd said. "My dad will go crackers —he cleans those himself, you know." She'd laughed and gone on doing it. How were things going with her up there, in Scotland, now, I wondered. Was she at this very moment, at 7.17 precisely, practising Missionary too? They were noted, the Scots, for adopting religious positions, stances, rather extreme. Calvinists. Something cold and austere, which wouldn't suit Fiona at all.

"Shall I put some music on? Would that help us all?" Pat was speaking; I could hear her voice but Douglas was blotting the view. Blotting out everything in fact, the central bulb, the beading on the ceiling, the thought of the long day ahead. The underside of him looked very red, poised as it was above me, like meat roasting on a spit—the blood had run down to the bottom. My legs were wide and welcoming; my breasts, in this position, lolled gently on each upper arm, their centres brisk and businesslike compared to the abandoned surrounds. Douglas snortled excitedly, a bead of something damp dropped from the centre of his face. I fervently prayed it wasn't his nose. His shoulders were raised higher than the rest of him, supported on my pillow by his hands, each side of me. He kept glancing down, towards his lower regions—to see how things were going I supposed. Was his missile to remain unguided then by hand? Would it know the way by instinct, like a homing pigeon? I shut my eyes and counted up to ten. When I opened them nothing happened.

"Should we give it a lead? Show the carrot to the donkey, Douglas?"

"Right! Here we go," he said. "Prepare for action." And leaning back and holding it with one hand, he lunged towards what all of us hoped was a hole!

Boomerangs take well up to half an hour before returning back to base. Douglas' took ten seconds. And an animal bellow of alarm. And a blow to his bollocks that must have sent his senses reeling, such that he might have reasonably believed his job in

Malta to be put in jeopardy from the need for hospitalisation. "Jesus Christ! What do you have in there—a concrete jungle or a jigsaw puzzle constructed from plaster and iron filings?"

Pat was peering anxiously over his shoulder as I lifted my head and looked down. All seemed as it should be at my end—no fighter's fist, no set of knuckles, no demon jack-in-the-box had emerged to deal his poor dong such a blow on the nose. I tentatively walked my thumb and index finger down to feel the tensile strength in that stretch of skin. It lay like a neat piece of plaiting, perfectly intertwined—no Entry sign hung anywhere. Oh hell on earth! No! Not again! I took the stoic sensible line, a nice no-nonsense approach. "What's up, then Douglas? Won't it go in?"

"Why not? Why won't it?" Pat bleated.

"She's dry," Douglas turned to me. "You're dry," he said. "That's why."

Dry? What, dry like certain Southern States or Sunday pubs in Wales? Or like your feet in well-shod shoes or under an oak in the rain? No. More like the dryness fear brings—as dry as a moth in a flame. As dry as my mouth in fact was now—where in hell was all that saliva? And all that oozing stickiness from before? "Oh, I'm sorry I'm dry. I don't know why, I was ever so wet a while ago." Even at 7.15. "Have you got a bit of spit to spare?" I found I was asking Pat. "Spit?"

Douglas turned 'Board of Directors'; he snapped his fingers efficiently, mopped his brow and settled on his haunches, his game erection resting on my thigh. "Quick," he said, "before this bugger disappears—some Vaseline is called for!"

Pat's eyes swivelled wildly around the room. "Vaseline! Um, Vaseline! Will Valderma do?"

Douglas started tutting and seized his weapon at source, high at the point of its growth from his trunk. "Ye Gods!" The mutter turned into a scream—I marvelled at how he'd managed to make that sound through such steadily clenched teeth. We seemed to have some minor emergency on our hands.

"Let's try again," I said. "I've got fifteen minutes left, before I get up and dress."

He sank as if in deep despair. "Do you mind going out of the room, Pat my dear?" he pleaded. "Perhaps that's what is putting her off."

"No, it's not, please. I like her here. I'm always like this I'm afraid. I've been told it's because I'm all tensed up and tight—just spit on it now, you'll see. . . ."

He worked solidly for the entire fifteen minutes—by the last five I was praying that he'd stop. Now I was sore as well as dry, and near to tears too. He'd gone, long gone, completely limp and lay back at last, exhausted. Pat was white and woebegone, her earlier radiance had disappeared—she looked like a social worker, whose case had come to grief. I tried to comfort them both as best I could.

"Never mind. Now can we have another coffee? I've got to get off to school. You two can stay and start again after a little sleep. . . ."

My day consisted of double periods. One lasted till mid-morning play, the next one saw through the morning till the school bell announced dinner. Another took up part of the afternoon which left a single lesson time to spare. My spare this afternoon was actually free as opposed to being occupied with Remedial Reading or dreaded Junior Netball.

I'd forged my fragile way to Earls Court Station, having carefully kissed Douglas farewell. I'd held my face well forward, not wishing to arouse him all over again. They were both in bed, he and Pat, by the time I'd left the flat. I'd heard them laughing before I'd reached the landing—but I'd trusted not over me. What the trouble was I couldn't imagine because as soon as my journey began, I felt as excited as anything. When I got back I'd ask Pat if mine was a medical case—Mark would know, we'd ring him. I had no one else to ask.

1 D were already in their seats up in my room when I arrived. I'd been a trifle tardy yet again it seemed. Good God, it meant that I'd be leaving more like eight o'clock, instead of ten past at this rate. Form teachers were meant to be in there first, with the register open, all ready to call their names. "Someone open the window, please. Who's Window Monitor this month? Pearl Buttons? Righto, Pearl! Not present? Well, you then. Do it.

Thank you!" Eleven-year-olds, but rising twelve. The heady age of almost there. An ill-assorted set, their skins still childishly transparent on the whole, except where adolescent acne was already taking hold. They already regarded me with respect; several inevitably sucking up, attempting to forge their places as my favourites. I ignored them and their sycophancies. Everyone says, Miss, you're the prettiest teacher—you should hear what they say in the playground—are you married—no, Miss ain't married—she ain't got no wedding ring on. Had I been like that with a teacher? Done such arse-licking until I'd turned her stomach? Probably, or then again, perhaps not. My head ached too much to remember. What had I said I'd do today—bollock them into submission—I still had ten new classes of children to come. Our school went up to a sixth form, and in each year except that sixth, we had four forms. But today, in this state of health, I wouldn't be up to anything, let alone setting myself up as a stalwart disciplinarian.

I stood, feeling lost, at my stock cupboard, before leading 1 D to Assembly. My first Assembly as well as theirs—since yesterday morning had simply been signing in. Christ! What would I do for first lesson? 2A, my curriculum said. It would be the bloody bright ones, well, brighter—on this day of all. The idea came in Assembly with eyes shut and hands clasped in prayer. "Our Father Which Art in Heaven, Hallowed Be—"

"2A? Now sit quietly. That's right. Good girls. Now this morning whilst I sit here trying to memorise your faces, you will use your time making patterns. Hands up, who likes making patterns? Yes, on squared paper like this—with no chance of it going wrong—all right, class? I shall mark them, of course, on the regularity of your shapes. You could do circles all the way down the page, in the coloured pencils that I'll be giving you. Yes, simple circles or even zig-zag lines—or come to that, you could outline the squares and fill them in alternately. Now, who can I rely on to give this graph paper, which is what it's called as I expect you know, this graph paper, one to each person? And if you finish it before the end of lesson, you come to me for a second and do it, the same if you like, but in a different colour." And in that way, I managed to struggle through the day, sitting before the nation's youth—setting them infants' work. The District Inspector would have eaten his shit!

In all the fuss and frustration, I'd forgotten to tell Pat that I wouldn't be back, not until later tonight. It was Tuesday today, my evening for St. Martin's School of Art, where Bernard Bolt, who'd taught me down in Brighton, held his evening class.

"Come," he'd said, "to cheer me up, they're an awful bunch of bloody amateurs. In any case, it'll help to keep your hand in—we've got a real live model. I know what you students are like, even the artiest of you—you leave and that's the end of it. Especially when you go into those ordinary schools, death and destruction. I'm surprised that you've succumbed to such a suburban impulse as having a nine-to-five job. You should have held out, you've got the ability. Spent your days painting and got a job at night, any old job, just to keep going. You don't begin to know half of it, you kids, about dedication, do you? When I was your age, I was starving in a Paris attic, but covering canvases as if my soul depended on it. Look at you, you—"

"I'll come! Okay, I'll come!" I said, just to shut him up. But he was right, of course, I knew that he was right. What bourgeois streak indeed was it to single out such a life—banked on one side by authoritarian headmistresses, and living on the other hand with pure suburbia like Pat, and even more, Fiona, when she'd be joining us. My father's influence, of course, whose else? And my own need to be like the others. Even going to Art School for a start, had set me aside enough. Had alienated half the people I'd been brought up with.

I made myself a cup of tea before I left the staff-room, still feeling under the weather, but on the road to recovery. Everyone else had gone except the other new teacher, Miss Einstein. I smiled at her. "How's it been today?" She was the one who'd been crying yesterday. I looked at her sympathetically, comprehending completely why children would play her up. We must have been surely about the same sort of age, but she was middle-aged already, somehow old before her time. The drooping shoulders did it, to hide the drooping breasts—they hung heavily over her belt, indivisible with her belly. There appeared to be no waist. Nothing there that dieting couldn't cure, of course. And nothing in the wide expanse of countenance that couldn't have been improved with cosmetics and the cunning artifice of somebody like Pat.

She creased her forehead and made a wan moue shape with her mouth. "They petrify me!"

"Oh, you'll get used to them—"

She winced and wrapped her arms around herself as if in abstract protection. "No, I'll never get used to them. They'll annihilate me first. I shan't ever understand how I managed to pass my teaching practice—I thought *they* were pretty awful. It was a pure fluke, that!" Her voice was lightweight, like a little girl's, at certain words even babyish. She must have been an only child, like me. But treated as one at home or else the youngest, perhaps. The accent was amazing, top of the class in elocution, careful in the extreme—which meant she probably had a background much like mine as well. But with more determination to disguise it.

"Well, at least today I didn't hear them," I said. "You are next door to me, after all." Not that I'd been very much of this world or capable much of hearing anything at all. But things seemed better now; I sipped my tea. She leant forward confidingly. "I let them just read round the class, a paragraph at a time out loud. Could hardly be called the art of instruction, I'm afraid. But I just wasn't up to it today."

"I shouldn't worry," I spoke cheerfully. "Nor was I."

"Oh?" Her expression lifted slightly. "Are you having troubles with discipline too?"

"Just with drinking. I had a heavy night last night—terrible hangover today!"

She looked impressed. "I wouldn't think of drinking mid-week. Not when I'd started a new job."

"No, nor would I normally." Was that true? Why wouldn't I, after all? This was my life, wasn't it? Other people did all sorts of things mid-week, new job or not. I'd turned in an inferior job of work today, of which I wasn't proud—but at least I had turned up! Didn't industry sustain a loss of gigantic proportions through people's misuse of their pastime? "Yes, we were getting up to all sorts of awful things, my flat mate and me this morning! Up with the larks—up to larks with the larks—sorry, rather weak! That's the way it is today. Actually, she didn't go in at all, and she's in a new job as well. Teaching. Her first term. In Essex, it's a bit of a traipse, she has to get up at six every morning anyway."

Miss Einstein shuddered. "Oh, I only come from Stepney, but that seems bad enough. How nice to be sharing a flat—" Now from looking wan she'd turned to looking wistful. I thought what havoc that swine Piers would have played with her 'naice'. "Where is the flat you're sharing?" She managed to inflect the question with a strange and sweet formality, the paragon of politeness, as if in fact what she was saying was "Would you care for a cucumber sandwich?" Had she turned from me, a child in her class, to write upon the blackboard now—I would have aimed an inky pellet at her arse. And pointed my tongue to make fun. The quality of her refinement provoked an alarming aggression.

I travelled to St. Martin's on the tube from Elephant and Castle, changing trains at Charing Cross to take the Northern Line and finish up at Tottenham Court Road. It seemed incredibly seedy there on that corner of Upper Oxford Street, with aimless unemployables leaning against the railings of the entrance to the station. And a general feeling of the flotsam and jetsam of the world. I hurried ahead down Charing Cross Road, in an effort to leave it behind. Our shop existed in streets which had that same feeling, and come to that, even the school where I'd now come to teach. Our flat, for that matter, was hardly impressive in its ambience—would there ever be a time when I might hope for surroundings which were a little more salubrious? It didn't depress me these days as much as it had once, probably because of having been to Art School—I'd learned in fact to look for other things besides the obvious poverty. But even so, those satisfactions—a certain light, a startling shade, the multitude of tones in just one colour such as grey, which could catch you unawares—these satisfactions were very much a private matter. I didn't expect that other people might share my special sight.

It hit me right away when I went in, even stopping as I did to visit the cloakroom first. The intoxications of pigment, sized and hand-primed canvas, hardboard, and the vinegar mix of turpentine and linseed oil, all rushed to my nostrils and reminded me of the world that I'd been missing all these weeks. I breathed it gratefully, I drank it up, I buried myself in it and mentally swooned like some rubber fetishist who'd stumbled upon a mackintosh shop! I smiled at myself in the mirror and into the eyes of two regular St. Martin's students with me. They both gazed coolly back but I didn't mind, it made no difference. In my time I had done the same. It gives a tremendous state of exclusivity—the being a full-time student. There isn't any need to accept the courtship of the commoner. Those ordinary people, the ones out in the world involved in merely mundane matters like the earning of a living. And art students above all, I'd even thought when I was one, carry their edge of superciliousness to an even greater degree. As if they really had been blessed with second sight and an inner understanding of the universe.

I went upstairs to pay my absurdly minimal term's fee and in addition sign myself on as one of Bernard's students. He happened to come into the office just as I'd finished and his face creased and crumpled with pleasure.

"Well, I'll be buggered! You actually made it!" He chuckled and gave me an affectionate hug. "Hey, what are you doing in here? Not actually filling in a form? And passing over spondulax? Here, give all that to me—" His voice dropped conspiratorially. "You silly child! There isn't any need for that—you sit in when you want. I thought I'd made that perfectly clear—you're to come to boost my morale. It's not a question of money! We let the parasites pay for you and I, the artistic likes of us! I'll tell you something—we've got a rum bunch this term. Come up and I'll introduce you. They could do with having a young professional to copy. We'll get you a good front seat. What are you doing today, drawing or painting? Not a bad model—a mangy little thing, like a Munch—all white and wispy—"

What a sweet chap, the old fellow was. Someone from another age. Fired by the flame, bitten by the bug, a devotee to Bohemia—but cuckolded by the Great Creative Urge. I'd seen his paintings, I knew his work, I'd curled my lip at the blatant lack of lifting inspiration. But he did all right, the old boy. He exhibited every year and had as much a name as his contemporaries in various stultified Art Societies. I wasn't sure if he didn't even have letters like R.S.P.P.—Royal Society of Portrait Painters or some such artistic irrelevance.

We'd reached the room in which he held his classes, it was already full. Bernard frowned. "The buggers can't wait to cast their images on canvas—to waste by the hundredweight their Winsor & Newton water colours, oils, gouaches, charcoal, pencils, paper—Christ!" He groaned. "Oh, would that Providence smiled her fickle smile on me and spared me this ordeal—"

"Now then, Bernard." I wagged my finger and pulled a mock prim mouth. "You know as well as me that this is a very nice number! No sooner than they'll have started and you'll be over to the pub. Unless you've changed, that is. There'll be precious little teaching that's going to tire you out!"

"Now, now!" He tweaked my chin. "It's not like that up here, you know. Not like trying to talk to your normal snooty student who hasn't the time of day to hear you anyway—poncing off the poor old Welfare State, trying to live the life of Toulouse-Lautrec with legs. No fear, these amateurs are quite frankly a paralysing pain up the arse! You've never seen such enthusiasm. Watch them. To a man, like dogs on heat, I promise you!"

I looked around for a drawing board and a wooden donkey on which to sit. I'd bring my paints with me next week, but this first one I'd spend on drawing. Then, having booked my place already in the front line around the model's dais, I stood up and allowed dear old Bernard to effect a few introductions.

"Oh, it's wonderful," I said, "to hear you again! Honestly, Fiona, it is! How did it go up there, and when did you get back? Come on, spill the beans! I can't wait!"

I heard her laugh at the other end. "We've only just got in. Ten minutes ago or so! But I shall have to be quick because daddy's meaning to be on the phone and I'm meant to be in bed. I've got masses to tell but it needs saying face to face for the full effect! Anyway, what I'm suggesting is that I come up to London this weekend—"

"And stay here? In the flat, you mean? There are only two beds but Pat's going home—I know that this weekend. So you could have hers—"

"Well, I tell you why—there's a frightfully smart party I've been invited to and I wangled you in as well. For Saturday night—that should give us plenty of chance to talk. It's tremendous stuff, honestly! You won't believe!"

The telephone had been ringing as I walked through the door. Pat was obviously out, there weren't any lights on anywhere. Unless she was sleeping already. I replaced the telephone and tip-toed down the passage to open our bedroom door. No. Nothing. No one there. Everything nice and tidy, including my bed I saw. She'd made them both again. The place was cold and uncomfortably quiet, it needed a human voice. I shivered and switched the little wireless on, and twiddled the knobs for some music. Songs for late-night lovers—nice for some, I said it aloud but entirely without any rancour. I'd enjoyed myself this evening. Going to see Bernard had turned out not a bad idea. "All set? Off to the pub?" He'd collected quite a crowd. "No, not me thanks. Not tonight." But they wouldn't take no for an answer.

He'd introduced me before the evening's work commenced. In fact had taken the trouble to introduce all the newcomers to his corps of faithful regulars. It was more like a club than an evening class. Someone had said so too—his name was Nicholas O'Dell, an Irish architect who'd just come down from Edinburgh. He'd been in London a week. I found him very friendly, with a thin, long, wiry body like a worm. Around twenty-seven, his hair the colour of sandy clay, and his eyes pale green like grapes.

"That's a bloody good drawing!" He'd come up behind me at half time.

"Oh, I was just thinking how bad—"

"It's obvious you're no amateur."

"That's probably exactly what I don't like about it—a cheap set of easy tricks. I haven't had a pencil, or a brush for that matter, in my hand for over a month. I always find I strive for effect when that's happened, to prove I haven't lost my touch." I looked beyond him and nodded towards the easels at the back. "Are you one of those?"

"Yup! I'm having a shot at oils—I've always had a yen towards them—but I'm making a hell of a mess. It's sliding all over the place. You could probably give me a few useful tips."

I smiled at such an obvious ploy. He didn't appeal to me in any way but I sympathised over the work problem. "Oils are a killer, I can still remember that from when I started. But I always found water colours even worse. You have to really know what you're doing with them. No second chance, no going over. . . ."

Other people now joined in, amateurs all, but every one with an opinion. All united by the binding bond of genuine enthusiasm. Knowledge. An intimate understanding of the chemical changes, the fugitive qualities, the effects of ageing and atmosphere, the out-and-out nature of the practical means employed in their self-expression was of total irrelevance here. Personal experience was the only prerequisite. Opinions based on that alone. Like my father on the subject of politics. "In my opinion and what I've always found—" That was how he had come to fascism and a deep admiration of Oswald Mosley, indeed. From a personal experience, so he claimed, which dated back to the thirties. "I'd managed to get this job cleaning cars in a garage—oh, don't look like that, my girl, there were graduates queueing up like the rest of us for anything in those days. Bloody true, there were! Buggers from Oxford and Cambridge glad to get milkman's jobs—" The isolated, though unfortunate, incident, had occurred in a London garage, when a Bentley accidentally ran over his big toe whilst he was happening to be polishing a windscreen. The quite arbitrary fact that the cigar-smoking driver appeared to be recognisably Jewish seemed somehow of special significance. It had triggered off the irrational and almost obsessive hatred of what he so often delighted in referring to as the Chosen Race. His emotional support of Oswald Mosley had led him to almost becoming an actual party member. But my mother had put her foot down. The only time she ever had in my own recollection. She said she'd leave him and take me with her if she had to see another single blackshirt goose-stepping up our garden path. It was humiliating to be Heil Hitlered with neighbours looking on. And extremely embarrassing to be seen stuffing fascist pamphlets down her pinafore pocket. He was to stop this nonsense once and for all. She wouldn't have it! Understood? And so, on the surface, he'd stopped. He surveyed the world and solved its problems, political and otherwise, from the comfortable platform of our shop counter. My mother still maintained, and I occasionally backed her up in it, that she wouldn't like to count the number of customers that he'd alienated and subsequently lost us with his views. A whole philosophy based on self-important ignorance and prejudice.

Bernard waved to me above his students', his amateur students', heads. He winked. But I didn't return the deprecating gesture or actually come to that, I couldn't quite share his contempt. It seemed to me to be quite marvellous that all these people felt the urge so strongly as to give up one whole evening, and obviously spend as much as they were spending on such grand equipment. One man, now working feverishly right through the break, filling in the background without the model there—he'd actually bought himself a proper, perfectly pleated artist's smock and was wearing a beret on his head to complete the pathetic picture. But, underneath, his pressed and perfectly tailored trouser-cuffs told a different story. We'd never worn artist's smocks at art school, the most I managed were my mother's old pinnies, or my father's discarded shirts, tied round the back of the waist by their sleeves. In addition to the artist's smock, this evening painter held in the crook of his arm at the fine appropriate angle—as artists are always depicted—an extremely expensive painters' palette with each colour in the spectrum squeezed round its edge like droppings in the bottom of a bird cage. But even so there was in his intensity something quite impressive. Bernard would try it on, I knew, pin-pointing this poor little sod—but I'd refuse to join him in his cruelty. We all returned to work. An hour had flown. I'd scaled the heights of satisfaction and descended to despair as I failed to match my image with my hand. Ten minutes before the end I'd torn my drawing up—the work of over two hours. But then in almost minutes I'd managed to capture in a set of lightning lines, almost exactly what I was after anyway. The evening had been saved—I had salvaged something.

Nicholas O'Dell had not been quite so successful. "What do you think?" He'd called me over. "What is your expert opinion?"

"Well, now . . ." I studied his messy canvas and held my head to one side as if absorbed in critical thought.

"Go on. You can be as beastly as you like, but give an honest opinion."

"The basics are there . . ." I didn't care to crush his boyish eagerness.

"Are they? Well, that's a start." He stood so close that I could smell his slightly sweaty underarms, it wasn't my favourite scent by any means. That's what I'd liked about Derek, how extremely careful he'd been regarding his bodily odours. After-shave everywhere despite the fact of course he didn't. Shave.

"Yes, what I mean is this—" and I gave the keen young architect a full five minutes of considered, though very kind, criticism. Turning at the end of it, feeling suddenly tired, I collided with the owner of the artist's smock. "Who was that chap in the artist's smock?" I said to Bernard later.

"Oh him, yes he's been with me quite a time, over a year I think. Strange chap. Some sort of an industrialist. Plenty of cash I imagine. Polish prick. I'd thought of trying to flog him something of mine—got no family, just himself. Has a chauffeur who comes to collect him."

"What's his work like? I didn't manage to see it."

Bernard held his nose between two fingers as if faced with a putrid stench. "Just like all the rest of them or, if anything, worse." We were sitting round a table in the pub, Nicholas O'Dell was on my right. Bernard removed his fingers from his nose and cupped his mouth with his hand. "What," he spoke in a loud stage whisper, "do you think of that young pup—a pushover for you, wouldn't you say?" And he threw his head back against the mirrored wall behind him and gave a bellowing laugh.

He was a pushover, Nicholas, I knew that all right. But nothing about him interested me. "What's the industrialist's name?" Bernard had stopped spluttering and now exaggeratedly dropped his jaw. "You don't mean to say that that old fart could stand a chance! Mind you," he suddenly became sober. "The money might not be half bad. You could give up that lousy teaching job and concentrate on your work, you idle bitch. Have you thought of capitalising on your obvious physical advantages? Not that any girl worth her onions would put up with an oldster like that in bed! Christ, if I thought for a minute that you would, I'd be trying it on myself! It's allowable now, you know, you're no longer my student—ethically and all that, I mean." And he lifted my hand, and turned it over to plant a kiss on my palm. I hugged him—he'd always been a favourite, the best one of our teachers, but as to anything further, I knew him too well for that. Too familiar for familiarities.

The flat felt so chilly, and so irredeemably unfriendly with no one there but me, that as I was undressing for bed I changed my mind and decided to have a bath. Back to the womb of warmth and comfort. The bottom of the bath was pock-marked with peeling enamel. I swept quite sizeable pieces into the plug hole, pushing them down with my finger-tips, before letting the water run. Our bath was much like this at home, stained with brilliant orange rust, streaked like an evening sky. If I could have chosen, I would have liked above all else a really sumptuous bath. Black with the proper shower attachment overhead, instead of bits of rubber hose that you had to squash on to the taps. This one didn't even have one of those. I went to the kitchen and brought back a saucepan for swilling shampoo from my hair. Then I got in.

I could have cried from the welcome the water gave me. You were far better off in water than walking around in the air. You opened out, you spread yourself, you surrendered, as it were. You felt in fact the opposite of how I'd felt—was it only this morning—with Douglas. I slipped for a minute completely beneath the surface, outstretched like a floating Ophelia. I felt my hair change character as it got wet. It dripped and clung to my eyebrows and over my ears, and opening my eyes, I saw that hair, much lower down, that nicely bushy shape turn darker still and even curlier, as if it had been permed. I crossed my legs at the ankles and carefully studied my navel. If I pushed hard with my thumb I felt a dull pain start inside and if I rubbed around it with the bar of soap, a tiny waterfall of bubbles poured down into its well. Lying at my present elongated angle, my breasts appeared to be as perfect as was possible. I looked at them dispassionately thinking how strange it was that two such perfectly ordinary pieces of flesh could excite such desire in men. My nipple gradually stiffened as I licked it with my tongue. The other one lay lonely and unattended, still flaccid on the other side. I lifted my hand and rolled the gristly little peak between my thumb and finger—within minutes both now stood proud and erect. I got up dripping wet to take a look in the mirror. I had to admit it made a pretty sight. If someone were to walk in here right now and plunge themselves into my pussy—I thought. I picked up the soap and rubbed it all over my pubic hair—it went white and whiskery with lather. I sat down again, this time with my knees as wide apart as they would go. What would happen if I pushed hard in there with a bar of soap? Might it get lost altogether? Could I close up? Conceal it inside? I rubbed it the whole length, starting from the clitoris end until I reached my bum. The trouble was you could be walking along with bubbles floating out of your bum like those metal rings that children dip in little pots of soap solution. People, passers-by, might well approach 'Excuse me miss, you seem to be making bubbles down below . . .' Yes, strangely enough I do, I'd have to say, it's simply a piece of soap that slipped inside in the bath. No doubt it will melt away in time—hardly a cause for concern.

A gnawing tenseness spread slowly around the area. I varied my movements now using the soap as my weapon and turning the tap gently to get an even warmer stream of water between my legs. What a way to end the day. Who needs other people? I sucked the insides of my lips and uttered several soft aahs. Then as the delicious feelings gradually escalated I quickly turned over on to my stomach and pressed my crutch hard down on the old enamel. There wasn't sufficient contact though the thrilling tension remained. So feeling that some peak of pleasure loomed suddenly in sight, I slid my arm under my body and straddling myself on my knuckles, worked feverishly through to the end.

I was asleep when Pat came in, and would have liked to have remained so, I'd taken such ages to get off. I'd somehow embarked on long-term planning of my classes, what I'd give them all to do tomorrow, and how I'd start to organise an after-school-hours special Art Club—to which girls with extraordinary ability could come. I didn't doubt that I should find at least a handful in that school. With clever coaxing and encouragement, probably even more. What Bernard hadn't been able to understand was that I actually enjoyed teaching, siphoning my own ideas through other minds. Tomorrow I would make up for my appalling indolence today. I fell asleep bathed in the smiles of Mrs. Pritchard and lifted to the heights by the congratulations of the District Inspector.

She'd put the light full on and was whirling around the room. "Wheee, wheee!" She went. "Wheee, wheee!" I buried my head in my pillow and brought my blankets higher than my eyes, but it wouldn't wash, she wanted an audience. It was half-past two in the morning! I gave in and rubbing my eyes, sat up. "I got him, kid, wow! Yes! I got him all right—no trouble!"

"Got? What? Who? When?" She dazzled me more than the light.

"Me. I got him. Had him. Ate him up. A piece of cake. No kidding!" Her radiance and the sparsity of hard fact set off a seeping irritation.

"Great," I said and prepared myself to lie down. I yawned. "Tell me it all tomorrow. . . ." It did the trick, she fell beside me on the bed and wrapped her arms around me. I smelt her perfume, Miss Dior mingling with Silvikrin shampoo. We'd have to go halves on a shower attachment. You could get the best ones from Boots.

"Roly. That's who, you fathead. I've just had him—old Roly Balls!" And she sat back to watch the information sinking in.

"Christ, but that's quick off the mark—no sooner the first than the second. What happened to dear old Douglas?"

She tossed the glorious mane impatiently. "Oh, we stayed in bed till twelve o'clock or so, then had a drink in the pub. Then I kissed him goodbye on the pavement. I'm sure I shan't see him again. But I thanked him for such an admirable service—"

"But where did you bump into Roly Balls?"

"Oh, well, I telephoned Mark, of course, and just wangled it on from there. Actually, I waited a while for you, it would have been better if you'd been there. Mark stuck with us and got to be a bit of a gooseberry, but"—she slid a lacquered nail along her lower lip—"it came out all right in the end!"

Now I was wide awake. "Pass me my coat, I'm freezing. Can you make us a cup of tea—and put the heater on? I'm buying a hot water bottle tomorrow. I'm certain these beds are damp."

At ten past three I persuaded her that we should get some sleep. "It's all right for you," I said, "you've been resting all afternoon, whilst I've been slaving away at school. Did you ring, by the way, and let them know at yours? I take it you'll be going in tomorrow."

"With a doctor's certificate too."

"That's clever, where from?"

"Roly, of course! On Guy's Hospital headed notepaper! It's useful that, isn't it? The Out Patients Department—there'll never be any check." But he hadn't seen her home. She'd had to get her own taxi. It didn't sound right to me, smacked a bit too much of Derek. 'You're okay on your own, aren't you? I can't be bothered to get out of bed—run quick and you'll catch the last bus—'

The light was out, but neither of us was asleep. I lay on my side to shut out the sound of her tossing, my weak ear to the wind. From very far away it seemed I heard her final words, and the subtly different note now the first hysteria had seemed to pass. "The funny thing is, you know, kid"—she paused as if not willing to actually put her thoughts into something as concrete as words—"that of the two of them, I think that Douglas was much better. I mean he really made me feel so extra special afterwards. Why do you think that was?" I gave a grunt as answer. "Though of course," she continued, as if now speaking only to herself, "to have got Roly after all this time of worshipping from afar. But I had to give him my number. He didn't ask for it afterwards. Bastard!" This time I didn't even bother to grunt. Not even in agreement.

I managed, of all things and for the first time, to find a seat on the tube. And I managed—more important—to be almost the first one in. Mrs. Pritchard preceded me, but only just, by the length of her Lilley & Skinner brogues. We smiled winningly at each other and she nodded her Marcel wave in matronly approval of my punctuality. "Nothing to beat an early start—" "Every time," I found myself agreeing, a shade too eagerly for comfort. And trailed off "as you say". But I'd had a very early training in the art of cliché; it was quite the normal method of communication in our shop. Words arrived unbeckoned, out of nowhere, simply to fill the discomfort created by a silence. "What a day!" "Yes, what indeed!" "This driving rain—" "Wicked weather—" She sailed above me up the concrete stairs from the senior playground, supported by a smudgy suede-gloved hand, the colour of coffee gateaux. It worried me, the way she slid it up the iron balustrade—the rust could easily ruin it. Perhaps one should suggest she run her other glove coming down, when she was leaving to go home. To even up each palm.

We reached the ground floor staff-room having left the problem behind. "Well," she laid a friendly, though patronising, rusty glove upon my shoulder. "This I fear is where you and I part company! Have a good day, my dear! Fight the good fight." I lifted my chin to the challenge. "And forge ahead." Something related to suspicion flickered across her face. But then it had gone. My guilelessness must have reassured. She patted me again. "Quite so. Quite so." And moved determinedly towards the room of her high office.

The brief encounter had exhausted me, I collapsed into the lower staff-room and peeled the orange I'd bought at Earls Court Station yesterday and now discovered, as spongy as a rubber ball, at the bottom of my bag. It filled the air and emptiness around me with a joyous pungent juice. I ate each segment slowly, one by one, waiting for the surge of instant energy. Pat had claimed that's what her breakfast did for her. I'd lain, barely awake this morning, watching her munch two Mars bars as she dressed. And three-quarters of a Kit-Kat as she combed her hair. "You don't deserve a skin like yours—or a set of teeth—with all that sugar, Pat," I'd said. She tossed it off. "Oh, it doesn't have time to do the damage. I burn it too quickly in nervous energy—'bye." And she'd gone.

Winnie Einstein, for various reasons, was the only member of staff so far that I'd got to grips with at all. This lower staff-room unofficially housed the fuddier duddies who'd been at this same school almost straight from college. Certainly long before the days of Mrs. Pritchard. They formed a tight conservative clique, a holier than thou attitude and a horrifying disregard for the principles of teaching. The upper staff-room, on the other hand, apart from lying adjacent to my own art room and therefore adjacent to Winnie Einstein, that staff-room, sparser and more spartan altogether, lacking the lumpy armchairs of the lower—all booked proprietorially in order of seniority anyway—that room was where I felt more welcome. One of the regulars came in now. Miss Bowen, Plymouth Brethren, who looked like something from Dickens. She also, unfortunately, shared the same floor as Winnie and myself, teaching by the book and a rigorous system of discipline backed up by the cane, teaching Religious Instruction throughout the school and Junior Maths to the Fifth. That was quite in order. I understood that there were girls in the Fifth who still couldn't spell their own names. This side short of educationally subnormal. Another reason to check your change in different shops like Woolworth's where most of them worked on Saturdays and would work there all week as soon as they managed to leave.

Miss Bowen lifted her equine nose and began violently flaring her nostrils. She pursed her imperceptible lips—I'd read that somewhere, something Laurence Olivier claimed—that your lips disappear as you get older. His had. Hers now were non-existent. The red corpuscles had packed it in. Had given up the ghost and refused to gather any more in any orderly line along her facial orifice. Her pale and creased and dusty skin stretched, quite unbroken, from one ear-lobe to the other, interrupted only by a set of rabbit teeth and the twin exits of her bony proboscis. It was raining outside, but she opened the window nevertheless and frowned disapprovingly down at my orange peel. She put her hand high up to a liberty-bodiced ribcage and spoke reedily in a thin, whining voice full of the gaseous fumes of which she was about to complain.

"I suffer so dreadfully from dyspepsia that I have to beware of even the very air I breathe. I apologise if I seem to over-react, but I haven't had an orange and certainly none other of the citrus fruits for something like fifteen years. The acidity, you see." She had hung her coat in the adjoining cloakroom and now rearranged her hair. "It's usually my habit to get here first," she gave a thin smile, "and have this staff-room to myself. I like to settle my stomach and organise the day. I find the quiet start invaluable."

"I'm just off," I said. And fled upstairs.

The day went well. Being so early, I also managed to organise myself, appointing a whole eager team of dinner money monitors, register markers, and, even should I be so late as to miss the whole of Assembly ever, I appointed a team of ten who should herd all of 1D into Assembly with the minimum of fuss. This I felt was essential if my life looked like continuing on its present course of burning at both ends.

Winnie Einstein was late; I could hear the hullaballoo from the sanctuary of my well-ordered calm. 1D sat waiting for Assembly Bell, their grubby nail-bitten fists folded at my suggestion on their uniformed fronts. Across the corridor I could hear the hysterical persistent whine of Miss Bowen who'd be more than pleased I knew to pinpoint the inadequacies of either Winnie Einstein or myself. "Not a word now, 1D, I warn you—I'm just going to see to 1C." And putting a squinting scrap called Sylvia Sound in charge, in the fleeting thought that her surname denoted the required dependence of character, I crossed the corridor to 1C.

The pandemonium died down slowly, starting from those nearest to the door. I stood there, proud and beautiful, magnificently menacing, pointing to no one in particular with my lifted arm. It always worked a treat, that one—I'd tried it before in teaching practice. It set up the ripples of a chilling nervousness, each child glancing straight from me to somewhere over its shoulder at the nearest neighbour in an effort to deflect attention. The next trick was the opening of my mouth, together with a lowering, dramatic lowering of the brow—as if to launch on a bellow to blow each eardrum up in smithereens. It worked. And it was working now. Small girls rearranged themselves from top to bottom, slipped into entirely different shapes. Wiped clean all signs of life from every single feature and stared almost in a state of unconscious terror at my face. Now I could speak.

"Now I can speak," I whispered. And carefully stepped across the silence as they strained to hear what I'd say next. But instead I swiftly called Winnie Einstein's register and took her dinner money in record seconds before the pealing for Assembly and the coinciding sight of Winnie herself appeared sweating and almost tearful at the entrance of the room. She looked at me with much the same expression as the dog wears in those illustrations for *His Master's Voice* except she managed to keep her tongue still in her mouth instead of lolling, as she might have let it, down to the fold of her chin. I wished she hadn't looked like that—I couldn't help it, it made me want to kick her.

But the work itself, the teaching part, the geeing-up of the children, and the carving out of vulnerable and soul-lifting slivers of imaginative creation, that went as I would have wished. Me or any District Inspector worth his salt. Only one child I managed to miss, to by-pass altogether, to not touch at all. "I think"—she'd sat there doing nothing long after the others, enthralled by my description of a forest scene in storm, had lost themselves in swirling washes of midnight blue and clouds the colour of cheese, and fearsome Hammer Film trees—"I think," she'd said to me conspiratorially, "I'll paint my bunny." And even then I didn't get it right. "Well," I'd said at the end of the lesson, "it's a very good bunny too." But she'd looked at me quite mutinously then, her mouth turned down in disappointment at my crass insensitivity. "It's not my bunny—it's my grandad!" "But you said, dear, that you were going to do your bunny—" She turned her back and answered short and to the point: "I changed my mind though, miss."

By the end of the day I had 119 storms pegged up and pinned and laying flat around my room to dry. And one old gent resembling someone's rabbit.

Winnie Einstein came into the room as I was finally clearing up.

"Good Lord," she said breathily. "My word, but you've been busy."

"Haven't you?" I felt completely knackered, but it would pass, I knew, that feeling, so much of it was backed by satisfaction with oneself.

"I can't thank you enough for what you did this morning—honestly I can't."

"That's okay. I only hope you'll do the same for me. I was early this morning, but I'm an appalling time-keeper normally. I don't care though. I like poor old 1D, but it gets on my nerves all this register lark, etc. I haven't done dinner duty yet—or playground duty if it comes to that. When are you? This week? And by the way, do old boots like Miss Bowen do those things as well?"

She shrugged. "It doesn't worry me too much. To be quite frank, I'd as soon do the duties as teach—"

"Why on earth are you doing it then? Why not take another job? Work in an office or something?"

She sighed. "It's not a decision I remember taking on my own, to be quite truthful. My mother was the keen one—well, it means you've joined the professional classes, doesn't it! That's all-important to her. And to be quite honest, even this is a disappointment. All my brothers and sisters did much, much better than me, straight through to universities, three at Oxford. All academics still—professorships and all that sort of thing. But I failed my first year at University College and ended up at a training college, barely scraping through. I knew I'd fail, you know, and I so dreaded it that I sat with nothing on all night in my mother's back yard with snow on the ground as she slept—so that I'd be so ill in the morning that I wouldn't be able to go and even sit the exams. But do you know"—her voice took on its baby lisping lilt—"I didn't even catch a tiny cold! Can you imagine that?"

Yes, I thought, I can, Winnie, with the sort of luck you have! She hung around until I'd finished then followed me to the staff-room.

"Oh Christ." I sank into a chair. "Can you get the kettle on missus?" and I smiled at her to reassure against the irritability in my voice. I'd sounded like my father. "I sound just like my dad!"

"Oh really?" I wished she'd keep her doggie palliness in some control instead of letting it out on such a loose familiar leash. Now she was pausing in some slow pose of concentrated memory, the kettle, that lift-me-up and life-giver—held limply in her hand. Instead of where it should have been by now, already on the boil. "Yes," she continued. "My father used to rule our roost with a Victorian air of attempted authority—when mummy let him, of course. I honestly think—it's the considered opinion of the entire family—that he chose to opt out of life because of her. She's the hardest taskmaster of all. Absolutely matriarchal."

I stared at the kettle. My throat, right through to somewhere round my navel, was dusty dry with blackboard chalk and too much talk. Each child today had had the benefit of my further education. I'd have to coax my larynx back to life within the next five minutes or else. I interrupted brutally: "Are you getting the kettle on or not?" And instantly regretted it. The blink came first and then a complicated crocheting of muscles round her mouth, which seemed in turn to radically change the angle of her chin. It jutted, that's all that could be said, like a constipated crocodile, and turned myopically away, making it now impossible to tell just what her mood might be. But I'd become a master-hand at moods. Merely from living with my father and simply from having to accommodate such swift, not even superficial, alterations in the lie of the land of Derek's changeable reactions. Cajoling was the sort of stock-in-trade I practised with my finger-tips. "Here," I spoke so warmly that I might have struck a match and lit the fuse between us. "Winnie. I can't think what I'm thinking of. There is no possible reason why you should put the kettle on for me. Here, you sit down and let me make the tea." She didn't turn at once, but only in the time it took to swallow and breathe again on a more regular basis. In actual fact it didn't matter much to me if she never turned again because by then I'd taken the cursed kettle from the limping hand and lit the gas and slammed the two together with the appropriate noise and cheerful vigour that one of Winnie Einstein's sensitivity might reasonably expect from someone like me. I had no wish to now confuse her further. She'd marked me down already in a register of her own—as I had already marked her.

We drank our tea together in quite companionable silence. I used the time to wonder what I'd do tonight and what, as well, to do tomorrow with my classes. And then I found before I'd even come to any decision on those two questions, my mind had leapt ahead to Saturday night and what I'd wear for Fiona's party. Winnie was talking. "Oh, I'm sorry," I said. "I was thinking."

"That's what I was asking. What were you thinking?"

"Oh. Things." Which would I choose to tell her? What topic would excite her most? "Well, to be more specific, I was actually wondering what to wear to a party I'm going to this weekend—"

An official of the Electricity Board somewhere had flicked a switch behind her eyes at the precise point of the word 'party'. "Oh!" She shone. "A party." The kiddie lisp was taking over. "I love parties. I've always loved parties. As a child I couldn't wait to pull the cracker and wear the hat and shake the jelly. You should see the way I shake a jelly." And laying her teacup on the table, and before I'd had a chance to swallow what tea there was already in my mouth, she'd stood up and was demonstrating in an elephantine movement her personal method of jelly-shaking. I burnt my tongue quite badly as scalding liquid hit me. I judged it fair to say that jiggling her jelly in this grotesque samba tango could wrench both mammary glands clean from her central trunk. But for an instant, as I stood, further nightmares seemed about to happen as she mistook my movement as a wish to join her in her wantonness. I hastily waved the approaching revolving nipples away. "Time for off—" And at my words she stopped as suddenly as she'd started, the disappointed child. My God, but that highly qualified and academic, intellectual, all-ambitious family of hers—those bright impressive brothers, those scintillating witty sisters, that matriarchal mother, and the dead dejected daddy—what indulgences they must have lavished on this littlest child of all. I looked at her and thanked someone, somewhere, for my own abrasive father. And what it had made of me, such that of the two of us standing there so similar in age, I was the one who patronised with my pity. And struggled somewhere not so far from the surface to control the sadism she so effortlessly aroused in me. It seemed that I had got the better deal.

Pat, it was becoming obvious, was able through some miraculous speed of light to actually arrive home before me. How, I'd said to her, I'd never understand. Was she bunking off the last two lessons, or what? What need was there to hang about, once the day was done? That's what she'd answered when I'd asked. And in any case, so she'd continued, what had I found to do out at Elephant and Castle that could possibly take until now?

"Oh, don't go on. You sound just like a nagging wife! I had to hang the paintings up, and clear my room and after that I had a cup of tea with Winnie Einstein. She did a little dance for me—a kind of cabaret." I laughed, preparing to elaborate further.

"I've made your bed again," she said, a trifle sourly before I had a chance.

"Oh did you? That was decent. You don't have to though, you know."

"I don't have to. No, I don't! But how do you think it feels coming in at the end of a day faced with the sort of mess that this flat is in—"

Oh, hell! Whatever could have happened! "What's happened, Pat? Is anything the matter?" Something was up, judging by her martyred mouth and the general air of injury.

"Fiona phoned!"

What was I feeling guilty about in that. She phoned. So? "When?"

"Just now. She said she'd phone again."

"Oh." I raised my voice deliberately to strike a chatty level. "Did you talk to her? At any length I mean? She's thinking of coming up on Saturday—"

"Yes. So she said." She tossed a titian lock which curled around her chin and turning violently to face me squarely, she almost spat at me. "Yes, so she said! And what she said as well was that she's sleeping in my fucking bed! But I'll leave it to you to tell her she bloody isn't! So there! I'm buggered if I'm paying half the rent for that stuck-up turd to filthy my bed linen—and in any case for that matter"—her voice became nearer to normality—"it won't have any sheets. I'll be taking those home for mum to do in the laundry. Along with all my washing."

I got in as quickly as I could, it seemed the easiest entry. "Oh, will you? What a good idea. I don't know what I'll do with mine, though I've seen there's a launderette near my school. I could take them in in the morning and collect them at the end of the day—that's if one of the women who work there will see to it all for me." I'd engaged her attention momentarily and lifted the lid from the siphon. "Otherwise, I suppose I could do it in my spare lessons, in that free time—" She stuck her lower lip stubbornly along the line of her upper. "What about a cigarette?" I said. But she shook her head without speaking. God! Was she going to sulk? That would make two of them in one day! But no, she'd decided to speak. And she'd decided as well to take a cigarette. I lit it for her and she inhaled, extracting the maximum amount for dramatic effect—I hadn't thought before how like Bette Davis she was. "You look just like Bette Davis, doing that, the half closing of the eyes. Or perhaps more Rita Hayworth. As she was in *Gilda*. You ought to think of getting a long cigarette holder. It would suit you. Honestly!" I'd scratched the surface of her vanity at least—the alley cat leanness melted into something more Siamese, but even so she wasn't prepared to relent altogether.

"No! I'm just not having it, that bitch sleeping in my bed! You should have heard the way she spoke to me just now! I mean to say, you'd think that pater knowing his precious daughter was planning to live in London—you'd think, since he's in the know—that he would have found a flat for her or us, after all—" She looked very pretty, aggrieved, in a truculent kind of way. Her lips were painted a primrose yellow sort of pink—a peachy, creamy shade I hadn't seen before. I pointed.

"New? Very nice."

She nodded. "Yes, new. Now, what you ought to say to her on the telphone is. 'Yes, that she can stay, but she'll have to bring her bed'—"

"Her bed! Oh, come on Pat! Her bed? How can she bring her bed? What up on the train? Don't be daft—"

"Not necessarily up on the train. Look, I've thought it all out! I'm not daft, and neither are you! This isn't going to be the only time that she'll be coming up and expecting to stay here, is it?

And what is going to happen, for instance, when I shall be here too? Where the hell will she sleep then? It's only by chance I'm going home this weekend—it being mum's birthday, I mean. No, what you've got to say is that she must provide a bed. And more than that—" Her voice had now become persuasive, even coaxing. Cunning. "Yes, really more than that—a—wait for it—double bed! It's obvious from last night, no not last night, the night before, with Douglas—it's obvious that we need one for when we entertain!" I looked at her. She had the business sense my father lacked. Had probably inherited it from her plumber dad. Anyone, anybody, given the right approach to life and money, could make a success of any chosen field. Of course what we needed was a double bed! A comfortable working surface. The space on which to relax. The extra degree of privacy. Privacy. Privacy where?

"I have to admit to you, Pat, that it sounds like a master plan. But where had you thought of putting it, that's if she comes up with the goods? Not in here—"

"No! Ye Gods, you painters—no sense of space—no inkling of design or the artistic appreciation of the possibilities in your environment! The kitchen. Of course! That's where we'd put the double bed, in the kitchen. We ask her for a bed-settee. To sit on in the day. And use at random any time, as a breeding ground for passion—turned into a double bed!"

"That's cute. In the kitchen. Of course. But will she wear it? Will she turn up trumps? I mean to say, you said yourself that Fiona is tight-fisted."

"It won't actually cost her that much. Two quid to be exact!"

"Two quid! What do you mean two quid?"

She stubbed her cigarette out triumphantly in the kitchen sink. The sizzle accompanied her smile. "I've bought it already, second-hand. They're delivering it tonight!"

It wasn't bad, I had to say, considering the price. It had about it a curiously affectionate air—as one who'd once been loved but now looked rather bashed about. Like a teddy bear who'd had to put up with too much hugging. "Oh yes, Patty—I can see all manner of naughtinesses taking place on this! Oh, what was Roly's bed like, by the way?"

"We won't go into that," she said darkly.

"Why not?" I could see she really wanted to say.

"Perhaps it was my fault—I shouldn't have looked—"

"Looked? Looked where? What at?" That was something she did share with Fiona, a wildly inquisitive nose. An almost manic need to know. Not something I went in for myself—for fear of finding something too unpleasant or disturbing, so I reasoned. In many situations, ignorance remained a preferable state.

"Stains."

I was pouring boiling water on some Bovril in a beaker. "Beg pardon, Pat? You saw some stains, you say?"

"On the sheets! There was no mistaking them."

I thought a minute. She must be meaning mucus. "Maybe he butters bread in bed . . ." But I knew what mucus meant. I'd seen it more than once, and not mine, either. On Derek's sheets, in Derek's bed. I might have pointed, many times, and made an issue of it. 'That mucus there. It's not one that I recognise—not one I've seen before—' A person's mucus is a source of pleasure to oneself, that springs in part from instant recognition. Another's mucus, on the other hand, raises a fearful feeling of depression. I knew how poor Pat felt. Though it could have been worse. In Derek's bed, I'd found an alien snotball one afternoon underneath the pillow. On my side. In the sun.

"Yes, stains, and what was worse, some stockings and a brassière hanging in the bathroom."

"Does he go in for dressing up? Many medical students do . . ."

She looked miserable. "These belonged to someone small. About the size of me—he'd never have fitted into them. You know how huge he is—" She was being unreasonable. Of course they belonged to another girl—there was no reason for him to be celibate. In any case she herself, Pat, had hours before been with Douglas. What did she expect?

"Some Bovril? I burned my tongue at school today, I couldn't cope with anything more solid."

She shook her head. "I've had a snack already. What will we do tonight? Roly won't ring, I know it." I knew it too and was trying to work out how to warn her not to bank on him anyway when the ring of the telephone interrupted before I'd even got there. She ran. She bounded like an arrow from the bow to answer it as if by saying he wouldn't ring, she'd altered the course of fate and made him do so. It was for me. Not bad, well, better than nothing anyway.

"He's nice," I said. "An architect. His name is Nicholas O'Dell. Bit niffy under the armholes—"

"Oh, very nice indeed!"

Wine, and bits and bobs to eat, come as soon as you can. What now? Why not! Just give him a chance to change his shirt, he'd said. So we hung around for an hour, just to make doubly sure.

It was straight through on the District Line to Notting Hill Gate, where he lived, sharing a pad with two others, two pals he'd been students with. Get out at the station and walk down Holland Park Avenue—it's the turning on the right before Holland Park, and we're the second house. Right at the top I'm afraid.

"It's a bit of a traipse, this, isn't it!" Pat was wearing her highest heels, though I had advised against it.

"They're only ordinary—well, Nicholas is—you don't want to overdress."

"They're architects, aren't they?"

"Yes, but Pat, we'll be seeing them just at home. It's not a party or anything special, after all. Only a get-together—all being new in London. Their flat won't probably be as flash as this—" I'd only said that to please her.

"Do you honestly think it's flash, our flat?"

"Well, it is, when you get inside. With all you've done, I mean. Painting the kitchen floor and hanging up your patterns. The approach of course leaves a lot to be desired. But I'm used to a sordid exterior, it doesn't distress me too much." I was lying. From the pavement, through the greasy green front door, along the depressing corridor before even descending our basement stairs to reach our own flat door, I was already finding to be indescribably dingy and bleak. Even to the point of neither looking left nor right at entry time or exit, but instead keeping a clear picture in my mind of what within seconds I should expect to see.

Leaving, the bursting blinding cloud-strewn sky above Old Brompton Road. And arriving, the warm oasis of our warren. "We're a bit like rabbits. You and I in our burrow. And will be even more so when we put Fiona's bed into action. Who do you think, Patty, will be misbehaving on it first? You or me?" Though come to that, why not Fiona?

We'd arrived already at the corner of our turning. She suddenly stopped and faced me, faintly embarrassed as she spoke. "Yes, that was what I was meaning to ask—what do you reckon was the trouble with Douglas?"

"With Douglas? Why? He was very good, wasn't he? You said last night he was better than Roly Balls."

"With you, I meant," she floundered. "You know, not getting in."

I'd known exactly what she meant. But what was there to say. Except the truth, of course. "I think I tense myself too much. Just at the last minute. I try to loosen up, you know—I think that's what it is. The more they push, the worse it gets. What do you think, anyway?"

"I can't understand the complication. He slipped in me like a spoon in jelly, but I tell you what he said after you'd gone, he said you—"

"Hold on now, here we are!" And we were as well, at Nicholas' number, and more than that was Nicholas hanging high above us and waving from the top-most window.

"The key," he said, and threw it down. I welcomed the interruption. Who wished to know, in any case what Douglas had bloody said!

The evening was uneven. Pat hated them all on sight, and what was worse, they hated her. She didn't speak, or hardly, for an hour. Which in the end turned out to be exactly right since she'd used up the time with imbibing a sizeable quantity of disgustingly sweet white wine. I'd taken a mouthful on arrival and had tactfully asked to be switched to the sourer vinegar red. Did architects not then earn so much? Not with the L.C.C. Oh, Civil Servants then, like us, I'd said. If you're working in County Hall. We get paid, or I do anyway—Pat was glaring sulkily over the street—I get paid from County Hall as well. That's where I went for my interview. I thought of the District Inspector and the texture of his skin and the way his filbert nails lay so gracefully in their fleshy beds. What finger-tips he had. His hand in mine. Nicholas and his two flat mates fawned upon me, their faces open and uncomplicated. There wasn't a line, a wrinkle or a crease, not anywhere on those facial canvases. The emptiness didn't endear.

The other two appeared to be marginally younger than Nicholas, the difference that National Service can make. He'd done his first before he'd started studying. But all three of them were really Peter Pans, believing their boyishness to be endearing to a girl like me. I could have told them right away that they were batting on a very wrong wicket. But Pat, on the other hand, had always seemed quite partial to that waggy, puppy-dog quality. I couldn't think quite what was up with her tonight—unless her haughtiness was just a cover up for far more complicated feelings. She might have been impressed, it now occurred to me, by the stylish simplicity of the surroundings. The house was very grand. The exterior, smoothly plastered to disguise the bricks, had been painted Persil white. And the heavy wooden carved front door had been brought back to natural gnarled finish by judicious use of a blow torch, and a sealing coat of varnish. Inside was painted white as well, all the way up the stairs with natural haircord carpet on each landing and neatly fitted over every step. I'd thought of our crass Axminster at home. A vitriolic puce and damson jam. Out from the Co-op and nailed to our stairs before I'd a chance to say aye nor nay. "What do you think then, girl?" My father had stood, with hammer still in hand. "Eh? What do you think—as the colour expert? Your old dad's not done too badly, has he?" He bent. "Not a bad pile to it. Almost as deep as a finger-nail, see! Should stand a spot of good wear, I'd say. Yes, what's the general opinion then—it's listed as Primavera, but I myself would call it more autumnal hues."

Yes, Pat had grown silent swaying up the stairs, now I came to think of it. And when we'd reached their tasteful Ivory door right at the top, her mouth had already shaped itself into a sulky bow. Perhaps she thought I might be blaming her in some vague abstract sense for not finding us a place like theirs. I looked around. They'd painted the ceiling throughout the place a harsh and shrewish acid green, and covered the floor on which we sat in a similarly coloured carpet. But not the sort of carpet that I'd really seen before. This one was like a highly superior home-made woolly one, with separate strands, thick and tufty like an elegant overgrown lawn. I touched it. "It's like grass, this carpet. Lovely," I said.

Pat, at the sound of my voice, drained her glass again and teetered towards us from the window. She looked down at the sea of green and, delicately, with one pointed high-heeled shoe, parted the fronds around one foot. "Scandinavian—bought from Heals. I know the firm—fucking expensive!"

We all looked at her, it was almost the first time she'd opened her mouth since arriving. From where we sat there on the floor, she looked to me—magnificent. Drunk. And randy, so I thought. I wondered which one she'd choose. Jim was who I'd put my money on. He seemed the most conventional of the three. The one who looked as though he had the cleanest vest and knickers. And socks and shiniest shoes. And tidiest drawer. The one I'd bet who cleaned his teeth and possibly even combed his hair before he went to bed. The other one, called Gerry, Gerry short for Gerald—I didn't think would go for any girl. Pat's brother might have stood a better chance, but I wouldn't have liked to put it into words. I wasn't ever that much good at divining deviations.

The atmosphere was warming up. Gerry put some music on, modern jazz—much the same as the Studio Club. Gerry Mulligan. "We heard some music like this the other night at a place called the Studio Club—in Swallow Street. Do you know it?" I turned to Nicholas. Pat stood above us swaying in a deliberate sort of way deciding who to settle on. The matter was taken out of her hands as Gerry, turning from a pile of records, neatly contained in a pristine record rack, decisively encircled her with a long loose arm as thin as her own, and rhythmically started to dance. I might have guessed that he would be the first to see her charms. Over in Pat's department, in Fabrics and certainly Fashion Design, there'd been a fair amount of stylish effeminate boys. At times it seemed to me she'd been surrounded by them—buzzing along the streets of Brighton. Bizarre and beautiful. Waspish, witty—all fragile, slender, supremely chic compared to the plebeian rest of us. We didn't have those sort of people in Painting. And I don't think they had them in Illustration and certainly not in Sculpture. She had exactly what it took to get on well with them, I thought. She understood much more than me about life's artificialities. I looked at them together and listened to Nicholas' question.

"The Studio Club? We've heard of that, the Studio Club. Hey, haven't we, Jim?" Jim rolled his heavy body over from laying on his stomach; he now lay on his back like me, both hands behind his head, supporting it whilst, like me again, he gazed at Gerry and Pat.

"They look good together, don't they?" I said. "Beautiful in the same way." Perhaps it hadn't occurred to them that Gerry might be like that. Or then again I may have been wrong. Nicholas joined Jim in shy embarrassed laughter. Their reaction irritated—it was as if I might have been casting aspersions on their manhood by my oblique reference.

We left at midnight at my insistence which strongly countered their own, and by then too, surprisingly or not—Pat's. "You can stay then if you like—" But no, she wouldn't, she'd come with me. They all would, in fact! They'd see us home on the tube. But I was tired of them by then. And even a little tired of Pat. I wanted the evening to come to an end and get back to my bed. It had been ordinary, that really was the only word to use. They'd been, the three of them, too much what I'd been used to for the past five years. If this was all that London had to offer I might as well have stayed at home—even with the Axminster on the stairs.

Fiona was meant to arrive on Friday. On Friday evening after tea was what she'd said on the telephone. But in the morning, she caught me just as I was leaving to say she couldn't make it. I didn't try to hide the disappointment in my voice. "You cow!"

"I honestly, honestly can't help it, darling!" She'd never called me darling, not directly, not before. It stopped me short. "You see, pet," she continued. "One of mummy's dearest friends has let her down over dinner, and to keep the numbers correct, I have to go instead. Something ghastly at the Grand—there's just no way around it!"

"But I've bought bread especially, and cream. And coffee instead of tea."

"We'll eat it tomorrow. I won't have breakfast till I get to you! We'll have toast and coffee. I'll get back in bed as soon as I arrive. You won't even have to meet me off the train. I'll jump in a taxi and be there before you wake up!"

I was still cross when I caught the tube and stood heavily all the way to Westminster on the toecap of a certain swollen gentleman to my left. Without saying sorry once.

But when I saw her, I'd recovered. It wasn't my way to stay cross for long. Sulking seemed to me a wicked way of wasting time. I'd said as much to Pat *à propos* our evening at Nicholas'. She appeared to be astonished even at the suggestion! Had claimed in fact, her silence at the start sprang quite genuinely from chronic shyness. That and the fact that she'd started her period unexpectedly at their front door.

"Couldn't you tell?" she'd said accusingly, as if I'd had X-ray eyes. "That's why I was standing up all night, in case it all came through."

"Wouldn't standing make it worse—on the principle of pouring? You'd have been better laying on your side like a bottle of vintage port."

"I couldn't afford the risk, not on their ultra-smart seating! Though I was all right as it happened. I took the precaution, in their toilet, of stuffing my bloomers with Bronco."

I was right about who she'd chosen. Jim was the one, as I'd thought. "The only thing that irks though, is that he likes you." She'd peevishly pressed her lips together.

"Me?"

"They both do. That Nicholas is mad on you. I as usual was left with the pooftah! Not that I mind that one, Gerry. He's a bloody good dancer, isn't he?"

I thought of them swaying so rhythmically together. Two slender bodies, so sexless and sublime. "Perhaps he'd do for your brother, Pat."

But she'd wrinkled her nose. "Oh, no! My brother wouldn't do for him. Much too provincial. Not pretty enough anyway! He's not like me, my brother. He's more knitted Fair Isle, if you know what I mean. And actual carpet slippers! Like an old auntie in spite of being so young. It's a different scene altogether from ours. You'd find it hard to believe we're related even." And she'd shuddered. "Oh, Christ! I'll be with the drip of course, tonight. I'm going to Brighton straight from school—so I shan't be seeing you till Sunday."

The flat felt funny without her as soon as she'd slammed the door. I lay in bed listening to her footsteps pattering up our stairs until she reached the ground floor immediately overhead. Straining my good ear, I could even hear the muffled sounds of the early-morning streets outside as she'd opened the heavy front door. But after the dull thud of its closing there was now no sound at all. You could die down here, I thought. I could pass out—whoof—and no one would know, not for the whole weekend. Not till Sunday when Pat came back and found my body. If Fiona weren't coming that was.

She'd rung, Fiona, at that precise moment. Exactly as I'd mentally said her name. Extraordinary, as I'd told her later. And arising from that minor revelation was something even more—we'd both agreed. It turned out that even down to the split second when dear old Douglas' defeated erection had boomeranged back on his bollocks, she, Fiona, was similarly engaged in sexual frolics all the way up in Scotland. And each of us wondering whether the other of us was!

"It's telepathy!" she said. "We're linked by metaphysical threads. Like twins out of the womb—"

"I saw a film called *Freaks* with Siamese twins in, in the college cinema club. And one of those was being poked," I said.

"With the other one looking on?"

"Well, no. In actual fact she turned her head the other way and did a bit of knitting. They were joined at the hip, I think. I can't remember now but I know they both had legs and arms belonging to themselves."

"She'd have been getting a bit excited then herself. Or not?"

"They didn't make that clear. Though she did shut her eyes when the chap shot off and I think that she did drop a stitch."

I'd had an early night the previous evening, on my own. Really early. Seven-thirty it was when I got into bed. Though it had crossed my mind to go out to the cinema. Michael, of all people, had rung to have a chat and enquire what I was up to. "What a shame," I'd said "I'm just rushing out this instant. No time to even swap good-days. Can you ring me another time, Michael?" And I'd slowly walked into the kitchen to make a cup of tea. The trouble was, a terrible lethargy had settled. It was more than disappointment that Fiona hadn't arrived, though that in itself was indeed contributing to my sense of anti-climax. It's this flat, I thought, that's it. It's giving me the willies! The walled-in claustrophobic feeling, being basement—with no windows. But more than that—the bloody quiet was what I wasn't used to. That's what comes from living above a business. On the premises of the shop. All nicely cocooned out back and down below and up above. Everything throbbing around the central nerve of the counter and the till. We had been offered a business once with alternative living accommodation, but my father had claimed my mother would pine away within the week without the boost of a busy shop bell, without the weight of spent loose change, or the shuffling impatience that spells full shop. So he'd turned it down before she'd say yes—in case. And I had to admit that at this very minute, I agreed with him. I'd have honestly given anything to be behind our counter now—rearranging Wrigley's Gums, tidying Cadbury's chocolates. Refilling rapidly emptying jars. Requesting firmly "Who's next please?" and "Come on, kids, decide! Or I'll serve someone else instead!" Instead of languishing in this Earls Court cell.

"What a senseless bloody time to ring!" my father shouted down the phone. "The shop is full, as you'd expect! What's up then? Are you ill? We thought you must be—not having heard. Can't you send us at least a card?" I could almost smell through the mouthpiece the poignant mix of confectionary and tobacco, could even tell exactly which wrapped hard-boiled sweets my mother was weighing out from the slithering cellophane kiss on the scales. Pascals, but possibly now perhaps their Buttered Brazils, not Fruit Drops after all.

"Sorry, dad," I said, swallowing very hard on my suddenly tender tonsils. "I'll drop a line and"—I finished in a rush—"perhaps come home next weekend!" I knew he held the line uncertainly at the other end. Torn between desire to continue taking money and keeping customers happy, torn between those and a natural feeling of wanting to find out more. "Oh, yes!" I added as bonus, "I thought you'd be pleased, dad. I went out with a barrister this week! Well, trainee barrister anyway—"

"You'll never believe this, Fiona, but last night being on my own in this place—I actually was *so* homesick of all things—that I got on the phone to my father!" We sat in our nighties in the new double bed in the kitchen. Each wearing a cardigan, with the gas oven turned up for warmth. She'd brought the double sheets from home but had forgotten to bring a pillow. I said later on we'd go and buy her one.

"Whiteleys, that's the place for pillows. So mummy's always saying. Household goods and electrical appliances—unbeatable bargains! You can make a sixty per cent saving on big bath towels and small tea cloths. She bought a shop-soiled toaster there not so long ago for under a pound, you know—"

I'd made no mention of the fact that Pat expected two pounds for buying the bed-settee on her behalf. I didn't think I could stand the strain of seeing her having to part company with her money. Not out of the blue, not without having been warned. But she'd brought me a little present from Scotland. Some barley sugar. "Oh, Fiona! How sweet!" An inferior make which even my father had refused to stock, for not being value for money.

"It's not one you sell in the shop, is it?" she'd asked anxiously.

"No," I'd answered truthfully. "It isn't."

But she must have doubted me because, before I could stop her, she'd impulsively unpinned a hideous shiny thistle brooch from her suit lapel and pressed it in my hand. "There," she said, "I think I'd like you to have it. I'd actually bought it for our old char. I was only wearing it until I see her this week. Now it's yours."

But the news she'd brought of her goings-on were more of a

tonic than any gifts. "Shall we get in bed with our coffee and toast before I get settled and start?"

It was patently clear she was no longer pure from the second she stepped through the door. "Fiona," I'd said, excited by the rawness of the eyes behind her shiny specs. "Stand in the light for me to see you better. There's no need to ask?"

"No." She glowed. "There isn't."

I had to admit to a pang or two when at last she started to tell me. Four lovers in a fortnight wasn't bad for a beginner!

"But who were they? Where from?" I asked.

"Oh, I didn't bother with names! I just had them one afternoon out fishing. One by one in the bushes. On a Friday. After an alcoholic lunch brought down by the gillies. But it's spoilt me a bit—you can see."

I couldn't see, not at all—she looked positively radiant to me. "What do you mean, spoilt? Leaving your L-plates up in the hills?"

"The having had so many all at once."

I nodded understandingly. "And the doing it outdoors. That gives an appetite—the open air."

"I suppose," she sighed and gave a beatific smile, "one might embrace the whole experience as rather a nice form of mass rape."

"A superior sort of gang bang—were any of them actual workers? I mean, the Lady Chatterley syndrome? Or were you all, as it were, social equals?"

"Interesting, that, though not so easy to answer! They hardly spoke you see. Just got on with the job and as I didn't dare to open my eyes for fear of embarrassing them away, I could only tell by the texture of the tweed. And there isn't much difference in that, or the fishiness of hands that have just held rods."

"Was one your father, do you suppose?"

"Daddy? Oh, dear, no! Daddy'd gone by then, old thing. He only was there a week. I stayed on by myself at Nathaniel's house. That's what I'm getting to next!"

I couldn't wait to hear about Nathaniel. I, without even meeting him, was already one of his fans. I'd seen every film he'd been in—which was more than Fiona could claim. He always played the sort of roguish country squire part. Or twinkling irascible Army colonels. Or some amused and knighted member of the medical hierarchy. A well-born establishment figure—the kind my father could have bowed and scraped to. But off-centre and anarchic enough to appeal to me. I crossed invisible fingers and silently prayed that Fiona might be generous enough to effect an introduction. There wasn't a chance. No hope in hell.

"It's not even that I fancy him for myself, you know what I mean. He's much too old for starters. But no one could say he wasn't a catch—a household name! And being one of daddy's dearest friends that gives it an extra *frisson*! You don't mind, darling, do you?"

I minded like mad, but managed with an immense amount of muscle control around the outer corners of my mouth to courageously conceal the fact.

"You see," she continued unawares, "I'd so loathe it if he fell for you, and it's ten to one he would. He's such a dirty old devil, you can't imagine, and terribly keen on tit! Oh dear—" She drew me close and pressed the hard steel of her spectacle frame against my cheek. "Even as I'm saying it, I sound so dreadfully dog-in-the-manger. And I know you'd be just the opposite in my position, which makes it that much worse."

Oh, yes. There was no doubt that I'd be opposite! What? With one of my father's dearest friends? You bet my nubile bum I would! I tried to think who'd qualify. An affair with which of them would carry, as Fiona so succinctly put it—that spot of extra *frisson*? What about old Wheelchair Willie, Ted Grunt's invalid uncle? My dad was fond of him, all right, if only for demolishing at darts. He'd come in for a lot of local criticism over that, not allowing Willie to win. An unfair contest, many claimed, with the board being too high for any invalid to aim. Let alone one like old Willie, who was not only hamstrung by the wheelchair's arms but in addition partially paralysed in both palms. Though active enough in other extremities. Nineteen National Health nurses already, he'd been through, who'd refused to attend him again. Even the women from Meals-on-Wheels were now, too, unwilling to drop off his parsnips and pudding.

He'd had me sitting on his lap some several years ago, on the boisterous occasion of his birthday. A knowing female neighbour has asked me afterwards how it had felt. "Much like the Chinese joke," I'd told her, "Confucius he say 'girl who sit on jockey's knee get hot tip'." And it had indeed surprised me with its snaky strength, so much so I'd feared for the contours of my loosely woven wollen skirt, and had sprung up in some alarm. I'd only recently ruined another garment in that similar fashion—from hanging it carelessly in the cupboard. On a peg which had stretched the soft material in such a way that, when I put it on, I appeared from certain angles to be sustaining a small but pointed hunch high up on my shoulders.

Yes, Wheelchair Willie would most certainly have been the most able and willing of all my father's friends to start a torrid affair with me. And I, without any doubts, could never have shown the selfishness that Fiona was now—about passing him on, so to speak. It wouldn't have crossed my mind at all to keep the undeniable *cachet* of a chair-bound lover to myself. Though on the other hand she probably wouldn't have wanted him anyway, since he was almost as old as Nathaniel. "What was the difference, then," I said, "with Nathaniel? Being that much older?"

"Oh, don't be silly." She sipped her coffee and sucked a glistening gush of Cooper's Chunky from toast to tongue. "You know."

"How do I?"

"Well, just guess. To do with the goolies, there's a clue!"

"The goolies," I said, "I imagine would, like the rest of the body in any person of advancing years—the goolies would have appeared more *gathered*, if that's the word. More knitted-up, more knotted, gnarled and wrinkled."

"Wrong!"

"More loose and less elastic?"

"Right!"

"What, all the time, you mean? No air in the balloon at any point? No sage and onion, thyme and parsley stuffing in the turkey? But surely sometimes, Fiona."

She'd finished her toast and started to lick the sticky tip of one thumb. "Well," she sighed, "that's just the thing you see. I had to work so bloody hard to achieve such minimal results. It seemed to me to be a ghastly waste of time—and all the talking got me down." She raised her spectacles from her nose, and, dropping them to her nostrils, looked at me steadily as if she were school-marm and me the attentive scholar. "You never heard such talking! A lecture a second, really! Telling me what to do and how to touch—though not so much by the end. He said I was such an appalling pupil. Not near enough concentration."

I looked at her and seethed. What gross unfairness, what wild injustice that I, who liked nothing better than to talk in bed, especially on sexually educational lines, was now to be denied this chance, simply because of her selfishness. It would serve her right if I gave Wheelchair Willie the A.O.K. in her direction. Tilted his wheels towards her well-kept house. Even pushed him myself all the way there, to present himself to her father. 'I'm here as prospective suitor, sir. Here to try rogering your daughter. I've heard that she's not such a big one for chat—well, the efficiency of my dick, sir, doesn't depend on discussion!'

"Though on the other hand, of course," Fiona was cheerfully saying, "I have to hand it out to Nathaniel. If he hadn't gone on quite so much, I would never have had them in the bushes. He'd whet my appetite. Made me curious. And knowing you were back here expecting me and England, or rather Scotland, to do its duty—well that put the tin hat on it, if you like? Hey!" She sat up and blinked, suddenly excited. "I wonder what we'll catch tonight."

I felt my envious resentment ebbing, just to see the smile she shone my way. She could do that. "Though one thing is certain, angel, eh? We couldn't possibly"—she glanced around and shuddered—"bring anybody civilised back here!"

I'd worked out what to wear already, that is till Fiona looked at it. Then I had second thoughts. "No, come on!" she'd said. "Don't joke! What are you really wearing?"

"It's what I wore to your twenty-first." I'd attempted a brave defence.

"Exactly!"

She'd delivered the brutal kick as crisply as someone else that

I'd once known, but I couldn't remember who for the minute.

"Which reminds me, now you mention my twenty-first—guess who's going to be there?"

"Where?"

"There. Tonight. At the centre of all the gaiety."

"Who?" But I knew who, just as I now recalled the all too familiar crispness of the conversational kick. "Piers?"

She laughed. "Right in one! He was up there too, you know, by the way. Up there, up in Scotland. Nathaniel claims to have known him man and boy, since he was six, so he said. I told him Piers had a thing about you—that's when I got the first warning signal. I believe they've formed mutual attachments in the past. Both keen on the same piece of stuff, despite the difference in years."

Now I felt well and truly flattered to think of them having discussed me! He was at least aware of my existence in the world then, Nathaniel. Might even have mentioned me to Piers. That spoilt it then, remembering back, to think what Piers could have said. "Oh yes, that one. A person of the people. A pretty thing, but—well, you know! Had a pleasant enough father, who as far as I could tell, suffered from multiple sclerosis. Always falling down, poor sod! Ever so slightly awkward, being a shopkeeper. Seemed bent on smashing up stock—" I felt suddenly, undeniably depressed, all sense of joyous anticipation seeping, draining rapidly away. As if somebody had pulled the plug out when I wasn't looking. I not only now had nothing to wear, but on top of that I'd have to put up with the scorn and ridicule of Piers and the like. Fiona could go alone.

"Are you certain, Fiona, that Piers will be there?"

"Oh quite." She said cheerfully. "*Sans* all possible *doute*! He's the cousin you see—of the host."

They paid in retrospect, the L.C.C., to keep teachers like me short and strained until our first pay. A full month's salary went automatically, when the month was up, into an account which they'd opened for me in the Midland Bank nearest to school. That applied to everyone. It amazed me, the organisation. The standard of efficiency required to move an operation such as that, with no loose ends out anywhere. My father banked our takings every Tuesday. Also in the Midland as it happened. I used to carry it to the bank in a big suspicious suitcase, which anybody would have been right in assuming to contain an awful lot of money. Money for the mortgage, so my father always stressed, in case I got ideas. Money to pay all manner of mundane matters to do with mere existence. And then anything left over ploughed immediately back into the business. I loathed that phrase—the ploughing back—with its biblical connotations. Linked so inextricably with the Reaping and Just Rewards. When all it meant, in actual fact, was him putting a face on with inconsequential commercial travellers. Ordering with authority! From the Representatives. The Reps, as he chose to call them. Not a breed to be revered I would have thought. But no, he found them extremely pleasant fellows. Full of the little courtesies of life. With company cars and cigarette cases. And shiny lighters of their own instead of matches made by Bryant & May or shabby boxes of Swan Vestas. It amazed me how very alike they looked, all with obligatory moustaches and haircuts which showed their ears. Until I worked it out that of course they were all meant to be Clark Gable. And once I'd stumbled on that fact I began seeing Clark Gables everywhere. On building sites and buses. Bartending and behind the wheels of lorries. All men of coming-on, middling age who would have had Clark Gable as the matinée idol when they were adolescents. The seediest fell far short of the ones who Repped our shop, and presented rather more an ageing Ronald Colman look about the gills. But one or two, more rakishly inclined, aimed even higher than Clark. As far as Errol Flynn, no less. With dimpled cheeks and dipping trilby brims. Those were the ones that I took to least of all. And my father tacitly approved my sour stand-offishness. "Nice enough chaps, these reps, my girl, but you're right to think to do better! Little or no education between the whole bloody pack of them! Smarm and charm, and a bit of a head for figures. Brylcreem Boys! No better, no worse. Though I'd be lost without them. And that's a fact—fair do's!" But mashers, which was really what those rakier reps were—I could tell from their line of chat—mashers had never been my line in any case. Except Derek of course, had he been born in different circumstances, he might have been termed a masher. It would probably stand to reason that any female worth her salt would get caught in the grips of one sooner or later. At some stage in her life. I reflected now that probably it was just as well that I'd experienced it sooner—with the rest of my days to devote ahead to higher ambitions and better beds. And cocks which fitted more comfortably.

"Pat's lost it by the way. With a bloke she brought back called Douglas."

But Fiona wasn't listening any longer. As if at the mere mention of Pat's name she'd switched off altogether. I didn't mind. It had struck me in mid-sentence that I'd be silly to continue. Certainly to go on to tell it all, including not only the implied intimacy of a threesome which she'd have obviously resented, but also to go into the complicating fiasco of my own failure at informal fornication. She didn't seem to have suffered such frustrations in that field. In fact the more I thought of it, the fourth of her fucks must have been pretty squidgy indeed. Like batting on a buttered bun. My dehydrated lower zones could well have made a welcome change in that steamy sub-tropical, cunt-clime of hers.

"Tell me," her voice broke through abruptly. "What is the state of your bank balance?"

The question startled me. I hadn't one as yet. How could I have without a salary so far?

"I've just been thinking that it mightn't be a bad idea for you to buy a frock—something, you know—" She tugged her nightie down and off her little rounded shoulders. "Strapless." I felt a sense of panic, knowing that I was about to be manipulated into spending money I didn't possess. "I'll lend you some. I'll let you into a little secret—Nathaniel gave me twenty-five pounds! For a handbag I said I'd seen in Bond Street. Made out of lizard-skin. Look, here it is—I'll let you feel—two tenners and a five." She pressed the crackling paper on my palms and sat back on her heels. Smiling, her arms wrapped right around her waist, hugging herself and her secret. "You mustn't ever say! You'll promise you never would. Mummy and daddy would do their nut. Accepting money from men. But"—she leaned forward—"I'll tell you something—

that has almost been the best part, this money. More than the sex I mean! The feeling, oh I can't explain—the feeling—sort of *kept*, I think."

I looked at the twenty-five pounds on my lap and thought of the things it could buy. What on earth would I have done with it myself? I couldn't for the life of me imagine. I'd probably have sent some to my dad. "Dear dad, here's this for you to spend on what you like. I've sold a painting! Yes, I have! So perhaps the years of training weren't in vain! I'm keeping some for myself—ploughing the profits back into the business, as you so rightly say! It will stand me in good stead, as in order to expand, I shall need new brushes and fresh supplies of paint and well-primed canvases . . ." Yes, that's what I'd have done without a doubt. Some showing off as if, say, I'd earned it with my talent instead of . . . "Do you look on it as untaxed earnings, then? Do you, Fiona? Tell me?"

She chuckled softly and dropped her chin to look at the rest of her body. "Well now—earnings you say! You know I never thought of it as that, but now you've put the notion in my mind . . ."

I laughed. "I didn't mean it seriously of course—"

She interrupted. "Well! Why not? Look," and in one wilfully childish gesture she pulled her nightie and cardigan up and over her head and threw them back on the bed. "Look," she repeated. "How much would you say I was worth?"

It was a dear little body. The titties tiny but tip-tilted like a child's *retroussé* nose. Set in the surrounding flesh like two firm yet trembling jellies. With curiously vulnerable nipples, more in the mould of rosy unburst boils. Lacking a head. She touched them both, holding each daintily between thumb and finger. I'd seen a painting once like that of two sisters. Early Italian? Tate? Or National Gallery? Twins, if I remembered right—holding each other's nipples. But they'd had something there to hold. Two sharp protruding points, not just a swatch of arbitrary tissue such as Fiona was offering me now. "Look. Look at these!" she said. "What do you think? Aren't they a washout! So weak and lacking in spunk!"

"Gristle."

"Gristle?"

"Yes, that's what it is. Do you remember that very young model we had? Maureen? Monica? What was her name? When we were doing Intermediate Life Drawing. She had nipples like that, I know, because we came in for heavy criticism over leaving breasts blank at the end. Not enough delineation. A shabby and superficial use of shading. When all the time there was nothing there, unless you made it up. Which then would have become a Work of Imagination. Quite a separate subject! Bernard Bart put it down to extreme youth. But she was about sixteen. Perhaps in your case, Fiona, it's been lack of sexual experience. Didn't Nathaniel voice some sort of opinion?"

I had such strong proprietary feelings now myself about Nathaniel—was harbouring quite excessive hopes in his direction, that even to think of him touching those undeniably enticing mounds of hers (despite their botched-up aureoles) made me prematurely old with envy. I felt as I had done, oh, long ago, in school when Rita Eaten had won the raffle instead of me. A mahogany letter rack, faced with Moroccan leather. That was the prize, I remember. It would have done a treat for my father's birthday present. But Rita had not been at school the morning they'd called the draw, so I'd been sent up instead of her to receive the prize in her place. Everyone clapped, of course. But it wasn't the same. Playing understudy.

"Nathaniel? Yes, he did. He actually did put the problem into words. If I recall rightly it was something to do with snobbery. Mine, he said. My snobbery. My nipples were something to do with that. I'm not sure now just how the two were linked."

"Inverted," I explained.

She let go of one breast. I watched it bounce down and then rise up again, not quite certain how long to take in shivering to a standstill. "That's it." She pointed in the air. For all the world as if an aeroplane had ripped the word 'inverted' through the backcloth of the sky. "Inverted! He said as well that what was wanted was a child. To properly suck them into shape. Can you imagine me coming back from Scotland and saying to mummy, 'Mummy dear, I do so hope you won't be cross. I'm going to have a baby. Why?

No real reason except to harden my tit ends up. Nathaniel has said it's the way'."

"You could go as a wet nurse to the poor. In places like the Gorbals—or out to British Guiana."

She stared at me. "What, not have a baby at all you mean? Just keep dipping them into milk, to give the taste?"

"Well, not quite that. You'd probably have to have your own, I think. No, what I mean is having had it, you could go on to become a wet nurse. The supply of milk does continue where there's a demand. The body rarely lets you down in that respect. And then you'd be assured of stupendous nipples for life! Like the steeples of Sacré Cœur!"

She frowned. "Not much of a social life of course—continually milking!"

"Possibly not the one you might envisage now, but Fiona—"

"Touch them," she said. "Yourself."

I didn't want to, felt no inclination, none at all. But if she'd said to me to kindly eat her ear wax, I would probably have done so. And begged to be given the recipe afterwards. "What these?' They gave me instant goose pimples to touch. Somebody could have put a patent on the extraordinary texture. Couldn't Pat's lot be taught a weft and warp to produce a similar surface? Spun from spider web threads and the under-arm fur of new-born baby mice.

She shut her eyes. A smile stretching slowly from side to side. "Oh God," she groaned. "It actually really gets me going. You know what I mean, down here." And she lodged a hand sideways between her legs, slanting backwards so the back of it, behind the wrist, rested heavily on her clitoris. The unashamed abandonment appalled me. Of course I understood that middle-class girls of Fiona's sort, brought up largely in boarding schools, were bound to be less self-conscious. Or even girls of Pat's ilk, where to walk from the bathroom in your bra and knickers in the bosom of your family, especially with no father on the scene, would be thought to be quite normal. But this obvious—*hedonism*! Is that what going away to school was all about? Did whole dormitories full of ripe, pubescent girls behave in this embarrassing way? My father would have demanded an enquiry.

"Is that enough?" I squirmed, trying like mad to match her smile and keep the conversation light and gay. I wanted to mention Whiteleys and whether they stayed open on Saturdays after the normal half-day. I still hadn't sorted out shop hours. Our half-day in Brighton had always been on Wednesday, but up here all regions seemed to suit themselves.

"That"—now she was speaking again, thank Christ—"is one of Nathaniel's greatest likes of course. Having two girls together. He has asked me how about it. I thought of you at the time."

The gas, I was grateful to see, was giving up the ghost—flickering lower and lower in the oven. The meter was running out of money. I stopped. "Loose change?" And started climbing off the bed. Stiffly, as if someone had punched me in the middle and emptied a tin of warm golden syrup in my open stomach. It oozed, or something did. It spun itself a tacky web amongst my tangled lips. It horrified me to notice that my whole body too appeared geared for action, so to speak. The entire circumference of my chest as pouting as an impudent pigeon's. Each starched and prominent nozzle pulling away in opposite directions from the feeble restraint of my fastened cardigan. I quickly folded my arms, a schoolgirl habit based on gossiping neighbours, washerwoman-style. To hide the tell-tale signs from my sensual companion. But she was gone, eyes shut, on a secret smiling journey of her own, legs now thrown wide, one hand well in. Plaiting and tapping furiously as if she were top toast of the typing pool—and abusing the office equipment. Would I ever learn, I wondered, adjusting the spectacles on her nose, to become so sublimely lacking in shame?

"This frock's a flop."

"Not if you think of the saving!"

"It's silly, Fiona, to ever buy anything at sale price. It's bound to be dud. My dad has always maintained that. They bring them in by the lorry load. Very few are genuine reductions! In any case they couldn't ever have asked full price for this. It's scarcely more than a skirt. Are you sure you found it in Gowns?"

"Gowns Strapless, certainly! That's the fetching part—the fact of it being being cut low." Her voice had acquired an accusatory tone. "You said you liked it in the shop. What's wrong then, now you've got it home?"

"It must be the merciless light, or this mirror. I don't know which. I look monstrous!"

But Fiona wouldn't have it that I did. Elizabeth Taylor in *A Place in the Sun*, that's who I looked like, she said. I could understand the lines on which she worked, but something somewhere was wrong. The dress had either just one flouncy petticoat too many or else it had several too few. And the top was designed with someone of more modest measurements than mine in mind. I tipped over such material that there was to a quite scandalous degree. "My cup runneth over, Fiona! I'm sure they could have me on indecency."

"They? Who?"

"People," I said miserably. "In the street."

"But it's a party frock—you silly fool. You'll feel different amongst all the others! It's just, I'm sure, that you're not used to showing such a sumptuous amount of flesh, that's all. Christ, what! At four pounds, seventeen and sixpence, for what is actually *haute couture*, I'd go dressed in a flag, the Union Jack! I'd be so pleased at the bargain. Doesn't it thrill you to think that those other girls will have paid an absolute fortune for what they'll be wearing tonight and you'll have gone in next to nothing?" Then she laughed and added, cruelly I thought, "Quite literally, I mean."

Was I stupid to trust her, I secretly asked myself, as if I had alternatives. Derek had always warned me over my blind acceptance of what other people said. 'Because you yourself have never worked on devious lines, that doesn't mean to say the rest of us share your Christian attitudes to honour, love and loyalties. Nor is there any reason why we should. Have you ever considered *that* before?' I hadn't. There was much actually that Derek fed me, or would have force-fed me, had I allowed it—that even in theory I thought shamelessly puerile and frankly pathetic. On a par with and as profound as the philosophy of our shop counter. If each had allowed themselves the self-indulgence, my father and my ex-fiancé might have had quite fine mutual debates. Not over-taxing to either.

Perhaps, after all, I had been doing Fiona an injustice to entertain any doubts at all, because certainly when she eventually produced her own intended party wear, it looked not unlike my own. And had, according to her, cost even less! She'd inked it herself as it hung in the store. Surreptitiously with her own small fountain pen brought specially for the purpose. "Parker 51. They're far the best. The flow is so much faster." So that the management had been forced into a further drop in price. "But if you ever try it yourself, be very careful," she'd warned. "Apply the ink—but wisely, where it won't show in the wearing—somewhere round the hem. Or waist, where it can be hidden by a belt. Otherwise you'll find the thing is unwearable. And don't be put off by assistants who might try to go one better and claim the ink to be the reason why the dress is in the sale in the first place. You can always call for the manager if you're feeling confident enough. It's never not worked for me so far. I'm thinking of starting on furniture—for when we get our own flat. But you must be careful, as I said. It's a wonder I haven't been caught. I take such appalling risks."

I knew she took appalling risks after ten minutes with her in Whiteleys. "Oh Fiona, don't! Oh please, "I'd whispered pleadingly. "Half of these shoppers are plain-clothes police. I'm sure of it. See that one there. She's been trailing us since we came in. I noticed her—" Her hand hovered over a bright blonde hairnet that quite obviously neither of us needed. I couldn't for the life of me see the sense of half she was taking. Was it due to her short sightedness or what? Though certainly I understood that kleptomaniacs never do lift articles that they may need themselves; that's not the impetus at all. But I'd be in a tricky position since she would keep dropping the stuff into the shopping bag I held. They'd have us both as accomplices. I shifted it now to the other arm, attempting to keep it out of her reach, and my usual bodily person much less accessible in case she took to my pockets. My whole future could be put in jeopardy just for the sake of—what? Two tins of Elastoplast. A tiny pale green satin pin-cushion, sewn in the shape of a pear. The spare part of a fruit-juice squeezer. And a bag of upholstery buttons. It didn't appear to be worth it whichever way I looked.

But afterwards, she'd shrugged when I asked why on earth she did it. "Is it a recent thing? Or not? When did you start? And why?" But I could get no sense from her at all. Nothing except an emotional outburst as answer—in which she turned the tables so neatly that I was the one who felt guilty by the end.

"I thought at least you'd find it fun. Join the spirit of the thing like a real friend. Honestly. It's like going out with a Girl Guide!"

"I'm sorry Fiona," I mumbled. "But I found it so scary, that's all—the almost being caught. A razor's breadth away!"

"But that's the excitement. The whole point. The kick—all the adrenalin pumping! I find it terribly arousing. No, really! I could get off with anyone after. It's the same sort of feeling as sex."

I knew which I'd choose of the two.

Fiona said we should go in a taxi, something I still wouldn't dream of taking. On principle, quite apart from the cost. I felt more myself on public transport—and of course, had myself felt more. I still hadn't got around to telling her all about that. Though such abortive titillation would probably not impress her overmuch, having neither to do with consummated lust nor the accumulation of unexpected wealth. Though, thinking about it, she, with her enthusiasm, might well have found in rush hour a chance to refine her art to the point where she would be equally practised in lifting cocks and wallets.

People who took taxis were, in my father's book at any rate, hedonistic, self-indulgent lounge lizards. The extravagant sort of spendthrift. Faintly shady cards who wore crêpe-soled brothel-creepers instead of straightforward lace-up shoes. Like Derek. Exactly like Derek, who'd chosen, alas, to take a taxi instead of walk the four miles back one night after he'd missed his last bus. My father had paid. I'd watched him counting out each coin with over-deliberate care. Into Derek's open palm and prayed that he'd change his mind. Not take the bloody money, none of it. But no—"Oh thank you very much. That's awfully kind!" My father's nostrils had flared with malevolent satisfaction. Another stick with which to beat. "The bloody tribe! The lazy, luxury-loving lout! Typical, that is, girl! You give a yid a chance to park his arse or else to use Shank's Pony!"

Sharing Fiona's taxi meant I now owed her, so she said, five pounds one shilling and sixpence. But I wasn't to worry, she wouldn't be charging interest rates, not quite yet at least! I got to the tip of my tongue the price of the bed-settee and a tin of Nescafé. And one lavatory roll. And bread and butter and the use of electric light—but no further than the tip. I couldn't have stood the chance, not taken the risk of a scalding rejoinder at that point, not now we were almost there. I had too many other things to think about, like not creasing my precious sawn-off party frock and not snagging my new silk stockings. I sat, most of my buttocks bare, against the cold seat of the taxi, only my flimsy panties between the leather and crotch. White, when what I usually wore was black. With a cheap white suspender belt to match. Cotton, covered with broderie anglaise. Mock. No brassière on at all. No need for one; in any case I didn't own a strapless one yet. The dress itself provided all in stiffened under-support. Strangely now, I did feel deliciously desirable, as Fiona had said I would. "Here, have a splash of this perfume, my darling—" her humour was all restored. And she dabbed it behind my ears and on both throbbing wrists. Then deep down in my décolletage. "And what about between the legs? You never know—a handsome stranger may lose his way and end up in the forest!" We'd both laughed very long and very loud. Holding our necks like giraffes, our heads high in the air. I'd never felt as close to her before, balancing so precariously on the frontier of the evening.

"You know what you should do, Fiona"—I felt emboldened by the intimacy. "Now you have the knack of extracting money from men—"

"What a neat turn of phrase."

"You should get someone like Nathaniel to come up with some contact lenses." (And a sculptural plastic surgeon to carve a slice off each ankle?)

"He wouldn't do it." She spoke abruptly. "I know. I've asked already. He says my spectacles are sweet. He insists they're part of me. And daddy would say as much as well. They seem almost to be in league."

"And what do you think yourself then?"

"Oh, I'd give anything to have them off."

"Well, it's settled then. Save up. You've squandered a fiver on lending to me for my frock. I'll pay you back, but that's not the point. It's an attitude of mind. What will it cost? It won't take you that long, not with large amounts like the twenty-five from Nathaniel—and anything else you might manage to coin. It will give you an aim. Don't you see?"

But I'd lost her interest again. A positive aim apparently was not what she was after. I couldn't quite see why myself. To aim for something—to take yourself to task and set yourself a goal was what it all came down to in the end—even if what it was was barely worth the having.

The house was huge, more like a small hotel with pillars pretending to be Doric columns, almost out on the pavement. The taxi had somehow approached it from Sloane Street. "It's obnoxiously smart, Lowndes Square!"

I lost her, head and tail, Fiona, when she started to talk like that. Why obnoxious? Why an adjective of that nature? Obnoxious meaning offensive? Objectionable? Sinister? Unpalatable? Uncomfortable? Onerous? She can't have had much of an English mistress in that smart school of hers. Not like mine. Old Turnstile. Her own *Roget's Thesaurus* she'd given me when I'd left. Falling apart in Penguin, with the price still in pencil inside.

Fiona pressed the bell so fiercely I farted. "I farted! Oh Christ! What now?"

"Whoosh your skirts and I'll whoosh mine. With luck we'll disburse it before the butler opens the bloody door!"

But out of nowhere a dinner-jacketed fellow guest appeared, darting in from the pavement to our side of the pillars. "Pooh!" he exclaimed. "I say! Wouldn't you think they'd clear the dustbins before the blasted weekend?"

I trembled with shame and social terror, but Fiona saved the day. "You blasted would!" she agreed in her best fox-hunting voice, and made an extravagant movement towards the basement area with her arms. "The offensive receptacles are in that direction, I would deduce—best if we face off this way."

He adjusted his tie and collar. "Percy's the name, Frentham-Withers. Puts one in mind of old Venice. . . ."

I hadn't really ever witnessed Fiona all out. Not no holds barred as she appeared to be tonight. It was a staggering display. I wondered that everyone she spoke to didn't shrivel and curl away. Except that they too were emoting fit to kill. Of course she must have been like that or more or less the same on her twenty-first party, but my time and attention had been monopolised there by Piers—or it didn't jar then quite as much. It sent me straight into a dull decline, much like Pat had been up at Nicholas'. I thought of that—but this scene was more daunting surely than the simple chic of their place. I'd never been so overpowered by such sumptuous surroundings—as if the people themselves weren't half enough to tear my tongue from its roots! They weren't unfriendly though. Not as clipped and cut off, by convention towards breaking obligatory ice, as affairs I'd been to of my father's. "Don't leave your bag in the bedroom", Fiona had said once inside, and then she'd winked. "In case there are people here like me!" "Oh yes," I'd answered. "Of course." She'd flitted off into the adjoining bathroom. "Just spending a penny. Don't go—" Go? As if I would go on my own! I'd looked around at the heavy mirrors hanging on every wall. Framed like ancient oil paintings, every one. In walnut, old mahogany and oak. Carved with cupids and entwined flowers. A chiselled cornucopia. Containing, as I turned to each in turn, the silvered shine of my own exquisitely bevelled reflection. My father had taught me to look for the bevel, the sign of a very fine mirror. Just as Fiona had since taught me all about cards—how to run over the print with your finger, to tell if it's stamped or engraved. "Does it really make that much difference then?" "Just the difference between two different worlds!"

Our host appeared to be a boy of twelve, but no—seventeen, Fiona said. I don't know why she hadn't said as much before. I'd taken for granted somehow that the person giving the do would at least have been grown-up. Not that it made much difference; the age group seemed to span a massive area. "Is that his grannie then?" I whispered.

"Yes, I believe it is," Fiona'd answered me to my surprise. And then, "Oh you should talk to her. She's an absolute riot I've heard. Really worked her way up out of nothing. Cockney, or so I believe." She didn't look directly at me as she spoke, but somewhere to her left of my right ear. I glanced discreetly over my shoulder hoping to register just whose eye it was she meant to catch. But there was no one there who faced in our direction. Perhaps she wished to tell the time from the turquoise Louis Quinze clock.

"It's half-past nine," I said. "Shouldn't we say hello to the host?"

She jerked her attention back to me and gashed her teeth in a smile. "Oh, what a good idea!" she gushed. "Though we possibly might wait for Piers before we go about introducing ourselves."

What did she mean? Didn't she know him then? Had we come here in fact uninvited? "Good God Fiona! Are we gate-crashers?" I looked around uneasily, saying it. And her shiftiness increased my suspicion. What a nerve she had—I felt a surge of admiration for her even so. And in myself a thread of defiance. "Well, while we're here then, we'd better make the most of it!" I looked round boldly, but she squeezed my arm.

"You've got it wrong, silly. We are invited. Of course we are. But I didn't want to tell you before in case you wouldn't come. Piers invited us. At least he said that I could come—on condition that I brought you . . ."

On condition! I stared at her. What me? Was I her card of entry? When all the time I'd been feeling so much on sufferance—like something the cat had brought in. The poor relation. A member of staff who'd managed to slip upstairs. It took me seconds to actually grasp the significance of what she'd revealed. I looked down at the crystal contents of my hands, and then further down to where I saw the deep pile of the rug on which I stood was playing havoc with my best suede shoes. Not as bad as if I'd worn my polished leather, of course. They picked up the pile like mad. I'd have come away with those in a furry tidemark all round the sole, like the salt mark left when you walk too near the sea. Nothing could get that off a pair of shoes. Not once the bugger had set. No possible shoe polish on earth could shift the stain. "I don't mind," I said. "Not a bit, now we're—"

But she cut in suddenly before I had a chance to finish. "Well, look who's here—talk of the devil, it's—" I knew without looking round exactly which devil it was, even before she'd so breathily said his name. "Piers!" And now for the first time she seemed to be relaxed. So that's what her put-on pose had been! Nerves! Well, fancy that! Piers tried to sweep me off my feet. Quite literally, from behind, with his two hands around my stiffening waist so that my elbow shot high into the air taking my glass with it. I held it fast despite the unexpected flight, but the laws of gravity controlled the liquid content. He dropped me as suddenly as he had that day beneath the ancestral stairs—and uttered an animal yap of discomfort. I turned to see that he was drenched, with a lump of melting ice caught up in his white carnationed lapel. He turned on his heel and left, followed by lighthearted hoots of laughter, and the unconvincing entreaties of his cousin, the host. But from then on, so it seemed in retrospect, everything changed for the better.

"I shouldn't worry about him, not at all. That's always been Piers' stumbling block—the fact that he lacks all humour. Especially when directed towards himself."

"But I honestly didn't do it on purpose!" I could see that he didn't believe me.

"H'm, he said you were a pretty spirited sort of girl—"

"Who, Piers?"

"And I fully agree! Quite super!"

I'd spent the last six dances with this young host and had long since lost sight of Fiona. For all I knew she may well have been had by the butler and seventy per cent of the guests—or even possibly gone home. Though I'd ruled that out as unlikely. His name was Ernest, Ernest Smythe. "Pronounced Smith? Or Smythe?" I'd asked for fear of giving offence. I'd read it first before either of us had put it into words. On the card he'd given me. Engraved with, what was more, a *deckle* edge. Another delight of my dad's. The deckle edge. Like bevelled. "Oh, what a delightful deckle edge, young sir!" he might have exclaimed. "Well, I'll be dammed! A deckle you say? I didn't know that before!" "Did you hear that, my girl? That which the young sir has said? He'd never heard of a deckle before, and doubtless knows nothing of bevel. It proves the point and goes to show that quite often the proletariat is more acquainted with the ins and outs of protocol and style than even the aristocracy!"

It was hard to believe Ernest Smythe was only seventeen. Was he really so young? Or so old? And how amazing that he too, like Nathaniel (I fluttered somewhere round my ribs as I even thought his name) knew already of my existence. But I had no curiosity now about what Piers might have said. It was enough that I was here and appearing so confidently to hold my own. The interest had started suddenly, right from when Piers had left. Ernest had approached and introduced himself immediately, and then had gone further to make both Fiona and myself feel more at ease now that our entrée had vanished. "This is my father. Father?" And he'd given I thought, a curious smile. "May I leave these young ladies in your care, for just a short while, as I mingle—" The father coughed and put a snowy handkerchief to his mouth. I watched him skilfully transfer a gob of loose catarrh and caught the fetid whiff of violet cachou on his breath. That's something I quite approved of, in fact. Making the effort. A civilised touch, to conceal the anti-social aspects of his phlegm. I smiled at him. The grannie Fiona had spoken of before could not possibly be his mother, I could tell. There didn't seem to be that many years between them both. She must have been on the maternal side. The mother of his much younger wife. I smiled again, wanting to make him feel a youngster such as myself could still find time to make old gentlemen understand that what they had to say might possibly still be of interest. Despite the generation gap.

Later, very much later on in time, I used to try to think back to that first impression. The one we both made on each other. If his interest had been kindled at that introduction of his son's, it didn't, I'm almost certain, appear to show in any way. His eyes remained remote and hooded behind his wrinkled eyelids. He nodded courteously enough and asked me to repeat my name. But other than that there was nothing. I remember how impressed I was by his extraordinary pallor, the skin so clear, it seemed almost transparent, lacking essential corpuscles. He was bald, completely bald, and there seemed no difference to the texture of his scalp. No demarcation between that area and his forehead. He was much taller than his son would ever be, even allowing for further growth. He was in fact the tallest person in the room. Was that the reason that he dominated? His voice surprised me when he spoke. With its lightweight quality and gentleness—yes, gentleness. He used it as an instrument, not just of speech, but in a further sense. To stroke. That's what it was.

Almost a week had passed before I heard his voice again. A long enough space of time to have forgotten its special quality. The telephone was the perfect weapon—it lent an extra persuasiveness, an even slightly sinister edge to the soft suede tones. It hadn't occurred to me at all, at any time, that he might choose to ring. But when he did, it seemed entirely natural that he should.

"Where are you off to?" Pat had passed me in the passage, home late because she'd been shopping.

"Oh, I'm out to dinner tonight," I said. "In a bit of a rush—"

"Who with?"

"I'll tell you later. Too complicated now!"

It had been like that in fact all week, ever since Fiona had gone, Pat and I hadn't been in once together. Life was becoming a social whirl for each of us in various ways. I'd have to start keeping a diary to preserve all the details for Fiona. I'd meant to say I wouldn't be here this weekend since I'd promised to go down to Brighton. My father had rung as well as sending a letter to say they were expecting me. But I wanted to go in any case, to go over the party with Fiona. She'd left so early on the Sunday, and had been so incapably drunk the night before that so far we hadn't had a chance.

"Dolphin Square, you'll take a taxi, my dear, of course. I'll reimburse you—Nelson House."

"Where is it, abouts? Near Earls Court?"

"The taxi will know, don't you worry."

Why hadn't I needed persuading? Was it normal to go out with fathers? Ernest had been phoning all week, but who could take seventeen-year-olds seriously? I'd thought at first that that's why his father was ringing, something to do with his son. But no, apparently not. What the hell was I going to call him? Colonel Smythe? Or, more intimate, Reggie?

The dinner was, so he said, in the nature of an introduction. Something he'd thought of today. Two very old friends of his had already been invited; he thought I might care to meet them. Not purely in a social sense, you understand, my dear. He is very involved in television and since you yourself are an artist . . . I couldn't see any connection at all between the two, unless he meant the man might like his portrait done. Or supposed I might care to paint scenery! People interpreted artist to mean so many varied things, from seaside cards to restoration of renaissance works. I'd suffered before from similar confusions. But even so, sitting in the back seat of the taxi, my eyes now anxiously on the clock, I had to acknowledge a mounting feeling of excitement. What cultured company might I expect to share tonight? What pearls of wisdom would assail my eager ears? I sensed adventure, something fresh afoot. A whole new chapter of my life about to start. How superb to be gaining experience!

"Nelson House, you said, Miss?" The taxi driver swung his head around at precisely the moment I'd chosen to adjust my suspender. "And very nice too!" he added.

"Mm, er, oh yes, Nelson House—whatever that may mean. I don't know Dolphin Square myself."

"Oh, well," he said conversationally, "there's lots of Houses in Dolphin Square, all named after admirals I think. There's Nelson, Beatty, oh who else? The whole bloody lot I believe. And plenty of dirty goings on in all of them, you bet! What's a nice girl like you doing there? Off to see a sugar daddy, eh?"

I went hot, then cold, all over. He didn't seem to be joking. Thank God my father was safely sixty miles or more away, he'd have booted me right up the bum! And sliced off the bonce of my sugar daddy! Bald or otherwise. And followed it up with his bollocks. I should have to be very careful of my step if I cared to keep out of trouble.

Dolphin Square turned out to be a rather luxurious block of flats, situated on the embankment. The driver dropped me off at Nelson House; I didn't care to meet his eye as I counted out the fare. And chose to ignore his parting shot, obviously intended as rather suggestive advice to do with being good or careful.

The hallway was deserted, thickly carpeted and discreetly lit. With anonymous looking doorways placed at regular intervals along a set of seemingly never-ending corridors. I was to go, so he'd said, directly to the lift, and take it to the floor marked seven. Then I was to turn left and place myself quite squarely before the second door that I came to. I did as I'd been told and saw before me the minute and shining microscopic eye. No other door had one. Why then had he? To warn of undesirables? Or not to answer if the moment was too intimate? More likely that. I'd been in bed with Derek when another girl had come to call. She'd nearly kicked the door down, screaming she knew he was there. And what's more with another woman. Another woman! Me, another woman? When I was meant to be the only one? But Derek had stubbornly sworn he didn't know just who the hell she was. "You mean to say," I'd said with heavy irony, "that the previous occupant of this place could well have been named Derek too?" "Quite possibly so," he'd actually had the nerve to answer!

I'd rung the bell and gazed ahead, chin up at a flattering angle, knowing of the scrutiny at the other side—but nothing happened. The silence was unnerving. It reminded me of the cell-like quality back where I lived in Earls Court. It would be difficult to know, if given money, exactly where it was I'd choose to live. Had I the chance. It wouldn't be here. Not in a grave like this. How nervous I felt, what nonsense! I pushed on the bell again, and still nothing happened. But then I noticed that the door itself was fractionally open. Was I meant to enter then? To stroll in like an unsuspecting fly straight into the soft-spoken spider's web? The door swung easily at my touch—it was exactly like a scene from Arabian Nights, so utterly unlike the passage I'd just left that I just simply gasped.

It was another world. Like entering a different sort of space, a separate climate altogether. Of touch and feel and smell. I knew instinctively that it was wrong to stay, but the spell was already too potent. I cleared my throat and took another step. The trembling heroine of a horror film? Could Colonel Smythe be cousin to Count Dracula? I never relished bite marks on my neck, especially not with going to Brighton tomorrow. My father's eyes were like a hawk for all that kind of thing. Was I foolish and asking for trouble? But trouble of what nature anyway? All that I'd come for was dinner. And assuming even that the kitchen utensils were dirty, all I'd end up with would be, at most, a spot of food poisoning and a dash of violent diarrhoea.

"Ah, you've arrived, my dear. Good evening." The voice set off such shudderings down my spine I almost slipped a disc. She's surprisingly young and otherwise healthy—they would have said at Casualties—to sustain such vertebral abrasion! Has she arrived from some volcanic zone? No? She maintains it was merely a greeting!

"Oh, hello. Yes, I'm here!" I said needlessly.

We stood necessarily close in the restricted space of the doorway. He leaned over and shut the door fast behind me. I smelled again that cloying scent of cachou on his breath. Was that his kick then—violets? Did he live on a diet of those? I couldn't wait to see what colour his tongue must be. Much the same as the tongue of a Chow, I thought. Theirs were always a dull purplish pink. Hanging out—quite unlike most other dogs—all the time, as if perpetually on the scrounge. Or perhaps it was a pale rose blue, the shade of a young sow's snout.

"Your cloak?" He meant my coat, of course, but cloak was more romantic. I smiled to show I understood the subtleties wrought by words. He touched my shoulder inadvertently—it didn't seem on purpose—as I shrugged the garment off. And brushed from there along the entire length of one underarm until he'd reached my wrist. I had my back to him, but even so the featherweight slithering touch on my bare skin was as unexpectedly intimate as if we'd kissed. He turned me round to face him, seeming to sense my confusion. "You mustn't be shy of me," he soothed. I strained to catch his words.

"All right, I won't," I whispered back.

"Let me show you around now," he said.

It amazed me in fact that when he did precisely that, there wasn't all that much to see. Not in terms of actual square footage. The whole place would probably, when I thought of it, have fitted three times in our flat. It's what he'd done with it that made the difference. Each wall, each odd and unexpected surface like table tops and tiny built-in cupboards, were covered in crystal mirror. Some split in tiny two-inch squares like multiple mosaics. Some smoked mysteriously in glowing greys and others reaching from the ceiling to the carpeted floor, majestically framed in glittering gilt and intricate carved ivory. Or hard flat ebony, black to match the velvet-pelmeted curtains at the windows. And black to match the thick fur covering the floors. The only deliberate colour now it seemed to me occurred on the ceiling where one gigantic painting of a nude occupied the entire area. It hurt my neck to look at it. He saw me straining back and permitted himself a smile. "What you're trying to do is sacrilege. Of course there is only one way to view that work of art. And that is flat on your back." I hadn't somehow been conscious of the bed at first. Not with so much else to absorb my eyes. And being black as well and similarly clothed in the same fur as the floor, it was conceivable that anyone might confuse the two. "Lie down," he led me to it. "And then look up. But," he paused, then added gently, "do take your shoes off first."

I squirmed inside with embarrassment, knowing I had a hole. Furious that in my hasty flight from home I hadn't bothered to change my stockings. "What limited life this hosiery has! But hardly the span of a butterfly—" Could I get away with such pretentiousness? Possibly not I thought. I slipped my shoes off with one hand and surreptitiously pulled the hideous hole right over my biggest toe, trying to grip the slack down with the others. Until the whole foot looked deformed. Then I lay down on the bed with both feet hanging out of sight over the bottom edge.

He smiled. "You're far too low," he purred. "Look here—come up much higher." He patted the many cushions at the top. There was no going against him. No way in which I could enforce my will or try to hide a thing. He *wormed*. Without exertion. I knew it even then, floundering foolishly about the trivial fact of the hole in my toe. As if our future hung in the balance of those broken silk threads. "Whatever's wrong, my dear?" I hadn't and wouldn't budge from where I lay. "I only wish you to place yourself in a more advantageous position. Nothing more sinister if that's what you're assuming! How could it be with dinner guests arriving at any second?"

"My stocking's got a hole in it. I don't want you to see!" I felt better as soon as I'd said it, despite the uneasy delivery. Funny how I'd forgotten how childishness felt. And what a stupendous relief owning up brought with it—always out of all proportion to the offence! I thought he'd laugh. That's what my father always used to do, start laughing as soon as he'd won. "You tell the truth, and every time it's best, my girl. Own Up could be our family motto." A crest above the Crunchie Bars, for customers to see.

But no. "How touching and sweet you are." He put his hand down on my knee and traced the through route to my extradited extremities. The monkey grip of my tense toes loosened. "Yes there," I said. "Can you feel it?" He said nothing, not a word, instead I watched in growing horror as he bent his head as though to actually—kiss it! Oh Christ Almighty, could there be a stink of something there as well? When the hell did I last wash those stockings? And my constant fight against athletes' foot (caught in Derek's bed, I might add). Would he know without looking under?

But I was saved now by the bell it seemed. Trilling at his sealed front door. My fellow guests? This evening's fate? He rose and tenderly helped me to my feet, holding one hand to steady me, as I put my shoes on with the other. "Come," he whispered in one ear. "Your little hole shall be our secret. I will remember it always—as the first gift you will have given me—." I took it he did mean my stocking. Though, strangely enough, each word he spoke was said in such a weighted and important way I gained the impression of weakness in myself, a sly disintegration. An awful readiness, an eagerness indeed to present myself for sacrificial slaughter. As if by even listening only to his sentences I was somehow mutely committed and on the brink of accepting whatever it was he wished to—to what, though? "That's just it," I'd have to confess to Fiona. "At that point in the proceedings, I didn't even know myself!"

But later on I did. Much later on. After the others had gone and long after I should have gone myself. But by then of course . . .

I wondered about telling Winnie, feeling the need to spill beans. She'd presented me with the perfect opening. "Are you ill—or on top of the world?"

"Beg pardon, Winnie?"

She'd cocked her auntie-ish head on to one side, and pursed her lips and narrowed what could be seen of her piggy little eyes. I thought how well she'd play in Gilbert and Sullivans. The Mikado. Himself. Or else the maiden aunt of Minnie Ha Ha. If such a person existed. "You look so—" She screwed her face up even tighter. But this time I chose, out of a sense of respect, to look the other way. It wouldn't be fair to compare the countenance of a colleague to a bleached and wrinkled dog turd. Those ones which sit on pavements turning white. "You look so—funny, somehow, I don't know. As if you are still asleep."

I was asleep in actual fact, still numbed and slumbering. I couldn't even pinpoint it myself. Could it be the effects of the sleeping pill? The first one I'd ever had! I hadn't wanted it, not at all. "No thank you. I never take pills, not even aspirins, as a matter of fact. I just don't trust them, that's all." But I'd taken it. Despite the lateness of the hour, or rather despite the earliness. "But there are only four more hours to go before I shall have to get up. I mean to say I'll have to go back to the flat to change. And to pack all the things I'll take home. I've got to take that case to school with me. I'll be going straight to Brighton from there—" But he'd placed his finger-tips to my lips and calmed me down with kisses. All over.

"What were you doing anyway, last night? Something rather special?" Winnie and I were queueing up together to be served the abysmal school dinner. Specials for staff, which just meant they were that much bigger. "Potatoes, miss?" "No, not for me. And not for you either, Winnie." I frowned at her eager plate, deciding against full confession, with me.

"Quite special. Out to dinner. With a television person and his wife. She used to be a dancer. One of the TV Toppers—" The kitchen-hand had caught my words, had stopped in mid-helping of a pile of swedes. "Ooh, TV Topper, miss, you say? They're really good. What legs!"

Winnie sighed. "My goodness, what a giddy life you're leading. Going out with such glamorous people."

We walked out of the kitchen towards the lower staff-room where we ate our dinner along with the other old fogies. I'd said to Winnie we ought to think about breaking unspoken rules and eat on our own upstairs. The food itself was enough to upset the system apart from having to put up with colic-making conversation too. There wasn't any real reason come to that why we shouldn't bring our own. "A bit of cheese and a packet of Ryvita. Or an orange and two boiled eggs. Much better than this muck, now, Winnie—"

"Perhaps we'll start on it next week. The hot food's such a comfort in the traumas of this teaching, don't you find?"

I didn't share the deep distress she was suffering with the girls. In fact in less than a fortnight now, or exactly a fortnight next Monday, my classes were going quite splendidly. Despite Mrs. Pritchard's first doubts. "Good heavens above"—she'd entered my room unexpectedly—"And whatever is going on here?"

"Collage," I'd explained, though barely bothering to turn. She'd looked bewildered. "It's better," I'd said as kindly as I could, but with a certain coolness, "to come and look when they've finished, Mrs. Pritchard."

"What confidence! You mean to say she just turned round and left?" Winnie could hardly believe it.

"But, Winnie, what you don't understand, is that we've just come out of training. You can't expect someone who's been in teaching since lord knows when to be up to the latest tricks. Especially not a Head, that is, who's preoccupied as well with administration. She knows that as well as me. If anyone's on the defensive it's surely going to be her. That's my view of it anyway."

It struck me forcibly as I spoke what a difference I felt at work. Here in this educational establishment I knew what I was talking about. My confidence sprang from knowledge and the limited experience gained from teaching practice. I had no fears, no doubts of losing a pupil's attention, simply because I cunningly constructed each lesson to lure that attention. They liked my classes. I taxed their hands as much as their heads and helped them form a definite link between the two. Winnie's was, so she thought, a much more difficult job. She made them sit quite quietly to absorb the knowledge. She fought to force-feed them with facts. My job was of my making.

But, last night how different I'd been.

The dancing wife had barely deigned to shake my hand. Her husband was only too eager. It didn't aid the evening. He'd asked me as discreetly as he could to give him my telephone number. "What for?" I'd asked in dumb naïveté. "I'm not trained at all for television." His eyes had slid towards our host, who was attending to his wife. That didn't please me either, very much. Why wasn't he here, sitting with me? The television man was scribbling something on a cigarette pack. "Call me." He said it curiously. Managing almost to make it a menacing command. And then, "Why haven't I met you before? Has Reggie been keeping you secret?" He lowered his voice. "The old devil likes to do that with the best!"

I hated him. I loathed what he was saying, as if there'd been others before. What was it then, some sort of syndicate? Where girls got passed around like goods. Chucked out of the circuit when soiled? I stood up. "Which way," I asked, "is the bathroom?"

The man stared up. "You mean to say that you don't know?"

"How could I? I haven't been in this place before."

Colonel Smythe had arisen now too and courteously came forward. "Can I help in any way my dear? Is there something I can do?"

"Your young friend here, this lovely kid, claims to have lost her bearings—" The television man insinuated cynicism. His glossy wife winked over her shoulder and then glanced back coldly at me. "The ladies' room," she said in an Anna Neagle voice, "is in the same place as the gents'!" And she jerked her thumb as direction like a hitch-hiker on the road. The false refinement of her voice fought with her words and the action. I liked people who were more in keeping, without all this social confusion. "Oh, and don't steal the jewels set into the taps! Remember the two-way mirror!"

They all three laughed. It couldn't be true! One of them had been in there already, and the rest of us hadn't been told to look. Unless I was to be the scapegoat. The unsuspecting victim of the evening. The sacrificial lamb then, after all. With the lavatory seat as the altar! What viciousness! What very funny jokes. "I won't go in there after all. I'll possibly go home instead." My second show of childishness within the hour. It felt an hour to me. Wasn't time meant to hang heavy when you weren't enjoying yourself? I'd obviously been there longer than an hour. How much more I had to learn about social ease and graces. About passing pleasant hours with people who had nothing in common. My father may have blustered his way and probably enjoyed it. But his aggressive charms were not my own. I wasn't invited for those.

I looked at my watch. Already past midnight. "Oh, I've got to be going. It's late!"

The dancing wife had looked at her loathsome husband. And from him she'd looked at our host. "Oh no," she'd shrilled. "I'm quite sure Reggie wouldn't like that. If anyone's going, it's us. Isn't it darling?" Her husband jumped awkwardly to his feet, his jowls jiggling in the process. I wondered how low his balls must be—right to the back of his knees, fighting for space with his buttocks. Why ever should the Golden Girl have married him? His wealth and position, I presumed. Fairly obviously not his fidelity.

I remained standing whilst they all three demurred and then the two of them eventually departed. The man had had the nerve to open my handbag now, I noticed, and slip his scribblings inside. I could, of course, have made a conscious and quite public show of passing the particle back, but something in me stopped, held back from doing it. Why should I be put in this position of dumb acceptance, like an animal? Like a horse accepting a saddle, knowing it would mean a ride. I wouldn't have ridden anywhere with him. Except home, of course, as of this minute. Back to my flat with his missus and him as a lift. They didn't offer one. Just went! I began to fret about my taxi fare, now we were alone. Would he forget, Colonel Smythe, to pay it? Reimburse me as he'd promised. I blushed to realise he'd read my thoughts. Had my eyes actually signalled avarice? Printed coarsely across each pupil—or just half the word in each? He fumbled in a waistcoat pocket and brought out a five-pound note. Then followed it with another!

My mouth must have dropped, my jaw swung lantern-like against my neck. I felt its bony frontier. He took my hand and smoothed the first note in its centre, then closed my fingers tight. "This is your taxi fare, my darling! And this"—he took my other hand now and repeated the procedure—"this is to cover your future fares."

"Then what did he do though? I can't believe it! A tenner before you'd begun? Is he a betting man by any chance, old Colonel Smythe?" Fiona's orchard was very cold. I wished we could go inside. I shivered and hunched my shoulders round my ears, deciding best how I could say it.

I'd tried to work it out the whole way on the train, but all I did was meander through the moments. Re-living liquid memories of that night, like someone mooning, moodily in love.

"Perhaps that's what it is, then! You're in love!" She'd meant it, Fiona, jokingly, of course. And I'd encouraged her in the sheer unlikelihood of the notion.

"In love? Oh yes, I'm sure. With Colonel Reggie Smythe? Of course I am!" But even as I'd made fun of the fact, I experienced deep disloyalty, a sense of some betrayal to someone who didn't deserve it. Perhaps I shouldn't try to put it into words at all. Why should I even tell her? Tell anyone at all. I supposed because of the money—I couldn't keep that to myself. Not from Fiona. I couldn't resist trying to impress her. A spot of showing off which she'd appreciate. That part of it was easy. That part of it was fun—the paying her back my debt. Whatever it was I owed. Almost six pounds, she'd said it was by the end. How in hell it came to that, no one could ever know! But what did it matter now. Now with my extra income. I had four pounds left for myself—or for genuinely taking taxis! Back to Nelson House on Sunday!

He'd shown me the bathroom when the Terrible Two had left. It was even more opulent than I'd have imagined. There were indeed fine jewels, quite genuine, set into all the taps—the golden taps, surmounting a golden bath. And a golden handbasin as well. And yes, a golden bog. I wondered what colour it went when flushed with a girl's menstrual flow. A rare exotic sight, no doubt, like a goblet containing rare wine. How difficult to clean, this place must be! Which scouring powder? Which? It was uncanny how he seemed to read my thoughts. "I clean this place myself, you know. Oh yes, I much prefer it, rather than have possibly unsympathetic people here."

I hadn't myself exactly found this evening's guests totally *au fait* with his style, but of course I didn't say so. Not then, at any rate. Instead I asked about his wife and where she fitted in. I'd asked already once before about her. After we'd been introduced at his young son's party. He'd vaguely waved his hand as if the matter held but little interest. "My wife? She must be in the South of France by now, I believe. She's motoring through from Rome. With friends." And so I hadn't pursued the matter any more. Ernest had told me anyway that they didn't live together, that his father kept a close relationship with the family by dropping in each day. But had for many years maintained his own existence. "Frightfully friendly, you understand. All completely civilised." I wondered how my father would feel if my mum took to motoring through Europe. She'd have to start some driving lessons first, of course. Enrol with B.S.M. And I think that he'd have probably put his foot down over that, let alone possible further junketings. A woman across the street had once had it off with a B.S.M. instructor. We used to see his car parked up the road, with the L-plates in the back window.

I shouldn't have asked about his wife, I knew it before he'd answered. The ghost of a frown had flitted across his face, the first time I'd seen him look irritable. The two were obviously clearly kept apart, this life of his—and her. He had no wish to mix them, even by mentioning her name. I quickly asked another question

"Tell me—is the mirror two-way?" And I opened my eyes ingenuously to make up for my insensitivity. The moment passed, his forehead cleared and his eyes creased up in a twinkle. His dentist was exceptionally good, or else they were all dentures.

"No," he chuckled roguishly—much in the manner of Nathaniel, I was reminded. The impression gave me a thrill. And so now was the proximity, sending signals all over my body. I looked at him, demanding silently that he return the gaze. He did. We faced each other quite squarely. A head-on collision, m'lord. No chance of side-stepping, no opportunity to swerve. On centre all the way. He took my hands in both of his and brought them to my chin, then tilting down from his great height, he lowered his lips. And kissed me.

His mouth felt dry and dusty, like crinkled tissue paper. A touch of velvet on my own. Each firmly shut, like boxes holding treasures. Withholding trembling times and a vulnerable closeness. So far so good. So very good. He, in his wisdom, broke away, as I was wanting more. I would have liked to stay just as we were, the paunchiness of his stomach so solidly wedged against my own. Something safe to lean against, something substantial in life. Oh yes, I would have stood there like that through the entire night Two statues frozen up like snowmen.

I watched him turning towards the golden bath and saw him twist the tap—the one with the ruby on top. It caught the light, the crimson stone. Red for danger. And red for stop, of course. And dark, rich roses, meaning love. The back of his neck looked like a reconnaissance chart, each thread-like line looped finely to another, in contrast to the skull-like smoothness of his scalp. I didn't mind his baldness, not a bit, it made him appear more eccentric. It gave him the look of a nursery book Humpty Dumpty. I could guess that his arms and legs were probably quite thin in comparison to his body. "This love of yours for the grotesque—preoccupation with peculiarities—is far from healthy, I feel! Normality is not to be sneezed at." Whoever had said that to me? Any number of people might have. Hidebound ones. I thought of Nicholas' friend Jim, and I thought of Pat's Douglas. Both fine, upstanding, Anglo-Saxon specimens instead of . . .

"I'm running you a bath." I must have looked dazed and stupid, in contrast to how I was feeling. "Before I put you into bed." No question of asking me first. The second man to put me in a bath. Did I suffer from serious B.O.? I hoped that he'd go out, to let me undress on my own. Not hover around assessing all my underwear like nosy assistants in shops. "I'll leave you now, to undress on your own." Oh God, could he read every thought in my head?

The steam was clouding up the mirrors; I surveyed my nudity through what looked like a fine sea mist. And then I stepped into the water. The surface of the golden bath felt much like normal enamel. Perhaps it was, but sprayed this way. How devilishly clever! How cunning! Hey, dad, how about spraying this bath of ours gold? And the lav. And the larder. And the lino. And my larynx—what about my larynx? The girl with the golden larynx—I could go as a Carroll Levis discovery. I saw from staring straight ahead at the mirrored wall before me that the door, the bathroom door, was slowly opening. I slid beneath the surface of the water, as if its scented transparency might hide my bountiful curves. It seemed so much, much more erotic me lying here quite naked—and he completely clothed. So formally, as well, was what it was, with pin-striped trousers, and dense black coat and waistcoat complete with watch. Rigged out like a city gent, but without the finishing bowler.

I smiled at him; I felt quite at my ease, and wished to tantalise and tease, knowing I looked quite good. The heat of the water had turned my body pink, toasted it up to a tender degree, softened the surface to taste. I felt the sweat form on my face and lifted one hand to wipe it, at the same time licking my upper lip. He didn't move. He didn't say a word. Just stood there looking down at me. Stunned, I supposed with my beauty! "I'm stunned, I suppose, with your beauty!" Oh Jesus Christ! It was going beyond a joke! I looked at him and at the strange expression on his face, for all the world as if it had been frozen. Carved from granite, very grave and ancient with regret.

And then—a terrible sob leapt, strangling, from his throat. Alarm sprang through my body at the sound. I sat up suddenly in fear. What was wrong? Was he ill? "What's the matter?" But he didn't answer, not a word, not one syllable of sense. Only a low groaning moan like an animal in pain, with rolling eyes and an agonised anguish on his face. Oh hell, was he having a seizure? Could it be a case of a coronary? Ye Gods, and me without my clothes on or a knowledge of first aid!

He fell to his knees, hitting his head on the side of the bath—hardly a reeling blow, but enough, it seemed, for him to feel the need to bury his face in his arms. I tried to still my mounting sense of panic and, slurping water everywhere, rose unsteadily to my feet. A rippling wave washed over his right ear; he seemed to be impervious, appeared now to almost be unconscious. No sound at all! I carefully stepped over the side and out of the bath. But before both feet were safely on the ground, he'd lunged himself towards me. I fell. I slipped and sprawled all over him. Now both of us were crying. Me just from sheer shock and fright. And he, it seemed, from—love!

He loved me! He'd lost his heart! And his mind had lost all reason! He wasn't sick, except in soul and spirit—he ached, had ached, for me from the minute that we'd met! He wished me now to tread on him, to treat him like a worm. Defile, destroy and defecate! To do whatever I wished. He wasn't fit to touch my feet. he wanted me to— It somehow didn't sink in at all—I couldn't quite grasp the switch. I couldn't fit the two together, this trembling jelly and the distant courteous stranger that I'd seen before. I shrank away from him. But where I went, he followed. Fell squirming around the floor, tugging the towel I tried to wrap around me. Oh dear. "Don't do that, please," I said. "You've not to. Stop!" But nothing, it seemed, got to him. He had quite possibly gone mad, but given time might recover.

"I can't be long now, Fiona. I promised my father, you see. In any case, it's bloody cold out here. Any chance of a cup of tea?"

"But you haven't told me anything at all. Not down to the nitty gritty."

I sighed. "It's difficult, that's all. I'm dreadfully confused, I think."

"But what about Ernest? You said that he's been phoning you—

are you going to see him again? And what does his father say about that? And when will you go there again?"

"That's what I mean, there's just too much to think about. Perhaps we can meet tomorrow." I couldn't bring myself to tell her all. I didn't want her judgement. In any case I needed time to examine it more myself. To try to work out just why I had found it exciting, and whether I ought to go on.

My father had met me off the train. "It's dead on time today! A fraction of a second short maybe, but nothing worth a complaint."

"I'm sorry, dad, to disappoint, I know you like a word—" He'd hugged me in embarrassment and to hide his smiling pleasure. It moved me, more than I would have been normally moved, to do with the state I was in. I felt his ear upon my cheek and smelt his shampooed hair. What little hair there was, of course—a running family joke. "Mm, you've washed your hair then, dad."

He took my case. "What, brought home all your washing, girl?"

"Well actually, yes I have. No drying, you see, in the basement. They can blow out in our back yard."

We took the bus back to the shop, the evening was growing dark and the street lights glowed. The bus was full of people going home just like ourselves. My father got into a chat with an old chap sitting beside him. "What do you think then?" he said. "Of the news?" "What news?" "All of it." "Which?" "Well any—take, for instance—"

I turned away and looked out of the window. It all was exactly the same.

I'd refused to do as Reggie had asked, couldn't quite bring myself to kick him. We'd never had a dog at home, and certainly never had cats—because of my father's allergy—and so the feeling of a *thing* around my knees felt very unfamiliar. I felt the need to air the leaping laugh that started in my stomach, from nerves, from nervousness, I now supposed. I couldn't cope, was what it was. And besides, it felt so ticklish, all his little lickings. He'd started slowly with my toes and gradually worked upwards. And then he'd guided me, like a big St. Bernard, from the bathroom to the bed—actually on all fours, bumping clumsily into furniture on the way. I didn't like to look at him. Is this how people were? Is that what happened then as they got older—a return to the animal kingdom? Was my father at this very moment playing mongrels on heat, with my mother?

The fur on the bed was nice; the feel of it against my naked flesh. Neither of us spoke at all. He whimpered, salivating by my side, then relentlessly moved downwards. A dumb and awkward animal, whose daintiness now surprised. I squeezed my fists together as he started, hoping I wouldn't giggle. His big and shiny head bent in between my thighs. His tongue licked left, then right, leaving a dampening trail behind it on each leg until it gently came to rest. To rest. To nest. To nestle, flopping, face well forward in my family treasure.

I stared straight up ahead and gave a silent greeting to the nude. What period then would she have been? Early, oh Christ, just when? A mishmash bloody awful piece of work. A fake. An obvious twicer. To me at any rate, with my insight and knowledge. A *Sleeping Venus* in the Giorgione manner with Titian tints but tits more Botticelli and a much more modern-looking face, in the mould of Manet's *Olympia*. I wondered if Reggie knew these things and how much he'd had to pay. The girl lay stretched in an idyllic landscape which might have been done by Raphael. It wasn't by any means or imagination my kind of thing at all. I favoured a franker kind of art, which started as late as Lautrec who, in his turn, was now superseded by my engrossed devotion to and preoccupation with the work of the German Hans Bellmer. Those were the nudes that fired my mind. Perverse and erotically surreal, not some weak pastiche of classical stuff. We didn't really have that much in common, I reflected, on looking around. The attraction of opposites? The mating of spring and—winter? Well autumn, at any rate.

He was still fully dressed, doing his chairman's duties. Putting his client completely at her ease. Relaxing me now. Relentlessly. I would have liked to wriggle right away. It felt so disembodied done like this. Lonely, with no one to talk to. His mouth was full; he couldn't speak in any case. He'd managed to prop his nose upon my pubic mound like a pottery pig on the mantelpiece. I thought of that and gave a smile up to old *Sleeping Venus*, but as I did, a piercing stabbing thread of something close to pleasure sneaked up from down below. It all felt very wet and dribbly because, of course, it was. It felt in fact not far removed from how it felt on trains with people touching me. It felt, oh, somehow awfully ripe and ready for the plucking. The old familiar tightening, the military formation of the muscles--that clenched and drawn discomfort wasn't there at all! I began to pay attention to the game.

The whole of Brighton felt freezing—depressingly, chillingly cold. My father refused to have the only heater in the shop. "A hazard," he claimed. "Not merely safety, but in terms of stock, you understand. Heat dries out the tobacco and would melt all the chocolate and cause the boiled sweets to bleed and stick together—"

"Boiled sweets don't bleed," I objected.

"They sweat," he said quite firmly. "Oh yes! They decidedly do. They're meant to be kept at a certain temperature, in conditions just-so for confectionery—"

"In conditions unfit for humans! Have you seen the state of mam's chilblains? No wonder trade is falling off. It's like walking straight into a fridge. And what about those silly gloves you're wearing? With all the finger-tips chopped off! People don't want their sweets weighed out like that, with old bits of wool in with them—"

I'd left his huffy, high-hunched shoulders and gone up to my room. They'd left it all exactly as it was; it made me want to cry. What poverty. What paucity. What shabbiness. What shame? No, not exactly shame, but just a suddenly seeing it as it was. Instead of as I'd remembered. My mother had had my quilted counterpane cleaned. It danced a riotous honeysuckle haze before my eyes. Beyond it pinned at intervals on the wall were my reproduction Degas'. What the hell had they to do with my current leanings? How long in fact, had they been there—since my second year in grammar school when my keenness was starting to sharpen. And my talents beginning to show.

Reggie had said I had talents last night. So far untapped, so he claimed. I couldn't fault him on that point—all I'd done was lie there. But lie there liking it in fact. "Am I giving you pleasure?" he'd said. I'd nodded and shut my eyes, then opened them shining, to show or give a show of bliss. As I'd seen actresses do on screen. How different was my situation here in his bed compared to the one with Derek. Or Douglas, if it came to that. How easy, how unreal. He'd risen and carefully wiped his mouth with the nearest thing available. A corner of the tablecloth, no less, which still sat on the uncleared table. I hoped he'd send it to the laundry now—the act seemed to me unhygienic. It now occurred of course as well that he would be clearing the table and washing up no doubt, since there was no one else to do it. A *pied à terre*, but with plenty to do with the hands. I'd have to put down my own foot over that. I wouldn't be used as a skivvy. There wasn't any cause for worry. I lay, a princess, on my perch while he played pauper and serf.

Afterwards, he'd excused himself and undressed in the bathroom. So that was it, there only were three rooms and the tiny space of the hall. The kitchen lay behind my head, and I faced towards the bathroom. I hadn't seen him nude, not once. Would I ever be given the pleasure? He'd returned to me in his pyjamas and on, reflection, I suppose I was pleased. But it made him more grandfatherly. How old was he, I was dying to ask.

"You know how old I am, Princess?"

I swallowed the surging saliva. "I hadn't given it much thought."

"Well. I am . . ." He paused. "I am three score and ten—come tomorrow!"

I did my mental arithmetic, my mind going wild at the sum. Cream crackers and cottage cheese! Three score and ten—that was *seventy*! "Many happy returns for tomorrow. Oh dear, I shan't be in town. Shall I send you a telegram, Reggie?"

He knelt at the edge of the bed. "Oh my darling child, say that again—"

"Shall I send you a telegram—"

"Reggie, say Reggie again. It's like honey. It's nectar to me in your voice."

I wondered just exactly what he meant by that. Wasn't my accent too much like his mother-in-law's? Ernest's grannie, who was such a card? "Reggie," I said it once again. And gingerly touched him on the cheek. I liked the way it was between us both, me being his big baby, but at the same time me controlling things. Me giving the directives. How subtle and seemingly swift the change had been. How hard to try to register those first impressions at the party.

"Tell me, Princess"—he kissed my hand, and placed it under his arm. I felt him warm both on my palm and on the other side. My blood ran much more swiftly so it seemed than his, but he provided solid river banks. "Has my young son been pestering you of late? Don't be frightened to tell me the truth—that is in fact the way I found your number. I watched him dialling, you see."

"And remembered the combination, just like that? How clever. I couldn't do that—" Imagine it though. *Seventy*. My dad could be his son. He probably would have liked to have been, especially if it made him seventeen. But how many years did that make it between us? "What since the party, you mean? Has he rung me a lot since then? Yes, sometimes twice a day, I think. He imagines himself in love." What gross imbalance there lay between the two. How old was he then, Reggie, when Ernest was born? Seventy, or sixty-nine to be quite fair since we were still in today—that much minus seventeen. Which made it—fifty-two? Or possibly fifty-one if Ernest were almost eighteen, which wasn't bad. Not bad at all. "How old were you when you married?"

"It's unimportant, darling thing. There's only you and I."

"And Ernest—"

"Ah, Ernest. What will you do about Ernest? Do you think that you'll see him again?"

"The trouble is, he's much too young. Too young to interest me—"

"I'd like you to."

I stared.

"I'd like you to, Princess. But of course, you must make your own decisions."

There didn't seem much point in coming home to Brighton, not after the first few hours. The school, of course, was centrally heated. And so had been Reggie's place. Home seemed as bleak as the basement in terms of warmth to me. And my preoccupation was with Nelson House and the beautiful taps in the bathroom, and the fabulous fur of the bed. He'd gently peeled it back like a banana skin and slipped me underneath his sheets. And then he'd slithered in as well and passed me the small sleeping pill. He hadn't taken one himself. "I prefer to not sleep," he'd explained. "I like to read and think of many things. I want to lie and look at you, my new and precious love." It probably was as well to take the pill, that's what I thought later. I never could sleep with any light on in the room, not even a little candle. And certainly not with someone staring over at me each time they turned a page. But he'd done more than all those things; I could tell that he had by the morning. The table was completely cleared of last night's festivities, in fact was laid for breakfast. Just for me. Smoked salmon and an avocado pear. "What, for breakfast? Meat and veg—or rather fish and—?" I'd spoken out of sheer surprise at the oddness of the offering. In coming days, at later dates, I used to laugh at that, me thinking it was odd at all. I can't remember—and did he also offer me champagne before I went off to work? I hadn't had an avocado, not before. And didn't know how to eat it. And when I did, I hadn't liked it much. "An acquired taste, for a princess. Like caviar and champagne." He'd called the car, one on his account apparently. "What, I don't have to pay him at all?" I'd let it take me to the flat in order to pick up my case. And change, of course, into my teaching clothes. And I'd let it wait to take me to Westminster, then I'd caught the bus on to school. All worked out with calm and consummate ease! Was that what age was all about? Or was it merely money?

Fiona saw me off at the station at the end of the awful weekend. It hadn't been a success. "You're strange," she'd grumbled. "Not, I don't know, not you at all. Is it something to do with Ernest's father?"

But it wasn't only my abstracted air. It turned out she'd gone off with Piers, from the party at Ernest's place last week. I didn't mind. "Good gracious me, why should I? Do you like him then, Fiona?" It seemed she always had, or so she claimed. But it apparently was hopeless. He'd never found her physically attractive, which made it so much more frustrating—the fact of his fancying me. I didn't know quite what to say. They'd gone to a club and got drunk, to return to Ernest's party for me. "Where was he though then—when we left?"

"Well, he'd seen you dancing with Ernest, and that was the final straw. He was so cheesed off and pissed that he sloped off on his own."

I was sorry now I'd said about Reggie to her. "I shan't see him again, of course," I said quickly. The train was arriving to whisk me away back to London. "Reggie, I mean. Ernest's father." I didn't want her telling Piers. I bought her a platform ticket. It wasn't nice leaving like this, with men and boys and life's experience seeming to come between us. "By the way, changing subjects, how is Nathaniel?"

"I haven't heard. I haven't heard a bloody word! Isn't it just the limit. I've dropped a line though, giving him your number—" My heart did actually miss a beat. "Yes, I've got to be careful down here. You know, with mummy and daddy. And even with ringing him up. I can't do it on our home account, I know that they'd somehow trace it. You don't mind, do you, I've done that? I can keep you informed of my plans. He comes down to London now and then. And he does know all about you."

I crossed my legs when I sat down and stared out of the window. A stranger, a man, of course, had helped me place my case. High up above my head he stretched; I looked with languid interest. How long ago was it when I had travelled up obsessed with the contours of cocks? When now I was so much more occupied with my own. Not cock, of course, I smiled at the chill wintry evening. No, cunt. My cunt. My criss-cross layered route that still as yet had not received the benefit. But even so, was starting to chirp and warble on its own and might soon start to burst into song.

Pat was lying in bed with Roly Balls when I got back. In the old bed-settee in the kitchen. Drinking wine and looking remarkably happy. I hadn't asked her how all that was going. What she'd been up to with whom. Perhaps she'd managed to tame the Gay

Lothario. Or was this a mere one-off? I looked at him; we hadn't met before. He winked above her head. I chose to ignore the intended disloyalty. Poor old Patty. A bit like me, with Derek. Everyone had known, oh long before me, and even then I hadn't believed. She obviously did love him to distraction. "Hello! Have a glass of wine with us. How did the weekend go?"

"A bit of a flop in many ways. I don't really know why I went." I took my coat off and sat down. "What a wonderfully cosy scene." Pat wriggled up to Roly and put her arm around his shoulder. He didn't acknowledge that she was even there, not by a single glance or even a flutter of an eyelash. What a curiously cold fish for a doctor. I wouldn't care to see him with a scalpel in his hand. He must run riot through the nurses of Guy's Hospital. What contrast there was between him and my own current bedfellow. "Oh, by the way"—I spoke as casually as I could. "Any telephone calls for me?"

"Masses! We took the bloody phone off the hook to get a bit of peace to be quite honest."

"Oh dear. Is it off the hook now?" Reggie had said he'd ring about this time. And there was always the chance of Nathaniel. I'd been thinking of that, of what I'd do if ever he got on the phone. Did I wish to be disloyal to Fiona back in Brighton by trying for Nathaniel myself? It didn't seem so vital any more, but then I couldn't guarantee just how I'd feel with his voice, that voice, at the end of the line. "Any messages then? I mean to say, did you write down any names?" Pat was busy trying to kiss the back of Roly's neck. I watched him shrug her away. It didn't work, she hung on like a limpet. Oh dear!

The list was what I knew before I read it, but Reggie's name wasn't there. And nor was Nathaniel's. It was Michael, and Ernest, and Nicholas. And Piers. Oh Christ! I replaced the idle receiver. It started to ring right away. Reggie. My pulses jumped with pleasure. He was waiting, he whispered in my ear. No other words were necessary. I dressed as if now off to school, thinking ahead to the morning. My single bed looked bleak and lonely, as indeed did Pat's. Her bed-settee had been her best idea so far. They could stay snug in there till tomorrow.

But Roly apparently had other plans. When I went to the kitchen to say goodbye, he was up and already dressed. Pat lay looking woebegone and lost in the bed without him. I thought her perilously close to tears. "Which way are you going then?" he asked. "May I share a taxi with you?"

I looked at him uncertainly, keenly aware of an awkwardness. "Oh," I tried to keep the coldness from my voice. "I'm not sure I'm in your direction."

"Oh, which direction would you think was mine?"

"Well, I'm going down to the Embankment. Towards the Tate, that sort of way—"

"What luck! Exactly mine." His triumph. He'd trapped me neatly. I sweated underneath my clothes, knowing how Pat felt. I'd watched Derek once responding too readily to another girl. And she flagrantly flirting with him. The bond was such across the room between them both I felt quite sick, quite bilious with my jealousy. An ugly coarse emotion, which twisted all my features. I didn't look at her, at Pat lying there. We both knew what his game was surely! The unfairness was I didn't want him. Not want or like him in any way. Too young for a start now, for me!

I wondered fleetingly how they would react if they knew who it was I was going to. He probably couldn't conceive that I might actually prefer to sleep with a geriatric, instead of a stud such as him. The thought reminded me of Reggie's lips and what they'd coaxed from my clitty. I turned away towards the door, to leave them to say their goodbyes. "I've got to be going, it's getting late." To my further disgust he followed closely on my heels, without even a kiss blown to Pat.

"Roly—" The pain and disappointment wavered in her voice.

"'Bye, Patty," I said. "I'll see you." I went with the minimum drama, trying to keep everything light. Perhaps that's where she was going wrong, trying to pin down the bastard. I'd probably made the same mistake. How much nicer men were like Reggie. "That was rather brutal, Roly." We stood outside the street. He hailed a passing taxi which didn't bother to stop.

"Bastard!"

"Exactly what I thought myself."

"What?"

"You are," I said, "a bastard." He looked up towards the sky and laughed.

"You cheeky little thing!"

I dug my hands deep in my pockets and looked at him disapprovingly. "Nobody should treat people as you obviously do—and least of all people, Pat." He frowned. I looked away and up the road. "There's one," I said. "Let's run!"

He tried to hold my hand first. Then he tried to kiss me. I kicked him hard and pinched his neck until he gave a bellow. The taxi slowed, the driver turning round and opening the glass divider. "Beg pardon, guv?" The interruption cooled him and seemed to curb his ardour.

"You've got a nerve, a bloody nerve," I said. "As if, even if I'd fallen head over heels for you, I'd ever do that to Pat!"

"Do what?"

"Do this!" I waved my hand between the two of us. "Do just what you've been doing. Or trying to at any rate. All that!"

He rubbed his neck and frowned. "My Christ, you're a little bitch."

I didn't bother to answer. He probably thought Patty a bore. And would have thought me one too I expect, if I had thrown myself at his feet. A boy, that's what he was, a greedy boy. When what I was used to was men. "You can drop me here at the corner." I leaned forward to the driver and jumped out as soon as it stopped without turning round at all. Roly must have lowered the window when I left. I heard him shout. "I don't give up so easily, you know!" But by then I'd approached Nelson House.

It was exactly as it had been on my previous visit, no one in sight, not a soul. And the lift as sinister and silent as before. The only difference was that this time Reggie's door was shut. He opened it immediately, almost as if he'd been standing behind it waiting. I fell inside, or felt as if I fell, so pleased was I to be back. Back amongst all that luxury, surrounded by sumptuous surroundings, bathed in the warmth and the glow. My senses swooned. Much more in fact than on the first occasion, knowing, I supposed, what further pleasures lay in store. Reggie stood looking at me, then crumpled to the now familiar position—on his knees. I stroked his pale bald head, it was really like patting a pet. He buried his face in my skirt and shook, almost trembling with delight and joy. We were together again. My sweet lover. "I've missed you so much. So unbearably. I can't tell you, I can't begin to explain how long a single day can be without you here. My Princess. My love. You're my life—"

I stood reflected many times, an infinity of me's. Young and ripe. Desirable. He, melting at my feet. Yes, Princess wasn't bad, I supposed—a bloody sight better than Bitch!

A fiver, he'd pressed in my hand, next morning, for taking a taxi. I didn't ask what happened to the car account. I supposed it was out of discretion. This way no one could link me up with him; calling a cab in the street, I might have been anybody. It suited me much better. I made on it, in fact, by taking the bus and pocketing all of the fiver. It meant leaving a little earlier, though still ended up making me late.

"You honestly push your luck with your unpunctuality!" What a whine Winnie had when she wanted. I'd run up several flights of stairs and fought for the breath to reply. "Mrs. Pritchard apparently has noticed. You ought to go easy," she warned. "Thanks, Winnie. I will look out. Phew, those stairs really wind you, you know."

"I don't," she smoothed a hideous half a mile or so of serge over an elephantine haunch. "I've never run up in my life. Not here or anywhere. It's not good for the heart!" Not if you're wildly overweight, not if you've stuffed a pint pot in a peanut, no.

"It might be good for the figure. It could count as curve control, Winnie."

She grinned. I wished she wouldn't. "I am actually on a diet. A new one I started on Saturday. Bananas."

"What?"

"Bananas. Only that. The Banana Diet it's called."

"It would be, I suppose. Fairly obvious."

"Faintly embarrassing side-effects, like passing an awful lot of wind."

"Passing? Breaking surely, isn't it? Or would the end make a difference?"

"What end?"

"That's what I mean, which end? Nose or knicker?"

"Well, burping I suppose, more than anything."

"I'd give it up. I'd let it go. It doesn't sound much of a diet. Oh, by the way—what are you doing with all the skins? Aren't they meant to be good for the complexion? Rubbing them on. Or is it avocados? It's avocados I think. I had an avocado for breakfast this morning, you know." The need to confide overtook me. I wondered what Winnie would think. I knew she'd disapprove of the money. I felt that instinctively somehow. It struck me now that Pat probably would as well, they'd both misunderstand my motives. They'd think as Fiona certainly thought, that old men meant only money. I didn't expect a single one of them to understand that with Reggie it really was love.

I thought I'd spend the evening in with Pat, assuming that she would be in. She wasn't when I got back home. Had she been and gone already? I put the kettle on; by the time it had boiled she was back. Back from the shop opposite, the small delicatessen with the sexy assistant. Male. We'd talked of him already. I'd thought how bold she'd been to ask which lavatory cleaner he thought best. They'd entered into a long discussion about which brand reached furthest round the bend. "Harpic," she said he'd said. I knew it was Harpic anyway.

"You're shameless. Honestly you are. You'll be buying your Tampax there next."

"They don't sell them. I wouldn't mind. I've never minded asking men for sanitary towels in the chemists."

"Oh, if I see it's a man and not a woman assistant I walk to another shop." She thought me over-sensitive. And she was probably right.

All was not well; I could tell by her face. "Hello, Patty. How's things?"

"A bit depressing, you know."

I decided to play it light again. "No, what?"

"You saw." She turned a gloomy face towards me at the gas stove.

"What, Roly? Yes, that looked all right. You seemed quite pleased with our old bed-settee." I walked across and sat on it, holding my cup of tea. "I haven't had a chance to try it out myself—" A spring or some subversive lump of stuffing bulged somewhere beneath my bum. I eased myself away. "It's bumpy, Pat. Did that get in the way? Or is an uneven surface more exciting?"

She poured herself a cup of tea and sank down beside me, sighing tragically. "Don't joke. I'm just not in the mood." The telephone interrupted what I knew was going to be a deluge of her grief. I wouldn't have minded comforting her. I felt so happy, so magnanimous and all-embracing in my present mood I could have run the agony column of the world. 'Dear Sad and Lonely—Why not stick your finger up your nose, then bring it down and lick it. It gives a very nice and salty taste—you'll find that you'll soon be smiling—' She put her tea down carefully on the floor in an attempt at false decorum, then sent it flying with her foot as she rushed to answer the phone. I genuinely hoped it was for her.

And it was in a way—for us both. Nicholas and Jim were wondering what we were up to. They'd been asked to the Studio Club and recalled that we'd been there already. Would we like to join them for a spot to eat? "Hold on." Pat had passed the phone to me; I covered it with my hand. "What do you think, Patty?" She shrugged. "Well answer, missus. They're waiting to know!" She bent to examine her nails, her shoulders slumped in deep depression, unable to make a decision. Going out was preferable, I could see, to staying in with her waiting, cross-fingered, for Roly the Bastard, to ring. He wouldn't. And if he did I had a feeling he would ask for me! "Nick, just had a word with old Patty here—we both think we're dying to come." Pat walked out of the room. I watched her bony pelvis swing from left to right. A pre-pubescent body. But with a woman's head. Would Reggie, could Reggie ever envisage love with her? I smiled. I didn't think that Reggie could, would, had ever or should ever love anyone other than me. It was inconceivable. Out of the question. He was mine. Yes, of course. All for me. "Okay, Nick. Got it. See you in an hour."

How long ago was it that we'd taken this route before? "It's only two weeks, you know. Two weeks to the day in fact that we last went to the Studio Club. What do you think of that?" I nudged her. "Pat?"

"What do you think?" she said ignoring what I'd just said. We sat on the Piccadilly Line passing the Green Park platform. The carriage was almost empty, so that each of us were faced with our reflections. Her face appeared, pale and tragic. A shadow really of her former self. "What do you think?" she repeated. "Of Roly?"

I studied the map of London's Underground system, as if giving thought to her question. "Well, he's bloody attractive, I will say. And seems very addicted to you. Doesn't he?" That way I felt, that way of wording it would give her, and her pride a fair chance.

"I don't think he is, you see. That addicted, I mean. Do you?"

"Oh don't you, Pat?" I'd carefully batted back. The train was slowing into Piccadilly. Situation unresolved.

We somehow got there before them, but only by seconds. Nicholas and Jim followed us cheerfully down the stairs. It was nice. I'd forgotten the smell. And the music. And the feeling of everyone being so much and much the same. Someone had painted, since we'd been there last, the entire reception area a particularly piercing pink. Which served as a striking background to the current exhibition of lino prints and lithographs. A students' show. From Camberwell School of Art. Organised by one of the members who happened to teach in Graphics. Pat thought them very good. I found them rather puerile, but her show of interest heartened me even so. We examined them, each in turn, after we'd shed our coats. Nicholas fell naturally in with me, and Pat accompanied Jim. How easy and nice it was with them. Not one of us on the defensive. Not one of us wanting to push too much, merely to make an impression. Pat spoke well and we listened. I fervently prayed she'd catch Jim. The club had served her well before, and in this light he looked not unlike dear old Douglas. His shirt was pink, his bow tie was bright yellow. The combination pleased her.

Of course last time they'd met she'd had her periods, I remembered. And looked a bit peaky and grey. Tonight the fine tragedienne role she played gave a chic edge to her prettiness. Like chocolate—the pull of bitter black compared to milk. I hoped he'd note the difference. We had a drink and then sat down to dinner, after joining the friends who'd invited them. And after all of us being signed in. They were nice as well, the other two. An architect, bearded, black-haired who looked rather feminine and fey, with a waistline not unlike Pat's and a nervously high-pitched laugh. His wife was shaped from solider stuff, from commoner clay. The combination was attractive. He set her off. The squareness of her face, the boyishness of her hairstyle, the severity of her suit. She wore a white silk shirt and a scarf tied like a tie. I thought her quite impressive. A journalist, they said, who worked on a woman's magazine. Well more than a woman's magazine, in fact—something like *Ideal Home* or *House and Garden*, whichever was meant to be the better of the two. To do with design—which made us quite a visual set of people. She was talking about a Finnish chair she'd seen and Pat had claimed Italians designed much better. They disagreed and Jim joined in as well, quoting the level of environmental awareness in the Scandinavian countries.

My mind drifted back to Reggie. A nagging worry surfaced again—not really worrying, but just a doubt, a question mark so far. Why was it I was so involved? What was his curious hold? I'd told him that I wouldn't come tonight. I'd told him that I'd spend it back with Pat. He understood, had asked, had rather begged, that when I thought of retiring finally for the night, that I should ring him first. I would of course, when I got back. Whatever time, he'd said. He didn't sleep, so I could always get in touch, all night. Perhaps that's what it was I liked. The knowing that he was always there, without being too demanding. That wasn't my worry. I hadn't seen his cock.

A superb pianist was going to play tonight, a Welshman called Dill Jones. A legendary figure in the world of modern jazz. The architect, Johnny, and Joyce, his wife, were becoming increasingly excited. Nicholas asked me to dance in the pause between dinner and coffee. He danced well; I idly supposed that he did everything well, or moderately so. What a very nice husband he'd make. I would have dearly liked to find him more attractive. But I knew from the feel of his hand as we danced that his flesh wouldn't mix well with mine. It sweated. It sweated cold, not in a—Latin way. Not flowing somehow. It didn't feel like mine. He held me tremblingly, his other hand too high up behind my back. I liked to be held dancing much lower down, in the small of the back in fact, and closer too. So that the erogenous lower zones were pressed hard up against each other. That way you could tell how your partner felt. I think he had an erection. It swung now and then on my thigh, which meant it must be pointing down, instead of up. Like boys. Derek had claimed that after the age of twenty or so, you'd be hard put to find them right up. Erections, that is up against the stomach, pointing towards their nose. He'd shown me, offering to measure to exact angle and degree. Nick's was hanging at 40°. I wondered what Reggie's would be. 0°? A surge of love came with the thought. A tenderness. A tear. "What a hell of a girl you are!" Nick suddenly squeezed with his clammy paw. But my legs were aching, I felt a dragging in my back just where his hand should be. As well I felt a thudding high behind my eyes of distant approaching headache. My periods were on the way.

"Oh shit, my periods have started!" Pat sat in the next lav to me. We, of course, were the only ones there.

"Oh hold on," she shouted back. "They've got a machine. I'll chuck you one over. Just a mo." I sat there waiting, reflecting how well things were going. It was in this very same spot, of course, that we'd decided on strategy last time. I caught the oblong cardboard container and unfurled the comforting contents. Two safety pins fell on the floor, I picked them up and put them in my handbag for future use. A wonderful object, the safety pin. So neat, so nicely designed. So, above all, streamlined and efficient. Functional. Though old-fashioned. They'd be hard put, this team of young architects, to aspire to design such as that.

"They've asked us back," Pat said. "We'll go, won't we? What do you think?"

I thought. If I went too, of course, then at the end I'd leave. But if I didn't go, there was the possibility she'd stay. "I'd go if I was you, Pat. But perhaps I won't. I promised I'd talk to Reggie tonight at some point or other."

"Oh, come. I shall be disappointed not to go. He seems quite keen tonight. Jim."

"I know, isn't it nice the way it's working out? But I don't fancy Nick, you see, that's the trouble. It'll go best with just you and Jim." She wanted to be persuaded, I could see. In any case I was right.

"I'm terribly sorry, Nick! You do understand, don't you though? I'm up at dawn in the morning on a special project at school, to do with a thrice-life-sized mural featuring amphibians—monster lizards, newts, toads, frogs, crocodiles, alligators—"

"I say, how very impressive. I'd really love to see that when it's finished. What lucky kids to have you as their teacher!"

"I shall invite you to see it when it's finished. We can have a special viewing."

"I shall hold you to that, remember!"

Oh hell! I'd have to do it now. Would the District Inspector approve?

I went home by myself on the tube. I didn't mind. I made them see I didn't. Johnny and Joyce had a tiny car, an open one which just about held the five. I waved them away down Regent Street and walked back to Piccadilly. Men murmured, passing, all the way. My own fault at that time of night. And men murmured at the other end, along the Earls Court Road. I prayed that they wouldn't follow. It would have been the easiest thing in the world for someone to force their way through our front door. I slotted the key in quickly and thankfully sneaked inside. Alone. The light in the hall wasn't working, which meant groping my way in the dark, down the stairs to our own front door. A dangerous hazardous path. Anyone could have been waiting for me at the bottom. The thought sent my heart to my throat. But no one was there. The flat was empty and, as usual, as cold as the grave.

Reggie was waiting. I rang him. He understood. Oh, how he always understood! It felt like talking to a father—not my father, of course! "Time of the month," was what I'd actually said, with no hesitation at all. He hadn't answered right away. "Reggie?"

"Princess." The single word flowed over me, securing me in his devotion. We talked, just talked for nearly half an hour, or more.

"I must reimburse you, my darling, for the tedious telephone bill." The bill? I hadn't thought about the bill! What, tuppence or tuppence halfpenny? I laughed out loud. How sweet. How very considerate! He'd probably pass me two pounds for that! His syrupy voice continued. "I don't want you at any time to have to think twice about ringing me, about visiting me, about communicating with me in any way—merely through lack of money." I shut my eyes and leaned against the wall, cradling the mouthpiece in my palm. Oh dear, oh dear, how wonderful this was. The basement had grown beautiful. Quiet, but with a perfect kind of peace. My period pain subsided to a rather pleasant sort of ache. An ache which merely made me more aware of what my body was. A woman's!

Seven seconds or so, but certainly not more between me tenderly replacing the receiver and the instrument shrilling again. I knew that certainly, about the time, because I'd just checked my watch. Ten past one. In the morning of course. Who on earth would it be at this time? Reggie. "Hello," I said softly. "Is this a second goodnight?"

"HELLO!!" The voice came booming through the room. An ultra-charming bellow. I choked. I couldn't speak at all. "HELLO! HELLO!" It came again, belonging of course—to—Nathaniel! He told me exactly who I was and what a cunt to have kept him waiting! Four hours in fact! From nine till now, he'd been ringing me every half-hour. I swallowed at the end of the dreadful diatribe and said I was frightfully sorry. I'd been out. "You've been in, you little liar! And engaged there precisely twenty-seven minutes! What the hell could anyone have to say at this blinding time of night, that could take so bloody long?"

He was wanting of course to find out if Fiona was up. "She's not here. Not at all. She's at home. She only comes up occasionally—"

"Who?"

"Fiona!"

"What's Fiona to do with this?" His voice had altered in its tone. Still fierce. Still angry. But now with some fun in it. It offered me a lifebelt thread of courage. Ye Gods, but he was frightening! Would I ever feel at ease? "Eh? What's Fiona to do with this? I perfectly know the set-up, she's in Brighton with mummy and daddy. And you're in London here all on your own. I'm coming over. Now. All right? No need for a special welcome!"

He'd crashed the telephone down before I had a chance to answer. A dreadful panic rendered me incapable. For several whole minutes it was simply impossible for me to take a step—in any single direction. The beds were made. They didn't look too bad. The room was tidy too. Pat had cleaned the bath, I knew. And cleared any muck to the dustbin. But God Almighty! Entertaining film-stars! At what was now going on for two o'clock! What would there be for us to talk about? Would I offer him tea, or what?

I went to clean my teeth, and run an old comb through my hair. And whilst I was at it there at the sink, I wiped both the taps with some Vim. She wasn't very good at doing taps, Pat. Much better at sweeping floors, and dusting horizontal surfaces, and tidying up as she went. But shiny, tinselly things like taps, and silvery objects like kettles, she never bothered with at all. I could see myself in them by the end. I could never quite do that in Reggie's. The gold was not a good receiver of the features on my face. Hell! Why did I feel quite this guilty? Betraying two of them, that's what it was. Both Reggie and Fiona, as well. Not, I thought defiantly, that there'd been any choice in the matter, my end. She shouldn't, I pursued it savagely, she shouldn't have bloody well given him the number and obviously—the address—in the first place! Or, come to that, told about me. But my heart was lunging around like a bat. I'd had a bat fly once into my hair, round at the back of my neck. In the gloaming when it must have thought I was a thicket. My father had made it an occasion to bollock me for not making the best of myself. "A daily comb and a good cut and that wouldn't have happened, my girl. Had nature intended you to look like an overgrown bramble, you'd have berries growing out of your ears. And a lot of bird shit on your brow—" But the sensation still hadn't left me. Two terrified, entangled creatures. Each struggling to extricate, to free itself from the other. They'd had to cut it off, my hair, to free the frightened bat. The first time I'd ever had it short. Some people did that to each other. Derek, I supposed, more mute, but in a similar state of panic, with me.

My panic still had not subsided. Where, for instance, was he phoning from? Nathaniel! I sat down on the old settee and said his name again, this time out loud. "Nathaniel!" Old me and Nathaniel! Wheee, heee!" The errant spring twanged with my childish jump of joy. He'd said that he was stranded! How was he stranded, here in London? A man with money like that? Couldn't anyone book into a big hotel at any time of the night? They weren't full up, they couldn't be. Not this far away from Christmas. Perhaps you had to have a case with you, some formal trivia like that. To show you wouldn't run off, not paying the bill. Though I'd read quite recently about a Hollywood star who had admitted to precisely that trick. For her and her children, when they were hard-up, taking their cases and leaving them. After staying at wherever hotel it was for months on end without paying. Judy Garland, wasn't it? I'd thought it awfully clever at the time. He meant to stay here for the rest of the night. Christ Almighty? And I had my periods! I'd wear my nightie, I'd be all right. And I'd wear my knickers as well. Of course. Just as I usually did. He must know women had periods. What did those others do? I could warn him of course when he came through the door.

When he came through the door, I warned him. It just jumped out before I could stop. Right upstairs, with him on the doorstep! With his case on the pavement behind! I blurted it, knowing at last what blurting meant. A stiff tongue and a set of rubber teeth, and lips as cold as snow drifts. But the words still clear as a skylark's song. I sang it over Earls Court. He stepped back, obviously enchanted. I had enslaved him with the frankness of my message! Not one iota, no, so afterwards he claimed! Merely reinforced the rumours that he'd heard. From Piers, of course, who else? And Fiona? In some rare disloyalty. Well, perhaps not rare. I ruthlessly strove at some reality. No one could help it, sometimes. Not even me. "What did she say? No, exactly. Did she mean that I—?" But all that searching came much later on. And by then I didn't care.

His luggage was exquisite, it really was. It shone in the light like a chestnut. My father had yearned for shoes like that. They sold them at Russell & Bromley. Punched with tiny little holes to make a patterned surface, the stitching showing all around the uppers. Shoes fit for toffs and no one else, he felt they'd suit him a treat. I'd thought of buying him a pair in two weeks' time when I had my first salary. "It's the time of month. I'm terribly sorry. You can't come in, I don't think—"

"Fucking Jesus, you've flooded the basement! What's it look like—the biblical ocean? A replica of the Red Sea?" I stared at him helplessly and stood aside as he swept into the passage, slamming the heavy front door behind him, with no consideration at all. The lights, of course, weren't working and with the street one now blotted out, we stood in total darkness. "A hell hole!" he thundered. "Pray God!'

I was petrified by the noise of him and overwhelmed by his presence. He was wearing, I saw before he'd shut the door, a massive coat like a cape. Or a cloak such as highwaymen might sport, and a deerstalker hat on his head. He was very tall. What, six feet two? Taller in fact than Reggie? He seemed to be much bigger in every way. His arms I felt, his thighs, his neck I imagined resembled hefty branches of a well-built tree. An oak. And Reggie a conifer, his hairless head a smooth and shining cone. Nathaniel was hairy; I couldn't as yet see his scalp but his beard covered most of his face. No sooner had it ended on his cheeks, it seemed his eyebrows had already begun. But in between this furry continent the salient features shone. Even in that shadowed light I'd recognised—I'd recognised—my master?

Cain and Abel. I put my mind to other things like that, to these comparisons, as I led him down, to me the now familiar stairs. He would have fallen had I not. And I was going first. The Education Authority of London's County Council had not been known to give employment to a caterpillar. A crushed though needy teacher. "She doesn't look, oh I don't know, quite normal—would you say? Hardly a figure of authority. The face appears quite, dare one say it, flattened! With a curious impression of coconut matting—" He tripped quite heavily as it happened on luckily the last step but one, but I'd managed to neatly step aside. The light shone out of our basement door and from it I witnessed his flight. The chestnut case fell crookedly to the floor as he went hellbent, in an effort at some balance, towards the basement dustbins. I didn't say a word. But the incident slightly unhinged him, I could tell. He'd made himself look a little ridiculous, and it surprised me that he'd mind so much. It somehow seemed out of keeping. A curious inkling of his vanity arose in me and that gave me a feeling of confidence. Well, not of *confidence* exactly. I still felt wormlike, cowering and what was worse, cruelly, cowardly young! I think now, looking back, that he intended that. It was part of the camouflage, a necessary strategy, the playing-out of roles. And I accepted mine then right away. Quite blindly in my ignorance.

He came inside, and put his case down in the kitchen, then ambled down our passage. I followed at a distance, studying the cut of his clothes. What would my father have considered him? An out-and-out bounder, or not? His clothes were unconventional, completely the reverse of Reggie's. He looked, what—Prosperous Bohemia cross-bred with Country Gent? With a spotted cotton hankie round his throat *à la* the Working Man. The working man on a building site, or a playwright's idea of a costermonger. He was of course a Theatrical Person, and was playing well, all sorts of roles. He turned and for the first time smiled. I honestly thought I might faint. There was such power and charm and geniality there. There was such underlying SEX! A huge and cuddly polar bear, with the cunning and guile of a wolf. "Tell me, child," he boomed. "How many bunny rabbits live in this hole? Are there others as well as yourself?"

Even in my half-dead, dopey, head in the clouds confusion, a warning sizzled inside. I didn't want him wanting anyone else but me! I couldn't risk even Pat. The sensation wasn't pleasant, and why at this especial stage? When nothing yet had happened even—excepting, of course, he was here. And I had dreamed and longed for just that much to happen. For me to be in touching distance. He advanced. He came towards me. I started to shake, I couldn't help it. I hadn't spoken more than half a dozen words as yet. Would he find me incurably stupid? A deaf mute like, who was it played the part? That actress in *Johnny Belinda*. Big eyes and not much botty on her? She copped it in the stables. I could, it seemed quite on the cards, be likewise in the kitchen!

I made him let me wear my nightie and my knickers. He laughed and said he didn't mind as long as I did everything I was told! I thought of Fiona as I opened out the old settee, whilst worrying would it support him, support us both. He brought out a bottle of brandy, which saved me having to make tea.

It wasn't a very romantic light, not even a shade on the bulb. I stood on a chair and tried to tie an old red petticoat of mine around it, one I now used as a paint rag. "Is it Christmas? Some fiendish festivity? Or a feeble attempt at a Maypole?"

"I'm trying to tone the lighting down a bit—" I floundered from my chair. My arms were aching holding them up high. The bulb had swung and hit me on the head. I felt a fool, as he well meant me to.

"Why not switch if off? A simple procedure. Watch." And he'd plunged us both into darkness, barely relieved by the furthest light in the hall. It worked fine, once my eyes had grown accustomed to the gloom. His was a shape you couldn't miss. Especially when he was naked. He'd thrown his clothes haphazardly to the floor. Reggie always hung his up carefully. We obviously, Nathaniel and I, had more in common, basically. His bare flesh glowed, he lowered it groaning on to the bed. The springs screamed out in protest. I apologised for them.

"We bought it secondhand, the bed-settee. It's not very comfy. I'm sorry—"

But he pulled me down beside him. "Brandy?" he said.

"Oh, thanks!" It burned its way into my chest, a fierce and fiery trail. I burped immediately, but managed to keep it back, swallowing hard instead. My stomach gurgled in return. I crossed my fingers in the dark. Praying he couldn't hear. He heaved around to settle himself more comfortably. "That's better—now child, let's chat."

He wanted it all, the ins and outs, from the start of my whole life story. With full details of sexual encounters. "And then? And then? Go on! Go on!" I didn't say about Reggie. Had I ever been in bed with Fiona? That was one of his very first questions.

"Yes, this one. The one we're in right now. But having breakfast, that's all." But saying it had brought it back—the wantonness that I'd witnessed. The delicate fur that she'd disturbed so frantically with her fingers. I couldn't say that to him though. No! Or how she'd offered her nipples. That texture though was unforgettable. I ran my thumbs over my finger-tips, lightly. Just as I'd done on her. "I've touched her though—" I'd said it to him suddenly. The words had just slipped out.

"You've touched, Fiona? Where and how?"

"Like this!" And I touched his nipples. I hadn't done it ever, not before, touched a man on his titties. It surprised me in fact how similar they were to mine. His hardened up right away. I stopped.

He offered me another drink. "You're a virgin then, I gather?"

"Am I?"

"We'll have to wait and see—unless you'll allow me now." I didn't want him saying that. He could tell he'd gone too far. "Come here, you silly little child. We've got plenty of times ahead. . . ."

Did he mean to see me then again? Given the chance. Without Fiona. We'd drunk, or rather, he had swigged, about half of the bottle of brandy before getting down to business, as he chose to call it. "I challenge you!" Is what he said? "Here! Have my set of tools!" And he'd drawn himself higher in the bed and arranged me much lower beneath him and between the boulders of his knees. They lay on either side like rocky Scottish moors. I knelt, a nervous animal, between the two, but comforted by his overwhelming kindness. He'd clearly see to my condition. Could obviously find a nice solution to it all. I had to wait just for the right circumstances, but till then of course, I'd try to do as I was told. And endeavour to raise an erection.

I thought of Fiona, what she'd said—how thankless a task hers had been. But that was not my own approach. Was it something to do with my teaching? Dedicated to the life, the one of total self-sacrifice. How opposite to my Sweet Princess role with Reggie. Though perfectly possible for me to encompass both. Each end of the scale, I thought. Adaptable. That's me.

He left at some ungodly hour, long before Pat came back. She found me sleeping in the kitchen. "Hey, who's been here? Have you been entertaining?"

I tossed up whether to tell her, and decided I'd better not. "No, actually I haven't. I'm only sleeping here because it's warmer. . . ." I could see that she didn't believe me, but if I told her the truth, I knew she wouldn't be able to keep it to herself. And certainly not from Fiona.

Her night, she said, had been heaven! Roly could spin his own balls! That was good at any rate. We breakfasted together, both sitting on the bed. "I'm seeing him again tonight, yes, I'm coming to the class."

"What, Bernard Bolt's?"

"Is that all right? Do you think he'll have me in it?"

"Is Jim joining as well then?"

"We thought we would together."

"That'll be nice. We'll all go to the pub after."

The tube was packed, even more than usual, due to a fault on the line. I hung upon a strap in front of a line of seated men. No one offered a seat. They never did, I'd come to expect that they wouldn't. They stared at me and at my outstretched shape, but I ignored them all. Lost in my thoughts of the night. There was a poster on the platform at South Kensington, with a blown-up drawing of Nathaniel, publicising a film of his now currently on release. I could go and see that tomorrow. And nudge my next-door neighbour. "See him! That star! We've slept together! Oh yes, in my back kitchen. On a very old bed-settee. Two pounds ten or thereabouts. A bargain. Secondhand."

Fiona was right, he was bloody hard work. The brandy perhaps caused paralysis. It wouldn't have made much odds that I had my periods or not, I somehow felt. But even so he'd taken me through it step by step. "That's it, start there, just at the tip. Christ Almighty! Let go! Not like that!" My grip was like a navvy's, so he claimed. A navvy's fist holding a hammer! But when I tried the other way it was more like a dropped stitch in knitting. "No! Much too loose!" He wasn't circumcised, unlike Derek, and I had a job with the slack. I could have said to him, "Look here, this loose material is getting in the way! Can't you think of having a tuck in it?" He made me do it with both hands, one holding down the yardage at the base and the other tip tickling at the top. It was incredibly tiring, the only place to rest my wrist was on his crinkly bollocks. "Ouch!"

"Oh, I'm sorry!" I said. "Am I wrinkling them?"

"You girls," he thundered at one point, "make appalling mistresses! Both you and Fiona—what's the matter? How can you be so ham-fisted?" I didn't answer. The comparison seemed so unfair. She was short-sighted after all, with a preference for gang bangs. She'd failed her exams where I had passed. And passed with flying colours. I bent my head and miserably applied myself to his prick. I tried to think of it as something else. A completely different object like, well, like uncooked pastry, plasticine, a piece of pottery clay. It didn't work, of course, since they were so much stiffer. Until I felt like hitting it into shape. "Right," he said. "Well go on then, suck on it!"

One of the seated passengers got out at St. James's Park. I sank down gratefully, although it was only one stop. I could have bitten through it at one point. And swallowed it like an oyster. Making medical history? Would he have died from the fright? Or from critical loss of blood. "This chappie here has had his thingie bitten off! Poor bastard! See, here are the teethmarks. Clean through, resulting in seizure. Write 'Coronary' on the death certificate—rather more circumspect!'

He'd risen, however, at an amazing speed, once he'd decided to rise. And had shot his load without me even knowing much about it. I had to take his word that it had happened. Straight down my throat, so he claimed. I sucked my tongue, trying to detect a different taste. Custard cream? Sour milk? Something cheesier. I felt like shouting hip hooray, had he not shouted for me. A bawling yodelling, fit to wake the dead and empty all the cemeteries.

"Oh, shush," I begged. "You must be quieter"—once I'd emptied my mouth. The satiated sliver slid out of my lips like a leaking of lukewarm water. "You'll get me thrown out of this flat, like that. We're not meant to entertain men."

He'd put a large and hairy hand underneath each of my armpits and pulled me up towards his face and kissed me hard on the lips. It was the first time, in fact, that he'd kissed me, despite all our different intimacies. I kissed him back, liking it very much. I would have much preferred to start from there instead of to finish like this. In fact, I now felt quite aroused myself, ready for fun and games. But he was tired and wanted to go to sleep. He snored as loudly as he laughed. I got up to shut the door and bumped my knee against the bed trying to get back into it. "What in hell are you up to, woman?" He'd woken up immediately. "For Christ's sake, it's like Paddington Station. Get in, and go to sleep!" But when I did, he wrapped his bear-like arms around me, and cradled me like a baby. "You're adorable, little one," he whispered. "And I love you to distraction." Just that, and the way he said it, made me stay awake all night.

Bernard Bolt wasn't there right away, so we started the class without him. I volunteered to pose the model, since nobody else seemed professional. "Standing? Or sitting? Which would you like?" We ended with having her lying, curled round on the dais, in a faintly foetal position. One of the older of the old ladies claimed it to be too difficult, so I helped her to start in Bernard's absence. And from there went to help various others. Pat was late as well. Perhaps she had changed her mind. It was a shame because both Nicholas and Jim, as well, were there. And so was the Polish industrialist. I smiled at him. He courteously clipped his heels and formally bent at the waist. How Continental. He introduced himself—William, pronounced Vilhelm—and asked my advice on his canvas. I ran a practised eye along its surface. Oh, no doubt, yes, the best money could buy. "You ought to really work on cheaper stuff than this—it's a waste, paying this at your stage." I looked at him straightforwardly. He began to blush. With anger? But I continued. "I'll tell you why. It's because the results are misleading. This very good canvas is going to make your amateur efforts look better, which in turn—"

"Sweet madam"—his voice was icy cold—"this advice is quite

beside the point. Not at all that which I wish to hear. Better that you should—"

"Oh, excuse me," I interrupted him as brutally as he'd interrupted me. It took him by surprise. Bloody nerve. Who the hell did he think he was? In any case, Bernard had come. I gave a devastating smile and confidently walked away.

Nathaniel had asked to see my work. When he'd woken up. "Show it to me. Now," he'd demanded as he was dressing.

"Oh no, another time—"

But he wouldn't take no. He'd insisted. "You're good," he said. "You're bloody good in fact! How much for this drawing here?" He'd chosen the nude I'd done the week before in this very room with Bernard. The question had caught me quite off guard. I wasn't yet used to selling! Twenty-five pounds! He'd rolled it up and taken it under his arm! Twenty-five pounds! The same as Fiona! But honestly made—not like hers!

Bernard was slightly drunk, I could smell it on his breath. Brandy. It brought back Nathaniel. "You're late Bernard, where have you been? Propped up in the pub?"

"Celebrating," he slurred. "A splendid commission. A portrait. Means flying to Mozambique!"

"Mozambique! My God, sounds mad!"

"Five hundred quid, no less!"

He bought us a round in the pub and we cheerfully drank his good health. "I tell you what, I was thinking, you know—that I'll need someone to stand in for me on this evening job. I'll be off in a couple of weeks. It may as well go to you as anyone else. Would you like it, eh! Yes or no?"

"Who, me?"

"Why not? You know the ropes. It's a simple enough task. In any case you'd probably make a better job of it than me. My heart's no longer in it."

I bought the following round as a celebration of my own. A lecturer no less! My dad would be thrilled to bits.

Pat had missed most of the class—an unexpected staff meeting. I would have found it difficult to guide her drawing constructively. "Shocking, isn't it! I've never been keen on nudes. But never mind. It's the occasion that really counts." She and Jim sat hand in hand like a pair of well-blessed lovers. He stroked her hair and kissed her fingers, and held her drink up to her lips. Like a mother and child. He took care of her. She blossomed with the attention. Poor Roly Balls, not that he'd probably care.

I looked around me happily. Bernard was quarrelling loudly over the merits of Henry Moore. Nick stood at my elbow, eager to catch my every word. A friendly group with everything in common. But my mind was elsewhere. Drifting between Nathaniel and, yes, Reggie. Two days since I'd last seen him. Forty-eight hours without playing Princess. I'd telephone when I got home.

The line was engaged, which surprised me. Pat had brought Jim home with her. They sat entwined together in the kitchen. I felt very much in the way. I could go to Reggie, of course. With my nightie. And my knickers and sanitary towels. I thought of the beautiful golden bath and the silky fur on the bed. Pat, I supposed, would be dossing down on the bed-settee. Why suffer in solitary gloom? I picked up a pair of shoes which I'd carelessly left by the window. One of them was sprouting mould. A certain sign of damp. I coughed. A cold? The second time I tried the telephone was clear. "It's me," I said.

"My darling."

"I phoned you a minute ago—"

"I was talking to Ernest as it happens."

"How is he?"

"Enquiring of you."

"Of me? How would he know that you've seen me?" I was shocked.

"It would appear Princess, that someone's been indiscreet. . . ."

Fiona. It was Fiona of course. Who must have told Piers. Who in turn must have got on to Ernest. How paltry. How inbred and petty-minded.

"Shall I come over?"

"Oh, Princess," he bubbled with pleasure.

"So long!" I shouted in at Pat, but received no answering sign. I banged the door behind me in the passage, to emphasise my departure. Several taxis, empty, cruised along the street. It was good, this stretch of London, for getting taxis so quickly. Now that I was taking to the habit. I still had Nathaniel's twenty-five-pound cheque in my handbag. Sitting in the back of the cab I took it out for the thrill of seeing the famous signature. How tempted I'd been to show Pat. What a thrill! What a boast it could be. To Fiona above all, of course. But impossible. Frustrating that, having to hug this glorious secret to myself. Perhaps Winnie would have to be my confidante and friend. A deserted Dolphin Square, and eerily empty Nelson House, as usual. When did other people go in and out? Were they all night-livers like Reggie? Did sly seductions and Bacchanalian rompings take place behind each of those doors?

Reggie was wearing a pair of clean pyjamas when he opened the door. Nicely ironed and smelling of starch, of all things. From being packed next to shirts I supposed. They didn't put starch in pyjamas. Especially not pure silk. He fussed and flurried around me, taking my coat and making sure of my seat. "Have you eaten? Some champagne?" I surrendered to the luxury. And assumed my royal mantle. He wanted to know exactly what I'd been doing, down to the last minute, since we'd last been together. I thought about it. "Well," I might have said. "I've had a mouthful of famous dick for a start! And a splash of rare spunk up my tonsils. And a fistful of scrotum to boot—"

"I've done nothing of any importance at all—except, oh yes, I've got a new job."

He listened carefully to the details of Bernard Bolt and his offer. "I'm not sure you should take it. It's not the job for my Princess."

I stared at him. "Why not? I think it's marvellous. I'm flattered as a matter of fact."

"I'd rather you spent that time with me. I could pay you at twice the rate."

"Pay me? What, pay me like a prostitute?" I watched him flinch. "Don't be so coarse, please, Reggie!" He sank to his knees at my feet. I studied him rather disdainfully. "Get up!" I said it coldly, with contempt, for various complicated reasons that I didn't fully understand myself. He squirmed, but made no effort to get up. I prodded him with one foot. "Get up! Or I'll probably kick you."

"Kick me," he said. "I deserve it."

Winnie and I went out to lunch. Out to the pub up the road. We both felt outrageously naughty. "No reason not to, of course, Winnie."

She'd taken some persuading. "What if the children should see us? What if the girls smell our breath?"

"What, beer? A lager? Don't be daft. What difference would it make? Come on, let's both be devils. Live a little while we can."

Once inside with a hot shepherd's pie, I showed her Nathaniel's cheque. She couldn't believe her eyes when I pointed out his name. "No! Really! Honestly? I say. Imagine that—you and him." I couldn't have had a more impressed reaction if I'd written the script myself.

"It is exciting, isn't it?"

"When will you see him again?"

"Oh," I hedged. "When he gets back I expect." I hadn't bargained for that one. Would he ring me ever again? I didn't like to think that far ahead. "He'll be gone for a month, so he said—"

"Will he write?"

"What, to me? I shouldn't think so. These things are not so cut and dried as that, Winnie." Her questions irritated. She seemed to be missing the point.

"Let me look at the cheque again," she said. "Oh, I say, yes. It is awfully exciting?" Better.

I sighed. "I suppose I ought to put it in. Into the bank I mean. But I don't like to let it go. You know what I mean—"

She nodded. "I do, indeed."

Should I tell her all about Reggie? There seemed no reason now why not. She'd hardly spill the beans to anyone important. Her mother or possibly one of her sisters or even to one of her brothers. "I'm working with this rather charming colleague, who sleeps with this sweet geriatric. And when his gummy mouth's not on her muff, she jerks off this famous old film-star! Oh yes, we talk about it freely in the staff-room!" She shivered when I went into the details. "What's wrong? Are you cold?"

"Just excited!"

I looked at her with interest. "What, aroused?"

A daft expression settled on her face. "A little," she said demurely.

"You've got shepherd's pie on your chin. Can you wipe it? It's getting on my nerves." I wondered what a man might do with Winnie. Of course she felt, she had her feelings, just like us. Like Pat and Fiona, and me. But it hadn't occurred to me till now. "Have you never done it, ever?"

"Oh yes!"

"What, you have? Or you haven't?"

"Oh, I have. With an Indian waiter from the Old Bombay up the road. Under the counter—"

"What, just like that? You amaze me, Winnie. Where was your mother?" I was deeply impressed by the danger. "What if she'd discovered you?"

"It was all over before she'd even pulled the chain. He was fearfully quick. And clean. He wiped himself with tissue when he'd finished—"

"What did he do with the tissue though? Did he eat it to destroy the evidence? What a fascination with detail you do have, Winnie." She smiled, she seemed to be enjoying it. Well, I was enjoying it too. It never failed to surprise, Life, when you scratched beneath the surface.

"That wasn't the only time, of course. I've done it as well with an African—"

"You're very ethnic in your choice of partners—"

"Ooboogu."

"Beg pardon?"

"Ooboogu. Yes, that was his name. A fellow student, but a family man, with something like six children—"

"Quite a tribe."

"Exactly. I didn't want to become entangled."

"It's a chequered career then, Winnie. Not quite inexperienced, I'd say."

She drained her glass. "I'd like some more."

I rose. "My round."

"No. Sex."

I couldn't stop thinking about it or her or that, throughout the rest of the day. A shame. A waste. What could I do to help? No one I knew seemed to fit the bill. "You should join my painting class," I said, when I saw her in the staff-room.

"I don't paint though, or draw, or do anything like that. You have to be able to do it."

"No you don't. Don't be daft. They're all amateurs. No one can tell the difference, honestly. Only me. You won't be going in under false pretences. And it's nice. You meet people. Lots of men."

"On which night? Oh, a Tuesday. I can't come. My night for helping mummy in the shop—"

"Bugger mummy. And sod the shop. It's you we're worrying about."

Nathaniel arrived back much earlier than the month. Two weeks to be exact. The weather conditions had been unfavourable for filming. I knew of his arrival before he'd phoned me in fact. Fiona had been pleased to inform me that he was staying the night with her parents. With her of course, as well. With plenty of chance of a spot of slap-and-tickle and how's-your-father on the back stairs, or locked up in roomy closets. I stiffened when she told me and tried silently to control the irrational reaction. "That'll be nice," I said. "When's he coming then?"

"Tomorrow."

I could have said to her to please give him my love, that I couldn't wait to see him. I could have tipped the wink, passed on a piece of practical advice on the extraction of his seed. You'll find, I could have said, that if you wrap your tongue round your teeth, it lessens the hazard with stray pubic hairs. I'd gone through agonies of prickling discomfort once with Derek, when one of his hairs attached itself to the roof of my mouth, then slipped to the back of my throat. Nothing would budge it, not even ice-cream.

"Tomorrow tea-time. He's taking us out to dinner. East Street I expect. The oyster bar, English's."

"Oh yes," I said bleakly. "I know."

"My favourite. What do you think I should wear?"

"Let me think now—" A cabbage? An empty old bottle? A cushion, two ounces of marge? "I like your pink, I think." That makes you look very plain.

"Perfect. How clever you are. And sweet. I wonder how much he'll give me. I shall have to box clever of course."

"Of course. I expect you'll manage it somehow." When I put down the phone I felt sick.

It was quite unreasonable, of course, and I hadn't given him that much thought to tell the honest truth. Life with Reggie seemed so cocooned and comfortable. A regular routine, a fine adjustment of power and comfort and professional satisfaction.

The District Inspector had been to see me. He'd called in quite unexpectedly, in the middle of the afternoon. The room was in an uproar of intense creative activity, each single pupil deeply absorbed in what they were doing. Perfect conditions. Impressive. I hadn't seen him enter, one of the girls had told me. "Miss—" she'd nudged me, pointing shyly. "A man—" He'd smiled and nodded. I'd risen from the floor. We'd embarked on a complicated process involving wire and *papier mâché* formed and moulded into magnificent flying birds. I'd planned to hang these three-dimensional lightweight sculptures from the ceiling. A few were already finished and swung gaudily above our heads. We shook hands. "You seem busy. I approve," he said, "of your efforts. Explain them to me. What it is you're doing—" I launched into the complications of the craft. "Whose idea? Oh, your own? Mm, well done!"

Mrs. Pritchard had come up in the middle of things and smilingly looked on with a mixture of pride and suspicion. "I don't pretend to understand the ins and outs of any of this—" she waved an arm encompassing the scene. "But then, I'm just an old traditionalist, I suppose. Schooled in the art of perspective." The District Inspector smiled politely. I didn't say a thing. We waited, he and I, for her to go.

"Show me some other projects."

"Will you excuse us, Mrs. Pritchard?" She took the hint and went. I walked the District Inspector into my tiny stock-room and began to show him some work. His eyes, though interested in what he saw, rested on me with a warm amused detachment. Could I have had him? Probably. If I'd wanted to, but I didn't.

"I'm organising an exhibition called Art in Schools—"

"A straightforward, self-explanatory title—"

He laughed. "Quite explicit. In keeping with the confines of County Hall. In any event, I plan to stage it around Christmas time. I would like your participation."

"Oh, that would be nice." I spoke enthusiastically. "How would I be involved?"

"Well, these are early days of course. Nothing as yet past paper stage. However, I see you as having a section to yourself—"

"My own stand?" I'm very good at getting stands. You should see me working the Earls Court route. A real old pro at it now. And would you wish to use me as an exhibit too? Sitting bare-bosomed up on a dais with my drawers around my ankles?

"Yes, your own stand. And for several afternoons at least, a practical demonstration." Voyeurism! Within the limits of the L.C.C. Clerks queueing up for a gander. Secretaries staring, shy and sly. A riproaring misuse of the Rates. Could there be questions in the House?

I smiled. "Oh, I'd like that a lot."

Before he'd left, I'd told him about the life-sized mural.

"Featuring fearful amphibians? Yes, interesting. The curious colourings. Raw Umber right through to the Cadmiums. But would it be finished in time? I'd like to use it very much."

"I could start on it almost immediately. It will mean, of course, working after school. The caretaker is not too keen on that, I know. I've had trouble already with the Art Club."

"I'll see to it, I promise. We can't have exciting educational enthusiasm on a level such as yours hampered in any way by petty-minded bureaucracy!'

"Exactly, I agree!" We shook each other warmly by the hand, assuming conventional formality. And then he went.

"He fancied you, miss, didn't he?"

"Don't be cheeky. Get on with your work." That was the way to maintain discipline. Erecting a barrier between you.

I'd put Nathaniel's cheque eventually into my bank; it boosted my first salary no end. "What do I do with this, please? How do I pay it in?" I'd asked the woman in the Midland Bank, and I'd passed her the cheque to see. Her eyes widened at the signature, and she shot me a suspicious frown. "I'm a painter," I explained unnecessarily. "He bought one of my works."

"Oh, very nice too," she smiled, relieved. Yes, I had nothing on at the time. Not a stitch. I could have caught my death, of course, but he'd demanded a special showing. Rather early in the day. I never knew the light of dawn to be so northerly and cold. I'd choose a studio facing south, if ever I had the choice. "You need a paying-in slip, there's one on the counter, there." She showed me helpfully, as comfy and warm as an old tea cosy. Unmarried, I saw by her finger. Had never been even engaged, not even the faintest tinge of white on the fine, even pink of her hand. Women had to watch that little give-away sign if they ever took off their rings, pretending for various reasons, like new jobs or illicit relationships. Camp Coffee worked as well as anything else. A nice, neat strip of it rubbed in with some cotton wool.

"Have you seen his latest film? He's playing a randy Archbishop." She glowed. The bank was empty but for us. "Is he really as naughty to meet? I'd love an autograph—if you could get me one. I could show off to all my girlfriends—"

I drew myself up magnanimously and exuded, as one in the know. "I don't see why not. You must give me your name and I'll ask him."

" 'To Daphne—with love'?—that would do." When I left she was still simpering.

I thought about her, walking back along the Walworth Road. How could she live contentedly without the company of men? I passed the Men's Outfitters and stopped to study three chopped-off torsos wearing varieties of underpants. A baggy aertex pair. Some neat Y-fronts. And one patterned like Bermuda shorts. Two young housepainters, wearing spattered overalls, streaks of vivid emulsion, large patches of shiny gloss, stopped and nudged each other. "What's your preference, love, then, eh?"

"Something substantial," I answered pleasantly. And walked

on, my shoulders well back. Dignity incarnate. The awful thing, of course, it wasn't true. What I liked best was Reggie. Without a cock at all, or so it seemed. He worried sometimes over that, that I might feel dissatisfied and drift away. He didn't understand.

And nor did Pat. I hadn't brought myself to spill the beans. She was in love with Jim now, so she swore. And he, thank God, was head over heels for her. They spent each single evening now together, and this weekend, she was taking him home to meet her mum.

"Will you get married?" I'd asked. It seemed to have happened so quickly.

"We've talked of it. Do you know what—his dad's a Master Builder."

"No! Really? You possibly could amalgamate. I mean, your families, in business."

"It's nice."

"It's nice, I quite agree. You must have lots in common. Backgrounds matter a lot. Being similar, I mean."

Perhaps that's why Winnie and I seemed to have so much in common. Both brought up behind shop counters. Charged by the thrill of the till. My father had rung up. "Oh hello, dad!" I was on my way out to Reggie's. "This is late, for you to be ringing—"

"Business is bad. We're still open. I'm waiting for pubs to start emptying. Should do a spot with Extra Strongs. Last night someone pissed up the window. Really far gone, he was. And puked all over the pavement. I had to wake your mother up to swish it down with water."

"Oh dear." I shut my eyes and smelt my wrists. Reggie had bought me some perfume.

"What's wrong?"

"What's wrong?"

"I heard you sniff—"

"Oh, did you? Only smelling my scent, that was all." A silence fell. I heard the tick of Pat's clock. Not much in use these days. She spent most of her nights now at Jim's. "You don't mind, do you? It's just that much more comfortable than the old bed-settee in the kitchen—"

"Not at all." I could have said I didn't spend much time there, here, I meant, now any longer myself. Nowhere could compare with Reggie's place for comfort after all.

"How's mam then, dad?"

"Oh, much the same. How are you, my girl, eh?" We'd reached a standstill. He was sorry that he'd phoned. "Coming down? At any time?"

"Oh yes, of course. I'll let you know."

"You do that then—"

"Okay, dad. I will."

Poor sod. The miserable old bugger. I should go down and buy him his shoes. Or send him the money to buy them himself. Which way would he appreciate most? I thought of him when I got to Reggie's. Just as I thought of Nathaniel. He would have been deeply shocked, of course, had he known about either of them. He'd probably have been very pleased if I'd fallen in love like Pat. Though possibly not with an ordinary son of a working-class Master Builder. His delight in lineage would have been dealt a blow. So I really had nothing to report in the way of a Social Romance. No reason yet to get into Moss Bros. and dress up like a penguin.

"I spoke to my father tonight."

Reggie sat cradling my shoes. "Did you darling? What a lucky man—"

"Why lucky? He sounded quite sad."

"I meant, Princess, that any man who has the honour of conversing with you, is automatically placed in a highly favoured position."

"Don't be so silly, Reggie. You make yourself sound ridiculous!"

He bowed his head and kissed my feet. "It's you—"

"How is it me?" I kept a sharp edge in my voice. It was part of the game, as we played it.

"It's you. I feel so nervous in your presence—"

"Fill up my glass. And be quiet." I went back to reading my book.

It had occurred to me of course that in my present regime I might easily well miss Nathaniel. And so when Fiona had said he was passing through Sussex, I assumed that he'd then pass through London. And I arranged to stay in those few nights. The trouble with Reggie, of course, was that he never took me out. Since he barely went out himself. A trip to Lowndes Square seemed about his limit. "But what about films and things? And exhibitions and other people's dinners? And parties?" He had no interest any longer in any of these. I was now what he lived for. But he didn't make a fuss, not ever when I said I couldn't come. And the leash being loose proved much stronger.

Nathaniel rang early in the morning, before I'd left for school. The day after he'd been down at Fiona's. "Where are you ringing from?" The morning seemed suffused with blinding light. I answered the phone in bare feet.

He spoke in a lowered voice, the sort of one he should have used that night here with me. "Oh, where am I ringing from? Fiona's." She'd have knifed us both had she known. "I didn't want to miss you, little one. I'll be in London later. So keep this evening free."

"What time?"

"I'll ring you. Better still, I'll call. I'll have my car by then. Just be there—"

"Yes, but Nathaniel—" He'd gone before I'd managed to ask would he make it early or late. And where we'd be going. And what should I wear. But I walked to the station on air. His poster was still up I saw, passing through St. James's. I looked around and smiled at the weariness around me. How grey they seemed. How grumpy. How ground-down and how grim. I stretched my neck. Young and straight and strong. And when I reached Westminster, I flung myself joyously from the train leaving six solid stands in my wake.

Winnie was thrilled when I told her. "Perhaps it's love. Perhaps he's fallen for you! Is he married by the way, you've never said?" Trust her.

"Separated, I believe. But honestly, you know, that's not important, Winnie!"

"I like to know though, where in fact I stand. I said as much to Ooboogu Alarmi from the start—"

"Alarmi? What a lovely name. And apt I suppose in the circumstances. But you and I are different kettles of fish, you see, Winnie."

"Yes. I see that." She sighed rather wistfully.

"I'm not that keen on getting set up for the future. I like to live it now. Whatever *it* is—"

I got home rather late, but it couldn't have made much difference. He'd never have rung before 6.30. Surely not, that wasn't evening. Pat was out; I ran the bath. Just as Roly Balls phoned. "Hello sweetheart," he said. "I was hoping that you'd answer. Where's Pat?"

"Pat? She's out. She usually is these days. A hectic social life!" That should do him in, I thought malevolently. But no.

"Oh good! Well that's great! How about it?"

"Go to hell!" When I got back the bath was full, up over the overflow. I heard it pouring down outside into the basement drain. One of the things that we'd been warned about. Oh blast bloody Roly Balls!

I was ready by half-past seven, dressed in my very best. The topless creation that I'd bought with Fiona. I poured perfume down each arm and picked up the phone to check TIM. Pat's clock was several minutes slow. I started curdling with excitement wondering just where we would go. The silence was unbearable. I went out to sit on the lavatory and wait there for my famous date.

"What the hell are you wearing, child? The torn half of a Christmas cracker? Probably cost you a fucking fortune! Some money-making manufacturer scrimping on his material—should be hung, drawn and quartered—like hairdressers! All of 'em!"

"You're late," I said and, "don't shout!"

I'd been waiting for almost four hours and was not in the mood for his rhetoric. The back of my dress was badly creased from sitting carelessly whilst falling asleep with my feet in the oven. He'd woken me with his finger pressed continuously on the front door bell. Now we stood there on the step together. He'd been drinking. He swayed and in steadying himself managed to land with the force of one elbow against the entire panel of bells. I could hear them pealing fiercely throughout the pitch black building.

"Oh God! Now look what you've gone and done!"

He righted himself and stood up artificially as if to brisk attention. Then just as suddenly de-stiffened and subsided again into self-indulgent chucklings. "C'mon—I'm here to take you out. Fetch your shawl, we're about to get going." And he turned with a swirl and got into his car.

By the time I'd run down to the basement for my coat and to turn off the lights, he'd started honking his horn loudly enough to invite the risk of arrest.

"Are you fit to drive?" I got in doubtfully. He turned to look at me with great difficulty; the small interior of the vehicle enclosed him like a glove. The street lamps slanted sideways in on us, emphasising his bulk and etching the bearded impressive splendour of his face. Larger than life—that's how he looked. I prickled with pride to be with him.

"Hello." He stroked my hair. "And how are you, little one, girlie, eh?" My bones dissolved to biscuit. He put a heavy hand upon my knee and slid up to the tip of the mountain. He patted, an affectionate gesture. "All clear? Up here? The painters gone?"

I nodded, a child, responsive, speechless. How feeble, how completely spineless. I gazed at him coyly, like a fan, instead of an equal companion. Shouldn't I actually demand an apology? For his lateness, his lack of politeness, some evidence of normal decency expected of normal people. But he wasn't normal, not like Patty's beaux. And the choice after all was mine, to be with him rather than them.

"Peckish? A little foody-ponks and a drop of some drinky-poo?" A degree in philosophy, Fiona had said, at a startlingly early age. A brilliant scholar who hadn't chosen to turn to acting till well past forty, or so. I wondered whether to lisp back in return, to affect Winnie Einstein's delivery. Best not. Best shut my mouth and keep my peace, especially on his delay. Any questioning or pedestrian demands from me might well be construed as nagging. Not a pastime for lovely young women of the world, out with well-known actors. I blinked and batted my lashes, and settled back in the venal embrace of his bucket seat and prepared to enjoy my evening. In twenty minutes' time it was tomorrow. But let that mundane fact merely take care of itself—who knew what the morning might bring?

It brought, apart from other things, a confrontation, *the* confrontation with Mrs. Pritchard over my lateness, of course. She'd caught me sneaking in through Senior Girls, red-handed, right in the act. Her upper lip drew coldly to her lower as she peeled back the cuff of her shirt to examine the watch on her wrist. "Over half an hour. This really is unforgivable! However, here is hardly the time or the place for lengthy recriminations. This situation, the repeated occurrence of your unpunctuality, must obviously now be resolved. I regard it very seriously. I take it your class has had to call its own register, collect its own dinner money, and in addition, conduct itself into Assembly? Quite! Be so good as to call into my office at the end of afternoon school. I trust that you won't be late for that—"

The skin of my forehead had been fitted by skilled craftsmen, more accustomed to working with drums. The crisp staccato of her delivery bounced like juggling balls against its brandied surface. I'd have to find a milder drink than that if I hoped to hold this job and Nathaniel. I ached in every orifice—each pore, each nail, both eyeballs, every hair, pulsated with deep felt pain. But I swam still, gloriously light-headed. Exuberant and buoyant. The dehydrated crew of one small craft amidst a sea of trouble. That thought, that little piece of poetry, spun through my mind as she spoke. It made me smile, a foolish act. She stepped aside to let me pass. "Oh, thank you, Mrs. Pritchard." I could have sworn she was testing my breath. But I had got there just one jump ahead and blasted her with Extra Strong before running confidently up the stairs to my room.

Winnie was horrified. "How awful! How can you possibly be so calm? I couldn't, I'd have a breakdown. I'm dreading she'll get me in there, on discipline, as it is. Some nights I hardly sleep—"

"Don't be daft. How can she get you 'on discipline', with the shortage of teachers today? Any more than me on my lateness, what! When I'm spending so much extra time here after school, to enhance the reputation of this place and do the honours for the

District Inspector! With any luck she'll take my class away—but that's what I've been working towards ever since I started. . . ."

Winnie heaved a deep and trembling breath. Her blouse shuddered with internal combustion. Her belt strained on its over-worked buckle. I changed the subject. "How's the calorie count?" And stopped listening till after she'd told me.

"What's your opinion?"

"Sorry. About?" She'd startled me with her question.

"Sideways. Do I seem slimmer?" She'd taken in a baffling amount of breath and posed in profile like a photograph of Mr. Universe. I took my time in answering, studying the sucked-in stomach, and the gigantic proportions of the distended ribcage. Her cheeks grew very red, her little eyes bulged larger with each second. I watched a set of veins start pulsing in one temple. She could quite well explode. In months to come, long after this room had been redecorated, we might still come across stray pieces. I say, would this be Winnie Einstein's lobe? It looks to me like the left. See here, it carries fragments of a small gold ring. A family gift for her twenty-first.

She'd come to the end. I'd out-tested her strength. "You wouldn't do well under water, Winnie. Sub-standard lungs, I should say. Is it smoking do you think?" She'd sat down quick, puffing and woofing like a stranded whale, eyeing me sadly but unreproachingly.

"You don't see a change then?" she said.

"I think you've lost. Around the middle? Am I right?" I could see no difference.

Fiona had been caught. I couldn't believe it. With a ball of wool and a fish slice, slap bang on the ground floor of Brighton's biggest department store. They were suing to set an example. Nathaniel had been there when it happened. "What, with her, in the shop you mean? Actually there, by her side?" I felt the pang of jealousy, seeing the two of them strolling together, drawing admiring glances of recognition from other passing customers—'Good Lord! You know who that is, don't you now—that actor—what's his name? We saw him in that thing the other day—you didn't like it much—'

"No, no! You silly girl. I was there when the cops rang up. Preparing to leave as it happened—out on my way up to you. Hence the unpardonable delay, of course, in case you hadn't noticed—"

"Over four hours, I expected you about seven. . . ."

He buried his boffly chin into the side of my neck leaving a clutch of fluffy rice grains rolling down to my cleavage. He waved a fork, a glistening prawn fell to the floor; a passing waiter scooped it up even before it landed. We'd finished the wine, the first of it. "More wine," Nathaniel thundered. It came.

"Will they put her in prison? Or what will they do? Fine her? A cautionary word?" I couldn't begin to hear the worst. Poor girl, but it served her right. It wasn't as if she hadn't been warned, by me as a friend, any rate. I couldn't help feeling what a piece of luck it was that I hadn't been with her too, with my shopping bag as the dumping ground. And my undoubtedly guilty countenance to give us both away.

"Let's drink to Fiona," he raised his glass. "To little Fionapoo, come on now—both of us together." He clinked my drink.

"Fionapoo," I echoed, hoping they couldn't hear me on the adjacent table.

We'd been approached on and off all through the meal, by acquaintances and strangers. He hadn't introduced me once. I'd sat there like the unemployed, waiting to be noticed, trying to look pleasant and pretty. But in the end I'd given up and merely carried on eating regardless. 'Hello, old fellow! Fancy, you! I'm your greatest admirer, you know!' The Fiona saga came in dribs and drabs. A bombshell delivered as shrapnel.

"Probation, no doubt! With a fine I expect—and lots of the worst publicity!"

"In the papers? Oh dear—"

"Daddy won't be pleased. Though in all truth"—Nathaniel laughed and tugged his beard—"it might do the old devil a spot of good—pricking the demon pomposity. Poor little Fiona. By the time I left she was in quite a state. They'd apparently found all manner of things in her room—remarkable objects, bearing no relation to anything at all—"

"I can imagine," I said, remembering. The terrible thing was, of course, the most frustrating aspect of it all was that ostensibly I didn't know of this development in Fiona's Brighton life. Nathaniel was on the inside, had happened to be there. Would Fiona ring and tell me? Or would I, like the rest of the world, have to read it in the local papers. 'Local girl caught Lifting. Daughter of Respected Resident. Found with a Fish Slice and Wool.'

"Your drawing has been much admired, you'll probably be pleased to hear!" Nathaniel beamed at me. "If Fiona had persevered at Art, she wouldn't be in this pickle now I expect."

"Do you think so? I don't agree. It wasn't a case of perseverance. She would never have been any good—"

"Bollocks!"

I plodded on bravely. "Well, they said at our art school—"

"All rubbish—"

"Can I finish? May I please make a point?" I turned to him primly.

"Not if you're going to talk twaddle. Don't quote me some art teacher's shit!"

I shut my mouth. He'd touched on something. I felt my guts draining away. Is that how Reggie felt when I spoke sharply then to him? Weakened and wonderfully—what? Dismissed and harshly disciplined, dying to get back in favour. To be held in a *louche* lap of love. I stared at my plate, moving my jaws mechanically, trying like mad to concentrate on something else—on Fiona's plight, on the chance of old Pat with a bun in the oven, on Winnie with big Ooboogu—anything to halt and freeze the ducts behind my eyes.

"Girlie?" The kindly concern is what did it. A huge tear ran right down my cheek and splashed into my *Crevettes Sautées à la Crème.* "I'm not certain," I'd said, "that that's what I want. I've never been that keen on shellfish." He'd ordered it anyway. "It's got brandy in, be a good child and eat it all up!"

"I'm sorry." I bent my head. "Don't look at me. I'm silly."

He pushed his plate away and carefully placed his glass at the furthest end of the table, and doing the same to mine as well, he turned and in full view of everyone, folded both arms around me.

Then he kissed me hard on the mouth. There wasn't anything I'd have refused him after that.

She'd rung me, Fiona, in the morning, just before I'd set off for school. Minutes after Nathaniel had left, in fact. I jumped guiltily and tried to sound natural. "How nice. How're things? This is early!"

She'd been crying. All night, so she claimed, and half of all yesterday too. I'd never be able to guess, not from the whole wide world what had happened! It was just too stupid, too ridiculous to believe! I wondered whether she'd mention the fish slice and the fateful ball of wool. I'd be able to ask her what colour. Pale fawn? Something frightful like that. Duck-egg blue? Sugar pink? Blackbird brown? "I've been pinched!" She used a tragic key.

"Have you? Whereabouts?"

"In the basement—"

"On your bum!"

"Well, lower ground floor to be exact. Pinched for pinching—"

"Oh, Good Lord! Oh Jesus God! How awful!" I gave it all I'd got.

"My parents are—"

"I can imagine!"

"They searched my room, well, mummy did. Behind my back as well. She found the whole caboodle, from months and months ago. I should have brought it all to you." To me? My God! Why take this out on me? I didn't need the stuff!

"You should have thrown it all away—"

"What made it worse was that they found all sorts of things of their own—ashtrays from daddy's office, and boxes of paper clips—apart from that lavatory paper from the Grand Hotel, with Grand Hotel printed along it—"

"You're crackers to ever take brand goods of any kind, Fiona love."

"And different things from mummy's friends. A fearful row about that—all the labels I'd cut out from their coats. A whole collection, from Hartnell to Harrods—"

"What in hell would you do with those?"

Her voice descended to the depths of misery. "Nothing. Except rummage through them. Now and then."

"Oh Fiona." She needed help surely. If only to sharpen her choice.

"Your father should have got you contact lenses. Those glasses have misted your vision."

"The dreadful thing is . . ." Now she'd started to sob. I felt numb with guilt for multifarious reasons. It was obvious I'd have to be late! A risk of a bollocking from Mrs. Pritchard. I'd have to plead crisis in my immediate circle. The fatal disgrace of a friend. Yes, a casual thief! Specialising in miscellaneous objects of all description. The Curse of the Magpie, it seems! "Yes, the dreadful thing is," she choked, "that if I'm put on probation, and even if I'm not, the question of me coming to live in London can be forgotten now!"

Our plans up the spout. The future kyboshed. No twosome tap-dancing the town. "Well. Never mind. That doesn't matter now. It's you we're to worry about. Will it be in the paper, do you think?"

"They seem to think so, yes."

"Well, take your glasses off when they come for the photo. Outside the Court, after the hearing, I mean. You never know what could come from that—film offers, anything." It presented her with other aspects after all. I detected a new and optimistic note by the time we said goodbye.

He was filming, Nathaniel, all day today, playing a roguish old anarchist. A role he felt well-suited to. "Complete and absolute crap, of course—the whole saga from start to finish!" And he'd thrown back his head and gulped his brandy in one go, then broken his wind in my face.

I thought about what he'd said. I was sure it was absolute crap. Come to think of it, I couldn't remember anything he'd done that wouldn't be included in that same category. Nothing at all, not a single film. And he'd never been on a stage. What a waste, when with his brains and mind and magisterial presence and even just his—gustiness—he could have been a great Shakespearean actor if he wished. Falstaff. Sound and Fury. Anyone.

"Why do you do it?"

"What d'ya say? Did you speak to me? Dare to address?" And he'd taken a bloom from the bunch on the table and plunged it down into my bosom. The water dripped from the wet stem straight through the thin material. Water could stain, I wasn't pleased.

"Yes, why do you waste time on crap?"

"CRAP! C–R–A–P!" He spelled it out in a roar, emphasising each letter with a blow on the table, his fist bunched up like a hammer.

The Head Waiter hurried forward, horrified. Behaviour such as this, criticisms of this kind could be catching. Other people I could see on surrounding tables were indeed already looking suspiciously at their loaded forks. "The food is not to Sir's liking?"

Nathaniel looked at him in astonishment. "'S"delicious!" And to my horror now broke into song. "'S"delicious, 's'delightful, 's'delovely!" The whole room lit up. "Who?" He turned to me.

"Who?" I repeated.

"Who." He spoke like a querulous child. I wished to God I knew who bloody who was. "Who?"

"Mmm?" How difficult the old could be.

"You give up then, girlie? You don't know who?"

"I don't." I said wearily. "No."

"Cole Porter."

"Oh yes, of course."

Yes, he was filming at Elstree. Or Shepperton. Some quite famous place in the country. He'd left me early to go and get changed. "Changed? Changed, but where? Here in London?" We'd spent a bad night on the creaking settee. He didn't mind as much as me, but that was because he easily occupied the majority of space. I'd existed along his left arm. A mishmash of muscle and bone constituted a pretty poor mattress, as Slumberland may have discovered. My father insisted on 'interior sprung' as opposed to everything else. No make, just that. He'd have point blank refused to even sit upon our bed-settee, let alone sleep for seven or eight hours. "The spine requires especial cossetting. No human in his right mind can hope to stretch out on something the consistency of a city street and then hope to hold himself like a man. On two feet I mean, instead of four. You get my meaning, girl." It hadn't occurred to me that Nathaniel possessed a *pied à terre*, but obviously he did, if clothes existed such that he could get changed.

I'd lain back watching him prepare to depart. Fiona had rung just after. "Why couldn't we have slept somewhere else then, rather than here Nathaniel?" I'd asked as disarmingly as I knew how.

He'd started coughing, a major event at that time of the morning. Thank God I'd thought to shut the window, sound rising the way it did. He hammed it up, slapping his chest and throwing the leonine head first left then right, then finally forward and back to hang on his shoulder-blades. I addressed his well-fleshed Adam's Apple. I didn't see as many of those these days, it struck me, as I used to. We children used to pick out people's Adam's Apple; the really protruding ones, and persecute their owners quite unmercifully. Perhaps now everyone had more to eat. That's probably what it was.

"This basement can't be good for chronic chest conditions, such as yours Nathaniel—"

He gave a curdling whoop of First Grade Phlegm and Cream of Catarrh, a joyous, juicy timbre. Then spat out in the sink. I turned away. Good God Almighty, spare me this! I prayed he'd run the tap. "Can't we," I wavered, "if we meet again (never take nothing for granted, girl) sleep in another place?"

He spoke, when he'd found his vocal chords again. They lay, it seemed, deep in his stomach. And until the upper sediment had been removed, no word could escape from his person. I waited. "Tonight then, girlie?"

"Yes."

"I'll ring."

"Okay, but—"

"No but, you bitch." His croak grew faint. "You'll hear me when you hear me." Not, I thought mutinously, if it means waiting another four hours.

So all was uncertain for this evening anyway. Winnie offered to wait for the outcome of The Confrontation. "Don't bother," I said. "No, bugger it. I can give you the news tomorrow." And I'd set my special group of after-school pupils on the technical task of suggesting scales, and fins and fronds and lumps and bumps, all characteristics common to amphibious creatures. First to be captured in charcoal. Whilst I went for audience myself.

I dismissed it from my mind as I shut the door behind me. My strategy had worked. There was nothing more to be said. Her coolness, Mrs. Pritchard's, flew far above my head. I'd educated my brain to vacate the premises of my body whenever it was being used as a punching bag in punishment. I whistled as I went back to my room, loudly, to make sure she heard.

I was the last to leave, as usual. The caretaker twirled his keys, his tea was getting cold. "Have I time to telephone?"

"Where?"

"To a friend."

"Not from here. No, most definitely not. It would be more than the worth of my job to allow staff to use Head's own telephone. I'm surprised, Miss, you should be suggesting—"

"Goodnight." My father would have said the same. Abiding by the rules. That's what they're for—to stick to, given as guidelines, girl. But I took a different view. It could be said, it could be claimed that rules were there to be broken. There to provide alternatives to imaginative persons.

Reggie lay heavily on my mind. I'd neglected him, I knew. The thought of him alone and old, cocooned in luxury, cut off but in a sense—incarcerated, brought me quite close to tears. Many things brought me to tears these days. Many men, I corrected myself. Reggie. Nathaniel. My father too, perhaps him most of all. Did Pat pitch herself to high emotional states like this, with Jim? Would her mother manage to steer the *sortie* this weekend into talk of mortgages and such? And if she did, would tearstorms start to manufacture themselves behind Pat's neatly mascaraed eyes? Even Fiona's tears were formed on a factual basis—her contretemps with existing laws, antediluvian some might say, relating to property at large. But mine . . .

I'd meant to ring Pat, in fact, in case Nathaniel had called whilst I'd been here at school fostering teenage talent. Had she blown through the basement, as she was sometimes prone to do around this time of day, early evening? There was a phone booth by the bus stop on the Walworth Road. I went to enter it, but was slapped back by the acrid fumes of adolescent urine and some foul stench, like breath, which blew out from the very phone itself. I decided to wait. It was just as well, a bus, my bus, was rounding the bend. With luck I'd be back home, surely by seven at the latest.

She'd left a note. Two telephone calls. Piers. Reggie. And more. The more said "Am in the corner pub with Nathaniel, join us." I'd thought she'd signed her name in red. Purely illusion, of course. But both my eyeballs flooded blood, my body had come straight to the boil! How dare she! He! Both of them! Be in the corner pub! Without me, on their own together. Fiona I might have understood, she'd met him first after all, but—! Why couldn't he just have sat outside in his car? Or in here on the bed-settee? Waiting for me. Alone. I ground my teeth and kept my tongue well back for fear of biting it in desperation over their disloyalty. Like a mad dog. A mad dog on heat, I could have said!

It took me seconds to dump my things and deodorise my armpits. I sprayed like a slut, straight on to ten hours' sweat—the accumulation of a stressful day. I didn't care. I looked a fright. Hell hath no fury, neither doth it give the time to doeth the face and hair. I was out of the flat and in the pub in under five minutes flat. I started chattering right away, my teeth, my double molars, from tension, as I saw his arm draped round her slender shoulders.

She was looking beautifully demure, the cunning bitch, down at her Rosebud fingernails, High Gloss to match her mouth. She'd drawn an especially feline chin on today, a clever trick of shading using Leichner's Theatrical Range. Strange that her draughtsmanship was so concise in cosmetic areas and so extremely sub-standard otherwise. She'd even managed a realistic dimple, *à la* Ava Gardner in one cheek. I had to admit she looked ravishing. Her hair had grown even in this last month and hung like Tallulah Bankhead's. Not an idol of our day, of course, but one had to acknowledge the mane. I searched for some discrepancy—the one faint hope, the flatness of her chest. But even here the outlook seemed improved. She must have cottoned on to Fiona's trick and taken up Sorbo rubber. They had them now, the newest thing from the U.S.A. 'Totally Natural to the Touch!' I felt certain that Nathaniel had been feeling. They welcomed me with genuine pleasure, which heightened my own sense of chagrin. How could all be as innocent as it appeared? I hadn't told her about Roly. I'd put on a face re his overtures. Nathaniel waved me to sit down beside him and slipped that spare arm easily around me, just as his other—on her. Pat smiled happily, I played the ventriloquist's dummy and managed a stiffened version of the same.

"Been here long?" I cleared my throat. A dozen frogs of fearful tension were strangling my epiglottis. They squatted, oozing bile along my major arteries. Like traffic lights, all green.

"Since opening time!"

"You haven't!" The blood rushed from my toes and knuckles straight to the tips of my ears. I could feel them humming near my cheeks, hanging bright and alive, with a seeming life of their own, no part of me. Like the kidneys of a newly-slaughtered sheep. My nose went like that sometimes—the sign of acute indigestion. Inherited from my father, so he claimed. "Our circulation, girl—not quite like other people's. A sensitivity of the large intestine linked up with our mucus membrane. Stress. At all costs avoid it if you can. Especially with food and drink in the offing."

They were in the offing now, imminently so. A packet of crisps in one hand and a gin and tonic in the other. Pat had had three of them already, so she said now, standing up.

"Sit down," Nathaniel growled. And grabbed her skirt playfully. Pain skidded along my skin. He liked her. Hell!

But she tossed her locks, though looking at him still through Subtle Mink flirtatious lids and Fabulash perimeters. "Got to go—"

"Her boyfriend's waiting—Jim—an architect—awfully good-looking—" I explained over-quick, unnecessarily. Nathaniel was winking. Up at her, not sideways towards me. I bent, pretending to rummage in my bag, my Adam's Apple the size of a Grannie Smith. Had it been a Bramley, they could have made a pie, big enough to feed the whole of Dr. Barnardo's.

"She's gorgeous, simply divine! That little flat mate of yours!" Nathaniel turned to me enthusiastically, having followed the last of Pat's clocked seams right the way through the door. She might have been a bone, the first that Fido had seen after a fortnight on bread and water.

"Divine," I agreed dejectedly. The evening, tomorrow, this year and next. The whole of the rest of my life was being lightly crucified by his comments. This must have been how Fiona felt, imagining Nathaniel with me. That didn't help though, not at all. That wholly extraneous knowledge.

"What's up? Hey, girlie. Look at me!"

The Spirit of Dunkirk! A sense of humour then at least. After all, there was always Reggie. What shade exactly would my father choose—for those long-looked-forward-to shoes? I'd go, goddammit, down this very weekend and buy them in Russell & Bromley. "A bit of a change of scene then, dad, from Dolcis or the Co-op Men's Footwear!" "The working man wears his dignity in his soul, my girl, not on his s-o-l-e!"

"Nothing's up Nathaniel, that gin and tonic can't see to. Another, I think if you're ordering."

"Better! That's very much better! For a moment there I felt an unpleasant wind from the wearisome little green goddess. We don't allow that totally destructive lady in our presence—" He pinched my chin (that, lacking the lush Leichner touch). "There's enough to go round for everyone." I knew that. Yes of course I did, with somebody like Nathaniel. But I wanted to be the special few, which in my book included—well, allowed for—just me and at most his mother.

* * *

"Yes, look at me before I made the break and learn from my example. . . ."

". . . Bugger the bacon slicer—you know what he said was the matter?" A shrill and piercing scream sliced through the thronging playground. I looked at Winnie. "Oh, don't get alarmed. Doris Wellington going too far. Shall I sort it? You just get everyone in line, it's time to go in in a minute. I'll see you later on." I caught her arm and pretending to plead, to make her feel more important, lowered my voice. "You'll quite like the intimate details. Ring up mummy and say you'll be late. One evening doesn't matter here or there with bacon, that's the beauty—it doesn't go off." I hadn't convinced, I could see. I would have to be more provocative, raise a much riper carrot. "Vaginismus!"

She looked startled. "What?"

"That's what Nathaniel said I had!"

"He didn't! Whatever does it mean?"

I turned to walk away. "Tell you later." I spoke mysteriously over my raised right shoulder pad. "After school. Tonight. Eh, okay?" Now I was confident that she'd come. I felt the need to tell someone.

"You're not odd, there's a name for it girlie—Vaginismus. The medical title. The vagina goes into a spasm—"

"It's doing it now Nathaniel," I wailed. "Could you force it open, do you think? With your fountain pen—or finger, even?"

"Christ! Would you ask a fucking dancer to put his foot into a vice? I need my fingers, every one. They're part of my stock in trade—" And to illustrate his point he picked up a cigar and put it theatrically to his mouth, his fingers raised, the little one crooked, the way Fiona said you weren't supposed to drink tea. He tickled the tip of my clitoris. "Snap dragon," he chuckled. "Quite apt!"

I warmed to him at least for that, to speak so figuratively using a flower. He might have said a mousetrap. Or a set of rusty dentures. But being more mature, he understood.

"It hasn't always gone like that—I think it's the parts that bring panic, Nathaniel."

He raised his head and placed the cigar on the bedside table. Veneered in the manner of walnut. Walnut Whirls with a nut inside. One of our biggest sellers. When I had still been eating sweets I could polish six off in one sitting. Decapitating them like Gulliver would a Lilliputian snowpeak. I liked it here, Cadogan Court. Pleasantries with the Hall Porter. "Good evening, Sir, and Madam too of course. A certain chilliness I fear." I'd walked to the lift with dignity, as if I was Nathaniel's daughter. I might have been, the way we'd entered, laughing, relaxed, unself-conscious.

When had the demon needles begun to knit? How had the sealing wax come? He'd plunged his hand inside my skirt, the minute we'd got in the lift, popping the waistband button. Grazing the skin of my stomach with a badly clipped nail. We'd had a tussle around Floor 3, approaching his own, which was 5.

"Hold on, what if someone's waiting for this lift! I don't want to get out undressed!" But nothing it seemed would detract him. "All right then, I'll undo your flies! What about your shy chump chop shocking Cadogan Court?"

When the lift finally arrived we'd embarked on the friendliest of fights. "Get on, you fucking whore!" he thundered, "and leave a man's prick with its privacy."

"The same applies to pussies—"

"I shall piss on it—here in the corridor—"

"No, Nathaniel, now you're going too far!"

But he had, in the fire bucket. Straight into the sand, seeming to go on forever. With me in agony and shame, cross-fingered that no one should come.

The décor was thirties style. Early Fred Astaire. If Nathaniel had been Fred and I'd have been Ginger, we'd have danced to the bed together. We didn't. Not at all. Oh no. Nathaniel liked it on the floor.

He knew the Elephant and Castle well, that's why he drove me to school. And in any case he claimed it to be actually on his way to Shepperton. In fact there was the faintest possibility that he'd be passing on his way back. Would I care for a lift? Should he pick me up?

"No, don't. Please," I'd begged. "It's not worth it. I'll be back in the flat at some point." Was he saying he wanted to see me? Three nights in a row? Surely not! My bruised and bleeding ego had needed time to mend. At least an hour from that first gin with Pat, until at last I'd got my feelings under control. He hadn't mentioned her again. Perhaps that's how he was, a man like Nathaniel. The attention wandering, like an insect caught by colours. A bee, a butterfly hooked on scent and sight, but returning to base. Base being me.

The sexual side of things at Cadogan Court had frankly been a fiasco, just as the night before in those terms, had been non-existent.

"Yes, Brewer's Droop, you see, Winnie. And a state of semi-consciousness, brought on by the drink as well. So all he did on the bed-settee was have a bloody good sleep. They must have heard him snoring as far as South Ken. I had to sleep on his arm—"

"Yes, but last night—all this vagiswhatsits stuff—I want to hear about that!"

I pulled my coat on, purple cloth—"Christ, child! What's this made from—cellulose? You need a fur, some skin in weather such as this—we'll have to see about it." That's what he'd said this morning.

Winnie and I were in the staff-room—preparing to go and have tea. "I've spoken to mummy—she was awfully put out. I had to lie, tell her we had a staff meeting!" Winnie looked woebegone and worried. "I hope she won't check with Pritchard."

"She won't check. You're not a child. Good Lord, what mischief might you find from Elephant and Castle through to Stepney?" I pinched her arm comfortingly. "Blimey, you're surely let off the leash long enough to have a cup of tea." She shrugged unhappily. I studied her. "You know what, old Winnie, old girl—we should go, you and I, up West one day. And buy ourselves some new clothes. Our money's come in now after all." A frown was forming, hovering above her eyes. With drastic tactics, I could divert it before it landed. "Now that you're losing this weight I mean—everything's hanging off you!"

"Oh well! Now that you come to mention it, I could drop a size I should think. . . ." She beamed, we were in there all alone, and she lifted her arms in the air, sashaying round the room. In seconds she'd start snapping her fingers and yodelling a Spanish *olé*.

"*Olé!* Ah cha cha cha!"

"That's wrong," I said sourly, before I could stop. What right, after all, had one human being to dampen the high spirits of another?

"Cha cha cha! *O mia cara!*"

I buttoned my coat and gave up.

Lyons, Westminster, was where I said we should have tea. Welsh Rarebit, Winnie had decided she was having, and had already launched into a lengthy description of her preferred consistency of melted cheese, before we'd left the staff-room. She followed, I went first, out through the senior playground, so it was me who saw the Aston Martin first. I stopped. But she continued, banging her hefty bust into the back of me and snagging my stocking with her well-worn attaché. "Oh shit!" I said. Nathaniel broke into a deep bout of chuckling.

"Charming! The welcome one receives, this side of the River Thames!" He got out of the car, doffing his Deerstalker towards us.

"My stocking," I explained. "Not you. How sweet—Nathaniel, this is Winnie." The street, the school and all around was mercifully empty. He must have waited ages, or else just chanced his luck. "How did you know I was still here? The girls and all the other teachers have been gone for hours."

He gave an uncannily accurate approximation of the caretaker's normal expression. Winnie and I burst out laughing. "I asked, no, I enquired of the old retainer."

I glanced at Winnie. She'd turned an extraordinary raspberry red, with two shining buttons as eyes—somewhere in that mass of mute adoring flesh. Her mouth flicked up each side like a satiated beast, almost as if she slavered at the sight of Nathaniel standing so near.

He noticed, and now turned to her, always the professional charmer. His voice took on a deeper tone. "Ah, Winnie! What a pleasure this is!" I stood well back, in case she fell. She'd ruined one stocking already. He took her hand. She wriggled and simpered, not speaking. They didn't move, it seemed to me for what must have been several seconds but appeared to be more like hours. The whole scene was so incongruous in the particular setting. Winnie, like someone's maiden aunt, though so young and so fresh and unlined. And Nathaniel, the bluff old buccaneer, dressed as it were from a film set. A swift presentiment of unpleasantness, as light as a falling leaf, touched me, then departed.

The spell had ended, Nathaniel opened the door and we all three of us squeezed into his car together.

He'd see her home, that's what he'd said, right at the end of the evening. And he'd dropped me first at Earls Court, back at the flat, in order to call back later. "I'd rather sleep at Cadogan Court, if we're spending the night together." I'd made that clear.

"Don't fucking fuss!" He'd waved an impatient arm.

"But I'd like to go back to the flat at some point to change my clothes, that's all Nathaniel—"

"Sure, sure, child, shush! Christ!"

Winnie's eyes were larger than they'd ever been in living memory. He'd driven us straight to Chelsea, to a pub behind the embankment. I'd suffered pangs at the sight of the river. A few stretches further on Reggie lay waiting whilst I played the Gay Deceiver. Or would have done, given the chance. When we'd got into the car Winnie, for some asinine reason, had chosen to sit on my lap. I'd had to plead mercy at Millbank. And buckled right down on the kerb when we got out of the car to change over. "They've gone to sleep I think," I gasped. "My legs, I'm sorry Nathaniel—"

He'd roared from the wheel. "Where the fuck has she gone—back where she belongs—in the gutter!" The small car shook with his laughter. Winnie joined in from sheer nerves. She couldn't believe it still, I knew, that he actually was here in the flesh. She kept cavorting, tugging down her roll-on, tilting her mammary shelf, applying herself assiduously to his every word. She looked to me quite hideous. But apparently not to him. That's possibly what appalled me even more than the pain of Pat. Were all women equal in his eyes? Each there to be made available. Might my mother have stood a chance as well? And her blind old auntie Mavis?

"What will you have then, Winnie, m'lass? But first let me, or rather, allow me, to divest you of this, your outer layer!" He stood behind her in the warm interior of the low-lit pub and helped to remove her coat by undoing the buttons for her. The garment sprang apart with ease, but his hands remained where they were, firmly fixed on her solid front. She squirmed. They shook. And thudded through his fingers. He held on tighter than before. "I never thought to find such bountiful tits," he beamed. "Over a handful, each one!"

I thought I'd be sick all over the bar, vomit straight into my neighbour's vermouth. I say, barman, my drink has turned solid! The zest of a lemon, old chappie, not this—the whole of the bloody old grove! I headed for the Ladies. "Powder your nose? Winnie?" I threw back over one furious shoulder. She made no answer, none at all. Nathaniel had his head buried like a vampire in her neck. She stood, eyes shut, the angle of her face quite horizontal with the ceiling, its expression—bliss personified!

Two other pubs—before we came to rest, with Winnie sparkling like—like Andrews Liver Salts. It was the last time I'd help her on discipline or advise her on social improvement. Nathaniel flourished between the two of us, delegating favours quite equally. Our final watering hole—since all we'd done was drink—turned out to be a tiny but crowded theatrical club. At least I had plenty to look at.

Winnie continued to amaze. I began to see what might have beguiled Ooboogu and the wand that she'd waved on the witless Indian waiter. Music played. She stood, inviting Nathaniel to dance! I sat and watched savagely, my first time as a soured wallflower, as Winnie repeated the staff-room performance of wantonly shaking her jelly. A small crowd gathered to cheer. Of course they were all theatricals. She gave it all she'd got, encouraged by their attentions. I studied my drink. Dry white, he'd ordered for us all. A menu lay on the table—were we ever going to eat? I signalled a passing waiter and standing, shouted over to Nathaniel and Winnie on the floor.

Nathaniel was in the process, I couldn't believe it, of removing his jacket and shirt. People were cheering "Trousers down!" But Winnie was next in line. He lunged at her, his powerful body wet with sweat, and ripped her blouse wide open. Buttons popped all over the place. The blouse fell back, over her shoulders and slithered down her arms to the floor. She stood there like the proud prow of a ship, radiant and regal in her hefty, blancmange-pink brassière. The crowd went wild as a madcap pervert, bent on mischief, darted forward and undid it from behind. She dimpled, squirming "Dearie me! Oh don't! You naughty boy!" The lisp was becoming more pronounced with every word. Nathaniel beamed, his belly belching over the workman's belt which held his trousers up. "Whoa there, my beauty!" Winnie pranced in imitation of a horse. A thoroughbred but built on heavier shire lines. The last supports, cup D, strong cotton, were cast gaily to all four winds. She waved her Berlei like a flag. The people gasped. Her breasts were unbelievable.

I could have left, and might have done, from simple feline pique. I doubt they would have noticed. In fact, I'd even started searching in my bag to see how much I had in the way of money, and whether or not it would have run to taking a taxi over to Reggie's—

"Hello! It is you, isn't it?"

I looked up. Joyce, of Joyce and Johnny. Nick's friends from the Studio Club. She was wearing a pinstriped suit, with a collar and tie, as before. But her hair was even shorter. She looked like Peter Pan. "You look nice," I said. She shrugged, self-deprecatingly but with impressive confidence.

"What on earth are you doing here?" Her voice was intriguingly low. Perhaps that's what it was about her—an actressy kind of quality.

I pointed to the centre of the floor. "I'm with the cabaret—"

"What, Nathaniel?" She seemed surprised.

"I nodded. "Well I was . . ."

"He's a bastard like that," she laughed. "But never mind, come and have a drink with us."

Johnny wasn't there. "He's round with Gerry." Gerry? Oh Gerald, the young exquisite. Flat-mate of Nick and Jim. Joyce's 'us' was completely women. Each talking of auditions, past and present or taking place tomorrow. All actresses. "I used to go through all this shit," Joyce whispered to me. "Before I joined the world of journalism—it's soul-destroying stuff, as you can see."

I looked around; they didn't seem that much different to the faces in our staff-room, the lower staff-room at least. Or come to that, the countenances of my fellow travellers on the morning tube. More make-up, that was all. As Pat might look in fifteen years or so. But Joyce was different. I glanced discreetly, when I could, at the firm lines of her face. She caught me once, but paid no special attention that might have made me self-conscious. I felt like a shy first former with everyone's favourite prefect. "Oh, by the way, before I forget—we're having a party," she said. "Johnny and I were drawing up a list last night. We hope very much you can come. It's in our place, the new one, the house that we've just bought. To celebrate the move."

I'd heard all about the move already, and about the marvellous house. A simple terraced one, off Fulham Road, but ripped apart inside and redesigned by them both. Pat had claimed it 'unbelievable'. The height of modernity. Praise indeed from her.

Winnie now clothed again, dripping with sweat and delight, had been sent over to reclaim my company by Nathaniel. "I'll come," I promised Joyce. "In a fortnight? Yes, that'll be fine!" And I turned to Winnie. "I wonder you noticed I wasn't there!" As coldly as I could.

I'd had a bath and dressed again, waiting for Nathaniel to return. Forty-five minutes he claimed, it would take to drive Winnie back to Stepney. The time was now half-past two. I'd been waiting for over an hour. He'd invited us both back to Cadogan Court. "A threesome," he'd growled. "How about it?" Winnie had simpered, patently unsure of what to say. But I had point-blank refused. I knew who'd be worst off between the three of us. Me, as a fine sandwich filling, bordered by these loaves of bread. I had no wish to be enveloped, smothered, suffocated by Winnie's billowing breasts. Hadn't even Fiona's non-tips turned my stomach? Nathaniel was not pleased with me, or with my prim reaction. Winnie had grimaced sympathetically behind his back as if both she and I were still in league. But I couldn't forgive her disloyalty. How could anyone not see he was mine? They'd laughed as they were leaving. "See you later," I'd said to Nathaniel. He'd thrummed up the car as an answer.

Half-past three. Going on four o'clock. I thought of summer holidays I'd had. And how it felt to read I'd got Matric. "Well done, my girl! She's done splendid, hasn't she, mam? For that you shall have a watch!" His own. It hung too loose around my wrist, getting wet each time I did the washing-up, and banging against the bottles whenever I served in the shop, until it became a vicious bone of contention between us—and he'd taken it back, for some peace. I'd give a ring tomorrow, to tell them both I'd be down. Four-thirty! Was the phone not working? Had Nathaniel crashed his car? Not got through. He surely would have rung. I picked it up and dialled O. "Hello, could you test this line? I'm expecting a call and have reason to believe I'm possibly out of order." No chance at all. "Thank you, that's good. It's obviously working," I said with pretended relief. I looked at my shoes, still brown I saw—when would the bleeding show through? But I sat up, I didn't care; like Florence Nightingale I'd see the ordeal through till dawn. He was a bastard, yes I knew! A monstrous bloated bugger. Screwing the daylights out of dopey Winnie Einstein in the comfort of Cadogan Court. This very moment, at this precise second poised above her like a raunching, randy—. Five! Five exactly when it rang. To the tee. On the dot, smack on, with a shrill. My nerves were primed for shock, however. I'd rehearsed my reaction for hours. I picked it up.

"You fart-faced, unfaithful fucker!" I said. "If you think you can come for me now, you can stick that flaccid thing you call a prick right the way up your own arsehole!" And I put it back down with a bang. It rang again.

"The trouble is you see"—I was shouting now and spitting all over the receiver—"you're a sackful of shit in any case—no use in bed to man or beast—let alone to the female sex—but just because you're a jaundiced, old film-star hack whom no respectable repertory company, even, would employ, you think you can fucking pick and choose! Now sod off! You understand!"

Once more—the third time running! I picked it up, and this time simply listened, saying nothing. "Hello, love. Ted here. Ted Grunt, y'know, greengrocer. Sorry to have to keep ringing. There's been a bit of bad luck. I mean—" He paused. "Bad news, my love. There's been a fire, y'see. And. Well. Your mam and dad. I'm sorry to say. They're both dead."

Fiona paid for the tickets, the most expensive seats, so that we wouldn't have to queue. *Sabrina Fair* is what we were seeing. Humphrey Bogart and William Holden. But Audrey Hepburn was the real reason. Pat had said she was having her hair all cut off in the same style. Today in fact, in preparation for her wedding. "Mind you," Fiona said, following the usherette, "when you come in to all your money, I'll expect you to pay for everything, whenever we go out—"

"No change, you mean, in our relationship then, Fiona?"

She'd squeezed my arm affectionately and laughed. "No, but seriously, I do deem it an honour to be out with an heiress."

I could have wished she wouldn't talk like that. I might have said 'Christ, can't you shut your greedy mouth? My poor old parents are barely in their coffins—' But I chose to say nothing at all.

They were barely in their coffins. The firemen had claimed it a difficult task to salvage much in the way of remains. The blaze had taken hold and become sweepingly uncontrollable in what seemed seconds, so would-be rescuers reported. And I believed it to be true, knowing my father's insistence on sleeping with his stock. The bed itself was bordered on each side with cartons, cardboard and highly inflammable, of cigarettes and wrapped and packet confectionery. And being basement, their bedroom would have been first to go. Both police and insurance believed the cause of the fire to have been the paraffin heater and I would have agreed with that as well. The one was all we'd had, carried from room to room at my father's command. Always a hazard, I'd said so hundreds of times.

The film had started, Audrey's doe eyes swamped the screen. Fiona nudged. "Nice make-up, eh?"

"Yes. Pat's already doing it. Tickling the end of her eyes up. And wearing two lots of false lashes."

"Two lots?"

"Yes. Theatrical ones, one on top of the other to make them that much thicker. Didn't you notice them at the funeral?"

"No. I thought that was her mascara. It was running. Right down to her mouth. Not meaning to be bitchy."

"Oh," I said mechanically. "I thought it very kind of her to cry. And you. Well everybody really."

She squeezed my hand. "Out of sympathy. We're all upset when you are."

I stared across the sea of hats ahead. Was it only ten days since it happened? And not just that, but all the other things as well. I'd travelled in a state of shock, down from Victoria at dawn. And had travelled so, it seemed, from that time right up until the funeral, when they'd both been buried. A twin burial, exactly like a wedding. Riding tandem. Playing doubles. Not going it alone. I'd thought it best that, being my decision, to satisfy their wishes to the end. A Cemetery Affair in Consecrated Ground was my father's idea of a Do. With lots of mourners. Ted Grunt and half the Darts Team vying with all of the pub for the honour of being pall-bearers. Though whilst alive he'd spoken often of the Special Significance of Cremation. The purging by fire of the spirit. This way he'd had it both ways.

Fiona didn't like *Sabrina Fair*. We walked along the sea front afterwards towards her father's office. The Channel churned to our left, a gusty wind destroyed the curls we'd only just combed in the cloakroom. I'd been staying at Fiona's house since her father had so kindly taken all under control. I didn't think my father had a lawyer. A bank, but nothing more. They were, it seemed, the trustees of his entire estate. But Fiona's father was acting for me now. Six months or so, before the insurance would pay out the bulk, but until then it seemed that money was no problem. I couldn't quite, still, believe it. The implications were too wide and too significant to understand in one! I needn't, for instance, teach again. Not unless I wished to! I could pack up my job this minute, just like that! I didn't have to enter ever again that evil, dank, dark Earls Court basement if I wished! Rush-hour, buses, tubes, travelling anything but First could well be a thing of the past! My painting could take precedence now and if need be for ever—it didn't matter if they sold or not, no longer my means of support! Oh no, it certainly needed thinking about, there wasn't a short cut to that.

I would have liked to have advice, other than strictly professional. Nathaniel, for instance, his wordly anarchistic judgement. And Reggie. But both those avenues were closed. I'd decided that in these last days.

It was Piers who'd spilt the beans on Reggie. On Fiona's instigation. I'd told her of our deepening intimacy in a way to divert the talk away from Nathaniel. "What? That old lecher, Reggie? You can't mean it! No, never him!" And when Piers had arrived from his parents' home to pay polite respects to me on my sad bereavement, she'd urged him to vicious enlightenment. "Of course, duckie! Didn't you know! What, old Reggie? A lovely old pervert! Been practising masochism for many years! Has elevated it to the higher realms of art. Sordid in spots and has to take care—since a scandal—what—oh, six years ago? Drove a girlie to play it a little too hard—cut his cock off, some actually say! Why? Don't say he was trying to make you his Princess? Reggie's Princesses if gathered all together wouldn't fit in the Royal Enclosure—" I probably cried more readily over that than over my Sudden Losses.

No, she wasn't that keen on *Sabrina Fair*, Fiona. She'd found Miss Hepburn's choice of lover ridiculously unrealistic. "Who in their right mind, given the alternatives, would have Humphrey Bogart instead of William Holden? Answer me that now, who?"

The wind cut through my new black coat. "Who? Lauren Bacall for one."

"Oh well that, that's a different thing—she's his wife. I'm not talking about fact, only fiction."

We turned the corner. "How do you mean?"

She chose to take me literally and launched into a lengthy explanation. But I'd stopped listening long before it ended. I found I did a lot of that these days. What was it called—withdrawing into one's own brown study? Especially with Fiona. I barely admitted it to myself, but in honesty she bored me. Thank God we'd never shared a flat. I thought about Bernard's letter. Dear old Bernard Bolt, he was the one I'd turned to in the end. His reply had arrived this morning. Mozambique for Christmas! Well, why not? 'The colours here are fucking unbelievable! They'll blow your eyeballs out! You've come into a spot of dough, you say! So every cloud's got a silver lining—concentrate on your proper calling—get a bloody paint brush in that idle hand of yours. See how you like it at Christmas (80° in the shade!) And after then, well, who knows. . . .'

Fiona nudged me. "Hey!"

I turned to her. "Do you know what? I think I'm actually feeling so much better now, that I'll go back to London tomorrow."

Pat was in the flat with Jim, busy painting the kitchen. All white. They kissed me, both of them together and made me a cup of tea. "How's things?" I said.

A lot had happened since I'd seen them both here, or even since Pat and I had been together on our own. She was pregnant, which was why they planned to get married. "Not that we wouldn't otherwise," she'd whispered big-eyed at the funeral. Jim didn't look like someone with a shot gun at his head. "Mum knows. She doesn't mind a bit. She's mad about him anyway."

The all-white made the kitchen look much bigger, and much lighter too. Something had changed. They were putting the finishing touches. "It's different here, isn't it?" I looked around. Pat beamed and slid a smudgy hand round Jim. "Spotlights!" she said. "By Jim."

"They're great."

"But come and see the other room." She led the way towards the door.

"No, wait . . ." I couldn't think what else was different. "I know! The bed-settee! It's gone!"

They laughed and looked at each other. "He couldn't bear it," Pat explained. "He claimed it was highly unsanitary! Jam-packed with vermin and unmentionable secretions! We burnt it, out there in the basement—" She stopped abruptly, but I didn't mind. There were bound to be these cross-references.

"Secretions, you say? I'm sure!" I raised what I hoped was a quizzical brow. They both laughed in obvious relief.

"Oh yes. The thing we meant to ask you too"—Pat paused

obviously shy—"do you mind awfully if we put you in the kitchen on your own? We're about to bring your single bed through from the passage. We'd thought of living on here for a while, after the wedding, you know. Until we get sorted with mortgages and such, and getting a place of our own."

It was no surprise to me. I'd thought of it myself, how suitable the basement would be for them both. But not with me as well. Oh no! I wasn't that green. And anyway, I'd honestly be bloody glad to see the back of it. To get a studio on my own, or something. All perfectly feasible now. "Christ, be my guests. Of course not, don't be daft! No, honestly, what I'm after is a great big studio room or something, if you know of one—my circumstances have altered you understand!" I made my voice as pompous as possible, saying it. It was still, my sudden wealth, a source of self-consciousness, especially to me.

They did know of one, exactly right! No! Yes—the perfect answer! A beautiful place, if it was still to let, at the top of Joyce's and Johnny's! Where they were holding the party. You know, the one tonight!

Something jolted in my mind, some clearly forgotten fact. "Tonight?"

Jim spoke. "Yes. Isn't that why you've come back, we assumed—"

"No, Jim. I'd honestly f—"

"You're coming though. Isn't she, Jim, with us?" Pat spoke firmly.

"Of course she is." Jim turned to me. "We'll be off in a couple of hours. We'll have a drink first over the road. I'll ring Nick now, he can join us."

I surrendered weakly to their bland enthusiasm, letting their sun soak through me. I felt a twinge. 'What, dancing on our graves so soon, my girl?' Not dancing, dad—tiptoeing, truly, simply that.

I wore my black. When all of this was over I'd give my whole wardrobe to the Salvation Army, down to the last dark depressing stitch. And buy some more, a cloudburst full of colour—cerise and shocking pink. Viridian green and all the blues. A tingling tangerine—I'd blaze my way to Mozambique! Put nature itself to shame!

Pat wore white. Regardless. "Will you be wearing white for the wedding, Patty? Even though it's just in the Registry?"

"Of course," she answered confidently. "No one can tell. On the outside. That there's two of us in here."

Quite true. Well, come to that, no one could tell whether all the brides who opted to wear white were bloody virgins or not. I kissed her cheek and squeezed her bony shoulder. "You look lovely," I said.

"So do you."

I did, I knew. Sorrow, I'd say, did actually seem to suit me. It lent a fine mysterious charm, such that I could have caught anyone. Anything. Though these last two weeks, ten days, eleven or whatever it was, all that had bled into the background. Not uppermost in my mind as it had been before. Except at night, alone in my bed, eyes wide open in Fiona's mother's guest room. Oh yes, I'd touched myself in there all right, from the sheer need for some comfort. An animal urge, quite primitive, like a beast of the field. But without fruition. Each joyless, self-exploratory session. It was time I was touched by another.

We weren't the first to arrive by any means. Guests overflowed down the stairs. Nick relieved us of our coats. He hadn't come round, we'd met him there instead. "Would love to, of course, but can't, have to help Joyce with the glasses," he'd said cheerily on the telephone. It was nice to hear his voice again, just that had the feel of friendship. He greeted me now with a bony bear hug. "Good to see you, kid. Pecker up!" His ginger beard tickled my chin. I caught a whiff from his armpits. Perhaps we all should club together and give him deodorant for Christmas. Or not. It didn't matter that much anyway, the unfortunate pong.

"Good to see you Nick, too," I squeezed him hard. "Thank you for all your sympathy." They'd sent a telegram and flowers, the minute they'd had the news. A bloody sight more than Nathaniel had done. Or Winnie. Or Reggie. Or Ernest. A nice letter from Mrs. Pritchard though, and the District Inspector! I'd finish the term for sure, and complete everything for the County Hall exhibition.

We went upstairs, greeted by various people on the way, colleagues of Nick's and Jim's. Until at last we reached the top and arrived at the heart of the party.

It was quite difficult to tell in the superb but lowered light, how large the room might be. It occupied, anyway, the entire square footage of the house. Had clearly been built on a flattened roof, its ceiling, as it were, completely of glass. I felt uncannily at home from the minute I stepped foot there. "It's marvellous! It's mad! My God. I love it." That's all I could say.

Jim laughed. "Hold on—let's ask Johnny or Joyce. Cross fingers anyway that it's not gone already—"

"Oh dear, please do find out." He slipped away, and Pat followed. Nick had gone for a drink. I stood alone. And looked around. That's when I first saw him.

They found me underneath the coats, that's where I'd crawled to, they said. Asleep, and smiling, Pat claimed, who'd stumbled on me first. "You missed it all! The entire thing. Where did you get to?"

I shrugged and looked around. "Is it over? No, obviously not—these coats are still here, so there must be people—" A hardy nucleus remained, the sort who always do, to see it through till dawn. "I'll wash my face and come on up. I promise. I'm wide awake now!"

Pat had lingered back. "Are you all right? Really?"

"Yes I am."

"I saw you," she said, "going off. He looked great! What did you get up to? And more to the point, where?"

"Hello," he'd said. "And what are you?"

"An orphan." It was the first time I'd said it.

"An orphan, eh? That's sad."

"It is a bit."

"Let's dance."

"You have no objection, I take it? To misbehaving in broom cupboards?"

"None at all." I'd dropped my skirt.
"That's good." He'd undone his trousers.

"A remarkable ride!"
"Yes, smooth as silk."
And I laughed all the way up the stairs.